I0637291

An American Band

An American Band

A NOVEL

TRAVIS BURKETT

FORT WORTH, TEXAS

Copyright © 2024 by Travis Burkett

Library of Congress Cataloging-in-Publication Data

Names: Burkett, Travis, 1991- author.
Title: An American band : a novel / Travis Burkett.
Description: Fort Worth, Texas : TCU Press, [2024] | Summary: "Javier Espinoza manages a
    hungry young rock band without quite enough money to record their debut album. When
    the slog of playing their hearts out for tiny crowds in Texas border towns gets to be too
    much, a dangerous idea takes hold of Javier: smuggling migrants across the border for cash.
    He knows a thing or two about it, after all. He made his own perilous journey from a farm
    in Coahuila to the US at age eleven, surviving brutal coyotes and dodging authorities. So he
    and the band find a ramshackle tour bus and an alibi, and are soon plunged into the heart
    of Juárez, where the harsh realities of human trafficking, corrupt border agents, and ruthless
    cartels are waiting. "Travis Burkett knows these roads, these horizons, these fencelines, and,
    most importantly, the pulse and grit of the border he takes us back and forth across."—
    Stephen Graham Jones"— Provided by publisher.
Identifiers: LCCN 2023040924 (print) | LCCN 2023040925 (ebook) | ISBN 9780875658650
    (paperback) | ISBN 9780875658742 (ebook)
Subjects: LCSH: Rock groups—Texas—Fiction. | Concert agents—Texas—Fiction. | Human
    smuggling—Texas—Fiction. | Illegal immigration—Texas—Fiction. | Mexican American
    youth—Texas—Fiction. | Border crossing—Texas—Fiction. | Mexican-American Border
    Region—Fiction. | Juárez (Chihuahua, Mexico)—Fiction. | LCGFT: Novels.
Classification: LCC PS3602.U75586 A85 2024 (print) | LCC PS3602.U75586 (ebook) | DDC
    813/.6—dc23/eng/20230921
LC record available at https://lccn.loc.gov/2023040924
LC ebook record available at https://lccn.loc.gov/2023040925

TCU Box 298300
Fort Worth, Texas 76129

Design by Preston Thomas

to Shelbey,
infinity x infinity

Part I

I was left for dead in a border town

Where no one knew my name

I sold my soul in that border town

In return for life and fame

Verse from "Border Town" by
D. RIVERA,
J. WAGNER,
S. MONTOYA

Prologue

THE ROOSTER CROWED BEFORE THE SUN ROSE OVER THE scrubland. When it was just a pink glow in the east, silhouetting the gobernadora and giant yucca, Javier rolled over and pulled the sheet up to his chin. Even with his eyes closed, the boy could see the day beginning. His father was in the other room, putting on his jeans, work shirt, and boots in the dark and heading to the kitchen, where his mother, in her blue robe, was cooking migas with last night's tortillas.

The radio hummed to life. A nearby AM station played old rancheras in the morning, and Javier's mother liked to sing along while she cooked. After eating, without so much as a yawn, Javier's father left for another long day in the fields. Then his mother got Javier up to eat the eggs she'd kept warm on the stove. Javier grasped his fork in one hand and used the other to prop up his heavy head.

After breakfast came chores. The chickens were kept in an old wooden shed, which leaned a little farther north each year. The latch on the door had rusted out long ago, so Javier had to wire it shut each time he left. He let the chickens out of the ramshackle coop, scattered some feed, raked the mess, and collected the eggs.

On to the goat pen, bordered by the coop on one side and a patch-work metal fence on the other three. Javier gave the goats fresh water, milked the nannies, and opened the gate so the rest could graze on rogue weeds in the plot surrounding their home. Javier stood, with the basket of eggs in one hand and the bucket of milk in the other, and watched them head to the same weedy spot where they had stopped the day before. The kids bounced ahead while the old billy—Javier made sure to stay upwind from him—kept his slow assured pace.

The morning was cool and still, just a touch of breeze from the north. Javier stared off toward the horizon. Something wasn't right. He blinked a few times to make sure his eyes weren't the problem. Everything looked so big, so close, like he was seeing through a fish-eye lens. The low blue mountains didn't seem so far off anymore. Like he could hit them with a rock. The morning routine broke off, jagged.

The eastern sky swallowed up the sun. Rolling charcoal clouds cast an angry shadow over the farm. The chickens stamped inside the coop. The goats were spooked and tried to climb a hay bale, get to higher ground. Not rain but fog fell from the sky. It fell in streaks like smoke from a thousand burning arrows. Javier stared with his mouth open, the terror seeping in.

The streaks got thicker until he could see only objects closer and closer to him. His mother appeared at the gate. Her shoulders rose and fell with short sharp breaths. She spun around, searching wildly.

"Javier," she shouted.

And then he couldn't see her face, her hands, her shoulders. Barely an outline, gray on gray. "Mamá." He wanted to run to her but fright had seized up his joints. The sooty fog closed in. He could not will his legs to work, to carry him to the warmth of his mother's arms. And then it was dark.

"Don't leave me," the boy cried.

Chapter 1

2015

THE BUS READ SLY & THE FAMILY STALLONE IN BIG RED letters outlined in gold paint that sparkled in the sun, temporarily blinding passing drivers. Parked at a convenience store outside Laredo, it was as immaculate as a twenty-year-old RV converted into a tour bus could be.

It wasn't even one of their many names airbrushed on the side, but that of the defunct cover band it had belonged to before them. The bus guzzled fuel, wobbled when it got over seventy, and had some electrical deficiencies from being struck by lightning. Javier had gotten a great deal on it, but the band didn't know any better. After spending years in an addled Econoline van that had to be coaxed back to life every chilly morning, up was the only direction to go.

It had its charm. The engine had been reliable so far, and the RV was just handsome enough to keep people from getting suspicious. There weren't any major dents, and the clear coat was still in good shape. The polished chrome wheels glinted in the Texas sunlight and the bug guts had been scrubbed off the windshield. It wasn't a palace on wheels, but there was plenty of room for the four migrants in its belly, hidden in bulky road cases. So it did the trick.

The bandmates headed for the store's entrance. Squat, the lead guitarist, had been bouncing in his seat and asking if they could pull over ever since they crossed into Texas. He bounded for the restroom ahead of the others.

Half-lives of adrenaline still coursed in their veins, but the crossing had gone smoothly enough. Javier glanced at his phone. They'd be in San Antonio in another two-and-a-half hours. He'd told Adam they would arrive at his store around eight thirty. They were right on schedule.

Webb, the skinny roadie with an inexplicable potbelly, finished an unfiltered cigarette out where the concrete ended and then dieseled up the bus. He waited there, picking at his belly button like he expected to find something in it until the automatic cutoff thumped, then he shook the nozzle a couple of times, getting each drop into the tank.

Javier waited at the counter with his arms crossed. He sported a stubble beard. Not the carefully cultivated kind, but the kind that suggested he'd lost his razor about three days ago. He wore hip sunglasses, but he wasn't so much in style as style had caught back up to him.

"Pump three? That'll be a hundred and nine," the clerk said.

A thick tuft of black hair fell onto Javier's brow. He swept it back, revealing the lines etched into his forehead from almost two decades of dealing with immature musicians, tight promoters, and aggressive cops. Not to mention the new blemishes that had appeared since they began smuggling people across the border three months ago. Javier flipped through his wallet for the cash.

"Y'all a band?" the clerk said, nodding toward the bus.

Javier looked over his shoulder. "That's what we tell people."

"What kind of music?"

"Tex-Mex, I guess you'd call it," Javier said. "Rock 'n roll peppered with Texas blues, Mexican folk, and outlaw country."

"Huh." The clerk considered this. "Sounds like a dog I had. Part blue heeler, part Chihuahua, part I don't know what. She was a Heinz 57 mutt. Damn good dog though—so what's your band name?"

"I don't know," Javier said. "You'll have to ask them."

One of the clerk's eyebrows shot up.

"Tonight it's Vic and the Vaqueros," Dave, lead singer and trendsetter, said. "Hey, don't forget the water."

He set his pack of bottled water on the counter and Jeff, resident intellectual bass player, laid his on top. "I thought we were going with Mondegreen."

"I like the Vaqueros," said the guitar prodigy Squat, adjusting his belt. "Has a nice ring to it."

Marck, their newly hired drummer, added an armful of chips and sugary drinks to the stack. "Would it be too much to ask to just stick to one name?"

"Yes," the other three shot back.

"Look," Marck said. "Say what you want about my last band, but The Mudslingers' name told people what we were about."

"Yeah," Jeff said. "About how happy you were to be the house band at the corn maze."

"Ouch, bro." Squat punched Jeff in the arm.

"Whatever," Marck replied.

Javier shrugged at the clerk and handed over the cash.

Dave and Squat held their packs of water and waited for Javier to open the storage compartment. They kept watch on their surroundings with jerky owl-like movements. Javier opened the hatch and got halfway inside. He pulled a Phillips screwdriver from his pocket and unscrewed the vent from the big road case. He peeked in, but it was still too dark to see.

"Están todos bien?" he asked.

"Sí," a couple of voices whispered.

He took their piss can, dumped it in a nearby shrub, and handed it back. He gave them a whole pack of water, just in case, and then repeated the process with the people hidden in the second case. He'd done ductwork to allow a little cool air to get down there, but the cases' vents didn't let much pass through. He told them San Antonio was only one hundred and fifty miles away. *Only* a hundred fifty, he scoffed at himself. And the high was *only* ninety-seven degrees.

They were on US soil, but it still wasn't safe for them to be out in the open. La migra prowled these parts. This was the third group they'd taken across the border, so they more or less knew the drill. Javier kept the band focused and within their limits. While other coyotes packed trailers and gutted vans to cram people in, they stuck to no more than six a run. The road cases fit four and there was room for another two inside, underneath the floorboards.

The bus veered onto the highway and the bandmates plunked into their usual spots. Dave sat on the pleather couch, crossing his cowboy boots on a suitcase, as horizontal as he could be without actually lying down. Squat claimed the spot next to him, where he practiced scales on his Strat. Marck, the road-tested rock veteran, lay on the floor with his hands behind his head and closed his eyes. Webb pressed down the accelerator and smacked his gum like he could compress all his stress into it. Jeff sat at the little table, separated from Webb by a wood-panel partition, and Javier joined him.

"How were they?" Jeff asked.

"A little stiff, but they're all right," Javier said.

Jeff nodded. A cop car went by slow in the oncoming lane. Webb waved with two fingers and really tore into his gum.

"Do you have to chew that so loud?" Jeff asked.

"What?" Webb said. He kept smacking and frowned. "Look, you already told me I can't smoke on here. If that's the way it is, you're gonna have to tolerate the nicotine gum."

Webb kept his eyes on the road and said, "Thirty years I been working with bands, and you're the first to ban smokes. I roadied for Motör-head's Night Raids tour. Lemmy would smoke a carton of menthols when he felt a cold coming on. Never missed a show. He was already over forty. And what happened to the drugs? It's all vapes and Adderall with your generation. Kids don't know how to cut loose anymore. If you ask me, we ought to dismantle all these dadgum smart phones."

Jeff had already put his headphones on, but Webb was one to keep talking long after he had an audience. Then there was only the noise from the road and Squat's unplugged notes for a long while, ample space to think.

Dropping off the migrants wasn't the only thing on the night's agenda. They still had a show to play. They were a working band, after all. The coyote business had whispered promises of big bucks and out-law adventure, but it was still their side hustle. Music was the meat and potatoes. Maybe more like meat and potatoes for the soul—since they had barely been able to afford the diesel and fried burritos it took to keep touring before the cash influx.

Things were looking up though. They dreamed of what the money would bring: independence. Namely, better equipment and their own state-of-the-art studio, where they would capture *their* sound the way *they* wanted. No suits calling the shots. It would be the perfect place to cut their epic debut album. Unlike most young bands, they had no desire to sign with a big record company or be social-media famous. For the most part, they just wanted to have a good time and make music. Javier admired that.

The bus rolled on by the small South Texas towns of Encinal and Cotulla. Javier stared out the side window at mile after mile of parched, pale grassland. The Nueces River dribbled along exposed banks of mesquite. Sporadic purple-bloomed cenizo stood out like lonesome fireworks. Near the highway, an aging rancher used a propane torch to burn spines off prickly pear cactus so his cattle had something to eat and drink. Chamuscando, a technique for desperate times. He'd never seen it before but recognized the practice from his mother's descriptions. Her father had to do the same thing during a vicious drought when she was a little girl.

Javier tried to read but fell asleep instead. He looked up a long while later to see the San Antonio skyline on the horizon. The downtown buildings were outlined in blazing sunset streaks of blue and orange. The sharp Tower of Americas jutted up like a syringe you could use to extract the color from the evening and mainline it. He closed the book and sat his reading glasses on top. He rubbed the bridge of his nose and then spoke.

"We're about ten minutes away. All that's left is the drop, but we still have to keep our heads. In and out, no funny business."

When they turned down the alley behind AJ's Furniture at dusk, a man appeared in the headlights and motioned how far Webb should pull up. The brakes hissed and Javier was the first one out. He let the heavy compartment door down to make a ramp. There wasn't enough room for the cases to be opened inside, so they unlocked the wheels and rolled them out.

They were hell to move, and it wasn't just because of the people inside. Six-inch false bottoms full of cables and effects pedals hid the migrants from a potential once-over. The broad sides were fitted with sheets of alloy that Javier's research suggested could throw off the X-rays used for extra screening at some border checkpoints. They hadn't come across one yet, but life had taught him to stay a step ahead.

Javier popped the latches on the first case. He reached in and a small hand grabbed hold of his. A girl, about six years old, emerged. Jeff joined in, helping her middle-aged father onto the concrete. The others got the mother and son, a couple of years older than his sister, out of the second case.

The girl jumped into her mother's arms as soon as she got on her feet. The mother squeezed her tight and kissed her forehead. Her azure cotton blouse was rumpled from the two-hundred-mile ride. The father put his hand on the back of his young son's head and led him across the slab of concrete. He fixed his mussed hair back into a presentable part with his palm. His eyes fixed on his wife. Sweat shone on her face and bare arms. He grinned while their daughter pressed her face to his wife's ribs and wrapped her arms around her waist.

"Estamos aquí," he said.

They gathered for a familial embrace, eyes closed, taking deep, disoriented, triumphant breaths. Javier couldn't look away. They'd risked everything and made it to the other side. A minute later, the father approached Javier with the other half of their payment. Javier had counted it before they left, knew it was a little light. He shook the man's hand and wished him and his family good luck in San Antonio.

Adam, the owner of the store, hugged the family and said how glad he was they were okay. He ushered them in the back door and returned to thank the band for their help. He talked about putting the father to work in his store until he could find something regular, about the new opportunities there would be for the family in the city. He had told Javier that the Montezes were old friends from Nuevo León when he vouched for them.

"They were short three fifty when I picked them up," Javier said evenly. Adam looked back at him in confusion. "That's not much in proportion, so I didn't call off the run. But they owe it, and since you vouched for them, you owe it."

Adam smiled, but his nerves betrayed the gesture. "Look, they gave you what they had. Haven't they paid enough already?"

Javier took two swift steps into his personal space. Close enough for Adam to feel his warm breath. He genuinely didn't want to have to hurt him.

"It doesn't matter how much they paid. It wasn't what we agreed on," he said.

What they charged was fair, Javier believed, compared to coyotes who packed people in trailers like livestock. The coyotes who accepted credit but wouldn't hesitate to go after your family back home if the payments stopped. The coyotes who treated women like meat. Javier wasn't about to explain himself though. He took a half step back to ease Adam's mind.

"Looks like a nice store. I bet you get a lot of business."

Adam looked at him with his head cocked and his mouth open. "Uh, yeah, we do okay."

"So you've got three fifty in the register," Javier said. "How about we go get it?"

Adam's eyes darted down the line, from one man to the next. Dave had stopped playing quarterback when he discovered the Velvet Underground and the high school started drug testing, but he had once been referred to as "a gunslinger." Jeff was harmless, but you could squint and—between the wiry beard and serious brow—see how somebody might mistake him for a guy who wasn't. Marck once went down a flight of stairs face first—sloppy on codeine and muscle relaxants—and had a boxer's crooked nose to show for it. Squat stood as tall as he could, which was insufficient for reaching the nice guitars at the music store, but he was solid as a cannonball, bulging arms on display in his Spurs jersey. Though they looked the part of henchmen, they were as apprehensive as Adam. No one spoke, only stared, and what was left of Adam's confidence melted away.

"I'll take care of it." Adam retreated into the store. Javier followed and returned a minute later with the cash. He didn't say a word more about it, just added the money to the zip pouch with the rest of their funds and took a seat.

They headed straight to the venue from there. They normally set up earlier in the day, did soundcheck, but tonight they were coming in hot. They psyched themselves up on the way. For all their immaturity, you couldn't help but respect the intensity they approached shows with. They played hard, no matter if it was for a packed house or a half-dozen weeknight stragglers. And after getting the latter time and time again, it took a lot of discipline to keep that up.

They each had their own preshow rituals—Dave repeated tongue twisters like *Chester Cheetah chewed a chunk of cheap and chunky cheddar cheese*, Jeff put headphones on and wrote in his leather notebook, Marck found rhythm in the road noises and tapped his sticks on the edge of the table, Squat limbered his fingers up and down the neck of his guitar—but they all came together in the end.

"Huddle up," Dave said, and they did. "Where are we, boys?"

"San Antonio," they hollered.

"Woo hoo!" he howled. "That's right. Hands in."

They joined hands in the center. The custom went back to seventh-grade football, when Dave, Jeff, and Squat played on the B team together. They'd admit it was cheesy—something Coach Peterson made them do before each practice—but it came to mean something more. It was a reminder that a trio of misfit kids from West Texas could make it this far, that it was still all in front of them.

"Win the day on three," he said. "One, two—"

———————

After the opening song, Dave said into the microphone, "Feels good to be back in the Lone Star State. We've had an interesting day"—he turned and looked at his bandmates with a grin—"to say the least. But we're thrilled to be here tonight. Make yourself comfortable, or even better, work yourself into a frenzy. You're in for a hell of a show."

Dave didn't lie about things like that. The band's music—a mixed bag of full-bodied rock 'n roll, springy conjunto rhythms, cosmic country soundscapes, and Americana storytelling—was anything but boring. It didn't hurt that Squat was a guitar savant, capable of picking up any style or key by ear, or that they all had an excellent sense of balance between loud and quiet moments, clobbering crescendos and elegiac instrumentals that turned the wide-open spaces of West Texas into sound. All the bandmates but Marck, who came from Omaha three months ago to replace their last drummer, had grown up on the Llano Estacado—an area rife with flat farm land, big blue skies, and Tex-Mex culture.

It was a melting pot, the kind of place where Mexicans developed a hint of twang in their speech and white folks at least knew how to say "jalapeño" and "pendejo." The bandmates grew up in the shadows of local legends like Buddy Holly and Joe Ely as well as Tejano groups like the Texas Tornados and Little Joe y La Familia. Even Jeff, the only one of the original trio without Mexican heritage, had developed a love for the music and culture. He learned the dances at classmates' quinceañeras and watched late-night novelas to improve his Spanish. None of them were fluent, but all three knew enough to pepper words and phrases in their lyrics.

Next on the set list was a conjunto-inspired ballad the bandmates wrote together on their front porch a few months back. Jeff let his bass hang and pulled a harp from his pocket. He could play the hell out of a harmonica. And with some tongue-blocking finesse he could make one sound pretty close to a Tejano accordion. The real thing would be better, they all knew, but this had to do for now. Jeff played a lively riff to get it going, and somebody in the crowd threw a grito. The bandmates joined in and they all settled into the gentle bounce of the oom-pah rhythm.

The song was based on a Mexican phrase that literally said *there's no fart*. The English equivalent was more like *there's no problem*. Dave could turn on a dime. He often played the fearless front man, but here his voice took on a lonesome tone that made what should have been a joke song take hold of your heart:

> *No hay pedo*
> *That wasn't me you saw crying*
> *No hay pedo*

Don't know why you keep prying
No hay pedo
I swear I'm over you
No hay pedo, no hay pedo, no hay pedo

The Monday night crowd—a tangle of pretty girls in dresses and boots, bros in snapback caps, caballeros in Wranglers, old rockers in band shirts, and hip kids with big glasses passing around vape pens—was more energetic than you'd expect from a group that would fit on a school bus. The crowd and the band were in the zone though, and that counted for something. A college girl in the front row, with a thin leather headband and yellow sundress, held her cup up and sang along with every word.

These were the moments when it didn't matter that they still couldn't make a living in music without their illegal income. It didn't matter that they couldn't get anyone to believe in the ambitious Tex-Mex album in their heads. Hard work and the dogged pursuit of thousands of little ideas had brought them to a place where they could share their music with people who actually wanted to hear it.

They had fought tooth and nail just to get a little recognition in their hometown. An article in the *Daily Toreador* had called them "The Band with No Name," which wasn't technically correct but sounded pretty cool. They worked up from doing occasional shows in Lubbock to scattered gigs across the state. Even then, they never landed the marquee cities, so it was Corsicana instead of the Metroplex, Seguin instead of San Antonio, Bastrop instead of Austin. Gigs that paid so little they had to convince themselves they were worth doing purely for the experience.

So they got a big kick out of slaying the San Antonio crowd, seeing a cute girl sing along to songs they had written. It was one of those warm surging moments they wished they could hold onto forever. They were right where they were supposed to be.

During the encore, Squat climbed onto the stack and played a pulsing solo. When the end neared, he jumped into the air and played vibrato on the last note while he dropped to the ground with a flat-footed thud. It all came to a pounding crescendo and the small crowd thundered. The bandmates raised each other's hands at center stage like fighters who had won a unanimous decision.

Chapter 2

1984

JAVIER'S MOTHER DIED ON A MONDAY. MARIANA PÉREZ de Espinoza was thirty-three, and he was eleven. There wasn't much time between her diagnosis and her death, not even three months. The cancer had spread too far to treat by the time they found it. She'd been so strong and full of life that Javier couldn't make himself believe that the gaunt and colorless woman in the hospital bed was his mother. He cried into her gown and held onto her when he realized she was gone. Nurses rushed in and out of the room, and he remained.

It cut him deep. His father had left three years earlier. He said he was going to Texas to work on a picking crew, that working their little farm was no way to support a family. He always said he would have sold his plot if he could. He was supposed to send for Mariana and Javier when he got set up in the US, but they never heard from him again. If his mother ever found anything out, she never told.

That happened a lot in those days. Most men came and went with the harvest, but there were those who crossed over and never came back. Some kept sending money back home but never had enough to get their family over the border. Others started fresh in the US. Got a new wife, had new kids, while the people from their old lives were left to wither on the vines of old Mexico. Others didn't make it out of the desert. Javier had asked around about his father, but no one claimed to know a thing. He was just gone.

His father did leave an envelope with some cash, most of his meager savings, with them before he left. Javier mostly remembered the waiting. As the months went by, into winter and summer and back to harvest all over again, Javier began to realize he wasn't coming back. His mother wouldn't talk about him. She got tense and impatient with Javier's questions, so he learned to stop asking. With his father gone, Javier relied on his mother more than ever. The cash helped for a bit, but once she realized no more was coming, Mariana had to find extra work to support her only child, cooking at a restaurant in the nearest town and washing others' clothes on her days off.

The family lived on a parcel of an ejido, communal land for farming. Since his father was no longer around to work the land, Mariana had to use it herself or risk losing their share. The Farmall was in disrepair, its remaining paint pinkish with age. His father had always spent more time working on the tractor than actually running it, and they didn't know where to begin.

Mariana and Javier worked the eight acres with the help of a sturdy black mule named Ricardo, growing patches of maize and watermelon and black-eyed peas. They raised goats and chickens, and his mother traded milk and eggs for flour and canned goods in town. Mariana tried to keep the worries to herself, but Javier knew in that unspoken way that times were hard.

Mariana and Javier would get up before five to tend to the animals, then she dropped him off early at school and headed into work. Summers in Coahuila were blistering, but after school let out in June was Javier's favorite time of year. He loved those days, even though they were full of hard work. His mother sang sweet songs while they made their way around the farm, tending to the crops and each group of animals. The stillness of the day, accented only by his mother's beautiful voice and the occasional cluck or bark, filled Javier with joy. He felt God's presence more at dawn on the farm than on Sunday mornings at mass, which became less and less frequent after his father left.

Mariana had a hard time speaking at her sickest. It was like she couldn't collect enough air to get the words out of her mouth. She spoke in short gasps, which were hard to comprehend. One evening, with Javier at her bedside, she was adamant about speaking, but her illness had progressed so that even a sentence was too much. The last words she spoke to him were: "Mira. Biblia." Look. Bible. The words were like an unfinished riddle.

The day after Mariana died, her brother and his wife arrived. They greeted Javier with hugs and tears. It had been at least a couple of years since Javier had seen them. His uncle Ramiro had a steady job with the city of Aguascalientes and took pride in his role as provider. He was nice enough and brought gifts when he visited, but his knack for steering any conversation back to money repelled Javier. And he'd never liked Javier's father. Even before he left for good, Ramiro tried to convince his sister to leave the dirty ejido and come stay with them. Especially after she had her second miscarriage. Ramiro was convinced that farm life was to blame. She wouldn't hear it.

They held a wake at the house and some of the other ejidatarios stopped by to offer condolences. Ramiro said they should have rented a building in the nearest town, eyeing every meager object in their home with contempt. Afterward, Ramiro told Javier the plan: to take him back to Aguascalientes to live with them and their two kids. It was not phrased as a choice, but a command. They would leave the morning after the funeral. Javier had other ideas, but he kept them to himself.

His mother used to tell stories of the United States while they worked. She'd never been herself—it was mostly men who crossed for work in those days—but her father had been to Texas as a bracero. He used to regale her and her brothers with tales of El Norte. The work was grueling, and they were only welcomed as long as they provided value to the white landowners, but the place made an impression on him.

Mariana's father always wanted to migrate, but his wife, Javier's abuela, wouldn't have it. She thought the US only made trouble for people like them. Her words swayed Javier's uncles—neither had left Mexico in their lives—but Mariana had been enchanted by her father's stories. She told Javier about how there were more opportunities for people to be successful, and fewer opportunities to go hungry or get caught up in violence. In Texas, she said, Javier could get a good education and someday have a job that could support him and his own family. They talked about going. About how they would pack up and leave Mexico, but it never came to pass while she was alive. After, Javier was determined to get there.

The morning after Mariana's funeral—a blur of hugs from family members he hadn't seen in years, ay pobrecito!—Javier got up at four. He had placed his alarm clock under his pillow to ensure its buzz would only wake him. He left his room, not much bigger than the single bed he slept in, and tiptoed around, stuffing a backpack with a change of clothes, food, a canteen full of water, and the small gold-framed picture of his mother holding him as a baby that hung in the hallway.

There was pure joy on both of their faces, her eyes clear and full of purpose, his cheeks fat and dimpled. He swore he could remember that day, but his mother would say he was too young, he probably just created a memory from the picture. He'd argue with her. "No, Mamá. Me recuerdo."

Javier snuck to what had been his parents' bedroom and peered into the half-open door. His uncle was asleep on his back. He had thrown the covers off at some point, exposing his mound of stomach, which Javier watched rise and fall with an even rhythm. While Javier began to tiptoe backward, his uncle twitched and a loud snort came from deep in his throat.

Javier's eyebrows rose. He knew that he was caught. His uncle began to lift himself up but promptly rolled on his side and snuggled up next to his wife. Eyes still closed, he cupped his hand on her breast and started to breathe deeply again. Javier didn't dare let out a sigh, though he felt one inside.

He stepped out of the room and crossed through the kitchen to the back door. He was glad that he wouldn't be going to live with his uncle's family. He loved his uncle, but that didn't mean he had to like him. All the bribes in the world wouldn't convince him to join them. If he had to leave, and he realized he did, then he was going north, not south.

He hitched his backpack higher and stared at the doorknob. He turned around and saw the little table where he had supper every night, the wooden crucifix he and his father made his mother for her birthday years ago, the green and yellow tapestry with patterns that always reminded him of snakeskin. He didn't count on the place tugging back at him. A desire that he couldn't explain, but obeyed nonetheless, pushed him onward. When he turned the knob, it felt weightless as a dream. A brand-new world waited on the other side.

2015

The bus stopped at a diner near Midland around ten the next morning. Webb caught up on sleep while the rest ate breakfast: syrup-drenched pancakes and sausage, buttered toast and grits. Nursing hangovers, the bandmates were quiet. Javier forked a bit of a gravy-sopped biscuit into his mouth while Squat asked if he had heard the one about the nosy pepper.

"He's jal-up-eño business. Get it?"

A short burst of air that could easily be mistaken for a chuckle, but which Javier would say was definitely not a chuckle, came from his mouth. Squat nudged Dave.

"Told you I could make him laugh."

"That doesn't count."

After their first round of coffee they talked set lists for that night's show. Jeff thought they should lead with "Old News from La Frontera" to set the tone, but Dave wanted to stick with the regular opener. Squat didn't care as long as they let him solo a couple of times, and Marck eyed his sausage like it was an enemy spy, waiting for it to spill the conspiracy plot against his stomach.

"I'm telling you," Jeff said. "We need to switch it up, show that we have substance early on."

"People go see Bob Dylan's ancient ass for substance. They come to our shows to have a good time," Dave said.

"Is it a crime to have a good time and be mentally stimulated?"

"Only if you're a prick about it."

Marck retreated into his phone, and Squat drew spirals in the pool of maple syrup with his fork. They had all developed the ability to tune Dave and Jeff's bickering out, for a while at least. Javier picked up the check and got Webb a couple of breakfast burritos wrapped in foil.

Driving west, the oil wells were as constant as railroad ties under a train. Unsynchronized metal horse heads went down and up, down and up, sending the polished rod down into the wellhead, into the earth. Javier noticed a big roadside sign, PERPETUALLY PUMPING PETROLEUM, from Salida Energy Co. It sounded like a knockoff Dr. Seuss book that roughnecks would read to their kids at night.

A jackrabbit appeared at the shoulder of I-20, his hind legs larger and more powerful than the rest of him. He hopped—in the awkward galumphing way jackrabbits do—into the oncoming lane. He juked when he caught his mistake, but an eighteen-wheeler, huffing fumes at eighty miles an hour, pulverized him. It managed to hit the rabbit with all nine tires on the driver side of the rig, flattening it by the time the truck had passed, leaving dark bloodstains and fur on an asphalt canvas. Javier turned his back to the window.

They rode the flatlands into the Last Roadhouse, a small venue between Midland and Odessa that Javier had booked before. It had a slick concrete floor, made for cumbias and two-stepping, and rustic wooden booths selling beer. Behind the stage was a large black backdrop with hundreds of small blue lights. Javier pictured how it would look when the band took the stage, a starry night sky behind them, covering them in shimmering royal blue.

While the band set up, Javier wandered into the dressing room. He sat in the folding chair in front of a vanity mirror with Hollywood lights. A couple of the bulbs were burnt out, but the glow was harsh. Gray hair had gained more ground near his temples and over his ears. He saw a second chin that he didn't remember being so prominent. There were dark bags under his eyes and diagonal lines jutting up to make a teepee between his brows. The more he looked, the less he recognized. Who was this old man in front of him?

It didn't seem like that long ago he was in his twenties like the band, full of desire to make something of his life. He never settled for a nine to five, but he hadn't exactly chased his dreams either. Part of him said he should just be happy that he made it. That he grew up in the US with all the opportunities that didn't exist back home. There were so many that didn't make it, so many more that did but lived in fear of being ripped from their families and sent back. He wondered why he couldn't be satisfied with honest work and an ordinary American life, why it took being a coyote to light something inside him that hadn't blazed in so long. And now that he'd felt it, it wasn't something he could just give up.

He was in over his head, and the anxious part of his mind told him just how sideways things could go. The fact that yesterday's run went smoothly wasn't comforting. It just reminded him that nothing stays the same. Every success is temporary. In three days' time they'd be in Juárez, and that was a whole new level.

Javier's eyes unfocused and he gradually slipped into a waking dream. *Red and blue lights strobing. Green-sashed Border Patrol SUVs surrounding the tour bus. Howls and panic.* Then the air conditioner shut off, and there was only the faint noise of Squat warming up on guitar. Doubt struck a gut punch. Javier slumped into his chair, holding his scalp with both hands, and his fears bore down on him like the tide.

"Hello, I'm Dave Rivera." His voice flowed from the speakers like warm honey. "And we're the Dead Rabbits."

The changing names bit predated their smuggling days. It started out as a way to sucker in promoters looking for a certain kind of act— they used Skullcrusher to land a decent paying gig at a headbangers club, Greenbreath to jam Grateful Dead-style at a 4/20 event, Dust Bowl Dogs to do covers of Willie and Waylon and the boys at an old honky tonk. They enjoyed the role-playing aspect of it. It didn't always go well, but they picked up all sorts of styles and skills, and it kept them from getting stale. Now their sound had become a little more focused, but the names still changed. Javier wanted to keep it that way, said it left less of a trail. They had agreed, however, that before they put out their debut album they would settle on a forever name.

Dave spun around to Marck and nodded while he counted them in. *Two, three, four*. They played loud and fast out of the gate, having learned it was easier to go in like a cannonball and then rein it in than the other way around. Their opener sounded like a modern-day rockabilly song, fed a steady diet of trucker speed and Mexican radio.

And it did the trick. The crowd was rowdy, with roughnecks set on throwing down fresh paychecks on Michelob and frozen margaritas. They spun their girlfriends and drank and somehow talked over the amps booming into their faces. While the band tuned their instruments for the next song, one of them in a red paisley shirt and flat-billed hat shouted to "play some Cross."

"This next one will be a kazoo medley in E," Dave announced.

The guy arched his thin eyebrows. His round nose looked shiny and purple in the stage glow. He looked like he was staring at a math problem he hadn't studied for.

"Oh, my bad. I thought we were all shouting nonsense things. No?" Dave said. He motioned for Marck to count them in before the guy could respond. The guy plugged his beer into his pouty lips.

Marck locked in on the drums. His arms were all over the place, like he had six of them. The others backed off after the second verse and let him go to town with it. About the time he was out of gas, Jeff's smooth bass line took over and got the crowd grooving. They ended in a crash of sound, sweat glistening on their faces and arms underneath all those blue stars.

"Thank y'all. Drive safe," Dave said. "You're beautiful, Odessa!"

He said this even though he thought the last two words belonged together about as much as "diarrhea" and "entertainment." Inner beauty, *maybe*. The bandmates bounced down the corridor toward the dressing room. Marck's sweat had turned a big section of his white T-shirt transparent.

"Electric," he said.

After a series of backslaps, Dave turned his attention to Jeff.

"You *almost* laid down that line perfectly," he said, and Jeff's smile melted. "I mean—you did good, man."

Jeff's eyebrows squeezed hard in toward the bridge of his nose and his lips pulled tight. Marck and Squat each took a long, exaggerated step backward, as if to say that they were not laying bets on the cockfight about to happen.

"You're one to talk, David." Jeff locked eyes with him. "I'm surprised you even heard it. You were so busy winking at that girl in the crop top. And do you have to use that arrogant bullshit on every heckler? Can you ignore it just once? It's not that hard."

"I was just having fun," Dave said. "And I am sorry—that you're too insecure to take a compliment."

"Didn't you need help with that, uh—" Marck gestured with his thumb, looking for the word, any word.

"Yes." Squat nodded. "I do need help with that thing."

The two of them slipped down the hallway and out of sight.

Dave and Jeff stared each other down. Jeff broke first, his eyes dropping to where Dave's jeans were tucked into his black boots, the ones with the pointy roach-killer toes and sugar skulls sewn on the tops in neon threads of pink, orange, and green. Jeff stared down at them, but Dave could see the gears were turning in that busy brain of his.

"If you were half as smart as you think you are," Jeff finally said, "we wouldn't be in this mess right now."

"What are you talking about?" Dave said.

"In a few days we're heading to Juárez. *Juárez.*" Jeff raised his hands for emphasis. "To do some shady shit. Javier just randomly found this new middleman, somebody we don't know anything about, and thousands of dollars are involved. No need to be alarmed. How could any of that go wrong?"

"Javier knows what he's doing," Dave said.

"What gives you that impression? He was our manager, he just got us gigs, and now we accept that he's the mastermind of a criminal operation?" Jeff looked both ways after saying that. His gaze softened and he went on, "We don't have to go through with this right now."

"He's done this before. We all have now," Dave said. "What other option do you see? If we quit now, there's no way we raise the rest of the money. Matter of fact, we'll be hemorrhaging just by staying on the road and paying bills. You really want to half-ass our shot at making the album?"

Jeff shook his head. "Of course not. It was my idea, wasn't it? I just want to be smart."

"Me too," Dave said. "Nobody's trying to sugarcoat anything, Jeff. We're risking a hell of a lot on this." He paused and scratched his smooth cheek. "But I don't see another way."

Jeff bit his tongue. The door leading from the stage opened and the sound guy came through, always smiling and always in a hurry. Deep dimples framed his bushy goatee. "Great show, guys," he said without slowing down. They nodded and said thanks to the back of his head.

"C'mon. Let's get something to eat," Dave said.

They left Odessa at half past one and traveled northeast to Lamesa, where Squat had access to his grandparents' old ranch house. Their next show wasn't for a couple of days, and they decided it would be a good place to rest up and recover. Or stay up half the night jamming and partying.

Relaxation felt like an alien concept to Javier at this point. The usual forces of confidence and doubt waged their war in his mind. Before a run, he went from calm confidence to jittery indecision, around the bend and back again several times. It didn't used to be that way. Doubt and anxiety had come into his life gradually, until they finally told him one day: *We're in it for the long haul, buddy.*

That was all on the inside though. Javier's past had taught him that perceived weakness was real weakness, so he stood tall, made solid eye contact, and did his best to suppress emotional tones. The bandmates saw Javier as uninteresting, always in control. There was a lot they didn't know about him, and he liked that.

They didn't think like him either, growing up in relative comfort. Squat and Dave might have Mexican roots, but they were third generation, and that was a world apart from his experience. They hadn't felt the alienation, didn't understand being a fugitive on the run, feeling like the earth could be snatched out from under your feet at any moment. Javier sometimes had to remind himself it wasn't their fault. They were just a different generation.

They had their own obstacles. When Squat would mention his abuelo was a rancher, people often replied, "Oh, who does he work for?" A Mexican who worked his own land, that was a hard concept to grasp. Being mixed, Dave got it from both sides. Some Mexicans ribbed him for being a coconut: brown on the outside, white on the inside. Some white people assumed he was fluent in Spanish and under strict orders from the pope not to use contraceptives. That made dating a Southern Baptist preacher's daughter a little tricky.

The airbrakes hissed and brought the bus to a stop on the shoulder, followed by the words "stupid computer!" Javier made his way to the front, where Webb was pulling a pack of cigarettes from the glove compartment. The GPS unit lay with a crack across its screen near the foot pedals.

"I don't care about their rules. I need a smoke." He fidgeted with the lighter.

"It's okay," said Javier, trying to talk him down. "What happened?"

Webb threw his hands in the air as if to say *let me tell you about it.*

"This hunk of junk has a delay. It tried to send us on a shortcut, and now we're way off track."

Webb's squinted eyes glared out the windshield. His hunched profile, from glowing cigarette to thin graying ponytail, looked like a figure closer to the left-hand side of the human evolution chart.

"I'm a hell of a roadie. I set up and tear down faster than anybody. I'm a good driver too, but I can't do my job with horseshit equipment. The amps belong in a landfill and this bus ain't far behind. Maybe I'd be better off scrubbing toilets at Allsup's."

"I took a risk bringing you in on this," Javier said with no give in his voice. "I could drive the bus myself."

Webb's whole demeanor shrank. He slouched even further and his eyes dropped to the floor like those of a cowed-down dog.

"That was a joke. I need this, man," Webb said. Since he didn't have a stake in the band, he got his cut in cash after every run. It was the best-paying gig he'd ever had. "I used to could find any place in the lower forty-eight without even a map for guidance. I just felt it, man. Intuition and a natural compass. But ever since I turned fifty-five, it's like a third of my brain cells ran off to Florida. Now I'd get lost in a one-light town without these doggone things."

Webb picked up the GPS and ran his finger over the crack on the screen, diagonal and all the way across. He used his shirt to dust the device off and then gently placed it back in its holster, as if apologizing to it.

"We're at least fifteen miles off of 349. It would have been a straight shot, but now we'll have to go the long way around."

Javier patted his shoulder and said, "It's all right, Webb. We'll get there."

"Yeah, it's not so bad. I can figure this out."

Peaceful silence lasted about eight seconds until the robotic British GPS voice chimed in, "You have. Missed your. Turn. Please. Make a. U-turn. As soon as. Possible."

Javier was quick on his feet and restrained the skinny roadie with a bear hug just as he lunged at the GPS.

"I'll kill it. I swear, I'll pull the wires out its USB hole and eat 'em," Webb said, struggling against Javier's arms to get free.

Squat stretched his arms over his head, perking up when he saw the old house in the headlights. They had a couple of days to kill until the next show in Marfa, and when he suggested staying at the ranch they were all in. The Spanish-style house, ten miles east of Lamesa, had a red barrel-clay tile roof and bold archways. It had been home to his grandparents—the place Squat and his sister also lived off and on during childhood, while their mother was away working out her problems. Family was everything to his abuelos, but he wasn't sure they ever forgave his mom for leaving them behind, again and again.

Squat could hear his grandparents' voices again, speaking softly in Spanish, while looking over the weathered wooden bench on the front porch, where they used to sit and watch the sunset over the caprock. He took it for granted at the time. He realized more and more, now that his abuelos were gone, how much he'd failed to appreciate, always impatient for his mother to come pick them up and take them back to Lubbock, where there were more kids his age and ways to be entertained.

His abuelo, Pedro, first came to Texas as a teenager, eager to leave home and make a better life. He found seasonal work in the cotton fields and later made a hand on a vast ranch in Borden County. Even while working for forty dollars a week, he vowed he would have his own spread someday. He and his wife invested blood, sweat, and tears until they had some unwanted acres and a few cattle to call their own. Over the years they built up a respectable cow-calf operation with eighty head, a great feat considering where he'd started out.

Squat had forgotten many of his abuelo's tales, but the bare bones of their family story had been seared in his mind from maddening repetition. Their ancestors had lived in Texas long ago, on a ranch in the Rio Grande Valley, as far south as you can go without crossing the river. The border crossed them, was how his abuelo put it.

The Montoya family had lived in modern-day Texas when the Mexican government offered lands to white settlers so that they might provide a flesh-and-blood buffer against Comanche warriors, the plan eventually backfired, and the Texans declared independence. When many Mexicans were run off by the wars of the next decade and a half. The Treaty of Guadalupe Hidalgo granted the family US citizenship with an asterisk.

They remained through it all, until La Matanza. The Slaughter, that was the name given to the lynchings of Mexican Americans along the border at the hands of Anglo vigilantes and Texas Rangers. After all they had weathered, it was a series of fear-fueled murders that finally drove them away, across the river at last. Pedro was born there, a stranger to his family's old home.

But he was never one for nostalgia. Instead of becoming bitter over what his parents lost, he cut his own path, working relentlessly and saving what he could. He was proud of what he and his wife had built, the small piece of Texas they were able to leave to their daughters when they died.

Squat's aunts owned the property now. His mother had already sold her share back to them and blown through the cash. No one was surprised. His aunts leased the land out for drilling and wind turbines but kept the house, even though they lived halfway across the state in the Metroplex now. They told Squat and his sister they could stay there whenever they liked. Anna never took them up on it, being tied up in law school at UT. She got all the brains, their mom used to say, and Squat got the brawn.

The three-bedroom house sat about a mile off Highway 180 with only a dead-end dirt road connecting it to the rest of the world. There was a large sloped driveway surrounded by a grassless yard. In its place were gravel and cacti and chunks of pale red rock. A patch of prickly pear instead of green hedges. A thick cholla instead of a shade tree. His abuelo had loved the landscape and said that covering it up with water-hogging sod was like tearing down the Sistine Chapel to put in a McDonald's.

Webb placed a foot on the split-rail fence and lit a cigarette. Marck looked the place over like a museum exhibit. Jeff and Dave walked, arms folded, several paces apart. They stood by the front door, and Squat sprang into the air and grabbed the edge of the awning above them. Sliding to the left, he felt around under the curved tile.

"Bingo." He jingled the keys.

In the entryway a mural of a rattlesnake devouring a rat greeted them. The rat was in the process of becoming a large lump in the snake's midsection. The snake, sinister and lethal, was so focused on the rodent it didn't notice the hawk swooping down on it from behind, beak and talons ready to maim. The sky over the rocky rise was baby blue and bright except for a few brooding clouds near the right border. Dave and Jeff looked at the painting in awe.

"You like that?" Squat asked.

They nodded.

"A friend of my abuelito painted this for him." Squat brushed his fingers over the mural. "He told me that really happened. One day they were out working cattle and he went over a hill near the caprock and saw that exact scene."

All eyes were glued to the wall.

"He used to say it represented life. Just when you think you've made it, got it all figured out, a bird swoops down and tears you apart—or some shit like that." Squat took one final look and then showed his tired friends to their rooms.

The next morning, Squat took them for a ride around the property in the restored '63 Chevy pickup kept under a tarp in the garage, his grandfather's final project before the dementia settled in. It had been done up like the original green with white and chrome accents, quarter-sawn white oak rubbed with linseed oil for the long bed. Squat had learned to drive in it, back when it was spotted with rust and the transmission thunked.

He, Marck, and Webb sat in the cab while Javier, Dave, and Jeff rode in the bed. He drove down a bumpy dirt track where the buffalo grass and mesquite trees had been bladed away. There were a few scattered wildflowers in shades of purple, red, and yellow, but nothing like there had been in spring.

The ranch sat just east of the caprock plateau, where the flat cotton fields fell away, plunging you down into the mesquite- and cactus-tangled cattle country. The mesas, which Squat grew up thinking were sawed-off mountains, could be seen in every direction but west. They came up to a narrow caliche road cutting diagonally across the property, a path the energy company made to access the enormous white wind turbine that now loomed ahead. They all craned their necks when the pickup went underneath it. Even the white box that contained the gears and generator, compact in proportion to the long blades and tower, was as big as their bus.

Squat pointed out the open window to the spot he first learned to hunt, sighting his abuelo's old .22 on desert cottontails. He told the others how if he got one, his abuelo would make him clean it. He didn't tolerate killing for sport. Hunting was either for food or to protect the herd, and since a three-pound rabbit didn't exactly pose a threat to a one-ton Hereford, Squat had to dress what he shot. He retched the first time he did it, his abuelo standing over his shoulder and walking him through the process, but it got easier with practice. He would skin the rabbit, rinse it and his sticky fingers under cold water, and trim away the tendons and connective tissue and damaged meat. Then he would cut the lean stuff into nice little strips they would smoke and make jerky out of. It wasn't as tasty as grilled quail or a venison stew, but it made a way better snack than a Slim Jim.

"You're only supposed to eat them in months with an R though," Squat called out the window. "They get wormy in the summer."

"Good to know," said Jeff.

The bottom half of a slender coachwhip slithered into the brush. The property was rife with creatures: coyotes, jackrabbits, cottontails, javelinas, rattlesnakes, bull snakes, horny toads, hawks, vultures, roadrunners, and the occasional mountain lion, but no cattle. Not since Squat's grandfather passed four years ago. The grama grass and broom weeds had gotten tall and wobbly, and since no one tended to the pastures anymore, the mesquites grew denser all the time.

In the path ahead, Squat noticed something exciting and slid the truck to a stop. He stepped down the caliche path, approaching carefully, while the others watched from the truck. He returned with his hands cupped. He parted them and a spiky head peeked out. The others leaned over to see.

"All that for a horny toad?" Dave said.

"Yeah." Squat looked down at it in awe. It was the color of sand with dark spots, covered in spikes from its tail to the two big horns on its head. They weren't sharp enough to do any damage to your hand, but looked fierce.

"Is that thing deadly?" Marck said, leaning away from the window.

"They're harmless," Squat said, gently stroking its soft pale belly with his pointer finger. Its black eyes narrowed like a dog being scratched behind the ears. "Aren't you?"

"I always heard they could shoot blood from their eyes," Javier said.

"Not the Texas kind," Squat said. "I read something a while back that said there aren't many of them left. People destroyed their habitats, introduced these fire ants that run off all the red ants they like to eat." Squat bent down and let the lizard scamper away. "Be fruitful and multiply, buddy."

Squat threw the truck in drive and said, "I have one more thing to show y'all."

———————

With the bandmates carrying their instruments, Squat led the way to a small cinder block building behind the ranch house. He flicked on the breaker and they went inside. On a folding table was an older computer, audio interface, and a single monitor. There were cables stretched across the floor and a mic stand in the middle. Squat propped the door open and went around knocking off cobwebs.

"This used to be my abuelito's workshop. Now it's my little Abbey Road. Pretty sweet, huh?"

They set their cases down and walked around the room. Javier brushed his fingers across the knobs of the miniature audio interface. He used to be more hands-on with his bands, doing some of the mixing himself. Squat fired up the computer, opened his pirated recording software, and motioned for Javier to sit down. Javier grinned and tried to acquaint himself with the program.

"You've been holding out on us," Dave said, popping the latches on his case.

"Ah, it's not much. My tías let me keep this stuff here," Squat said. "Got a bunch of it at garage sales."

Jeff got his bass set up and laid down a rapid line. Instinct carried the others to their instruments. They plugged in and began to jam. Since lugging the drums out there would take too long, Marck had to adapt. He pulled his sticks out of his back pocket and sat down behind the others with the smaller microphone. He hammered out a simple bum-dah-dah beat on a five-gallon bucket and a hard-shell case. Dave strummed a bright chord progression and then it all clicked.

Squat let loose a beautiful flurry of notes that raised everyone's blood pressure. The band shared glances and nodded in rhythm for a few seconds before returning to their instrumental sanctuaries. Marck stared straight ahead, not even looking at his makeshift drums. He made rhythm on everything he could find: the low and hollow beat of the bucket, the metallic clink of the mic stand, and the solid thwack of the case. Javier turned up Marck's mic so the others wouldn't drown him out.

Jeff rocked his head back and forth with his tongue protruding slightly between his teeth and lips. Dave's eyes were shut and he tapped the sole of his left boot every fourth strum. Javier adjusted the gain and nodded to the beat. Squat stared down at his left hand on the fretboard in apparent astonishment, like it was the ghost appendage of a long-gone guitar god.

When Javier found out the first two songs Squat learned were "Malagueña" and "Hound Dog," it all made sense. That foundation still held up after all the other influences he'd piled on. Squat's style united electrified flamenco fingerpicking and the satisfying flatpicked solos of old-school rock and blues. It was all on display, and he coupled it beautifully.

The moment came as a great relief to Javier. He was able to let go and enjoy the music. He looked at each of the bandmates, trusting each other to feel out the progressions, keep the music flowing, and fill in with just the right amount of texture and style. About five minutes in, the music slowed, got quieter. Dave walked the concrete floor, strumming while facing Marck, then Squat, then Jeff individually for several beats. Nodding and strumming harder, asking without words if they were ready. Suddenly, Squat unleashed a hellhound of a solo that engulfed them all.

The band filled in the blank spaces around Squat's furious Latin note spree and together they rushed the horizon and hit the crescendo right in time. Then, as swift and natural as the music started, it stopped. No one dared to speak a word. They all basked in the creative wonder that still hung thick in the air. Javier clicked the stop button and the waveform halted. Dave draped his arm over Squat's shoulder. Jeff and Marck looked like kids when they gave each other a leaping high-five. It reminded Javier of what hooked him in the first place.

The first time he saw them play was at a grimy sports bar called The Dusty Dawg in Lubbock. It was early October 2014. They went onstage right after K-State had finished beating the Red Raiders like a dirty rug. Half the crowd had left at halftime. The ones who stuck around for the live music craved something familiar. Javier was impressed with the band's repertoire. They obliged requests for Josh Abbott and ZZ Top, peppering in their own off-the-wall covers of everyone from Lightnin' Hopkins to Calibre 50.

Javier admired their work from the shadows. It seemed like there wasn't a song they couldn't make their own. The strategy of most bar bands was to play songs that the drunken audience could sing along to, and while the crowd didn't know the words to "Mujer de Todos, Mujer de Nadie," they stuck around and cheered when they finished "Just Got

Paid." The band followed that with a string of energetic originals and somehow, by the end of the hour, they had the place rocking. Javier invited them to his booth after their set. They talked over the bro country pumping through the speakers, which seemed plastic and lifeless compared to what had just transpired.

He bought them beers and got their story. They were Tech dropouts with massive student loans. They had no savings—which were hard to accumulate, Squat admitted, when you take out a payday advance just to spend it all on stompboxes. The bar gigs earned them enough to keep the lights on in their cheap rent house in Arnett-Benson, where they had invented a drinking game called Gunshots or Fireworks.

Daywork, music lessons, and a ramen diet got them through the tough stretches. They weren't model workers, would never fit into the world of timesheets and memos, but they were completely dedicated to their craft. They would make it in the music business or die trying. He became their first manager by the end of the night.

Javier stared at the motionless sound waves on the screen. He wondered why they were so set on making all that money for recording equipment. Albums weren't as vital as they used to be. If you ever got established, the real money was in live shows. In any case, they had enough cash right now to get into a decent studio and cut an EP. If that wasn't enough to get them noticed, then maybe it just wasn't their time yet. Part of him wanted to scream at them, "You're young! Forget this whole coyote mess and just make your music. It may not happen as soon as you like, but it'll happen."

But he didn't say that, even if it was the truth. Because that would mean giving up a position he wasn't ready to let go of. Javier felt all the eyes on him and looked up from the computer. They were talented and headstrong but still needed so much validation. They trusted Javier to tell it to them straight.

Chapter 3

1984

MOST MIGRANTS TRIED TO MAKE IT ON FOOT. THE CROSSINGS in populated areas, the easiest to get to, often had officers lying in wait. Sometimes big groups would rush over all at once, thinking that la migra couldn't catch all of them. Sometimes they were right. Four young men from a nearby town tried that. Two were detained near the river and another got deported within the week. The final one found work picking peaches and pears on Colorado's western slope.

Charging the border like that gave a person about the same odds as a desperate boxer throwing a haymaker. Those who preferred a stealthier approach took to the desert, treacherous rocky lands that seemed to reach into eternity when the sun was at its peak. Truly wild country where death came in a hundred varieties, and the vultures and insects and heat could erase every last trace of a body. Traveling without a guide who had the paths memorized—even a boy as green as Javier knew that wasn't wise.

Paying a coyote to be escorted across gave a migrant the best chance, but it was expensive. They demanded at least three hundred American dollars per person, more if they took you by truck. Javier's mother had warned him about them, how most were cold and unconcerned with the fates of their passengers. The ones who stuck around had only one redeeming quality: being good at not getting caught.

Javier worked on his plan for crossing over but knew he had to get close first. His home in southeastern Coahuila was about 350 kilometers from the nearest border city of Nuevo Laredo. To get in range he would ride the trains. Mexican freight trains allowed migrants to move quickly across the country and avoid immigration checkpoints. People in search of better lives rode on boxcars for days on end.

There was a reason migrants called the train La Bestia. The Beast. Javier heard the stories about people who tried to stay awake for as long as possible but eventually nodded off when no one else was watching. They were bounced from the train, sucked under the wheels, and chewed up before anyone realized they were missing. La Bestia just chugged on into the dark night. Others didn't duck when they should have—under a tree branch or the concrete arch of a tunnel. Dead on the tracks either way.

Riding on the tops of train cars was illegal, but since most locomotives hauled fifty or more cars, it was almost impossible to police. Javier had heard other stories, that if the federales ever did make a bust, they would only target a group of people. They knew they couldn't catch everyone, so they targeted one or two specific cars. They cornered passengers, roughed them up, and shook them down for anything valuable.

Even the ones who made it still had to cross the border. La Bestia could only get Javier close. He tried to put that out of his mind while he trekked to the nearest train depot. The midday was warm and dry with the faint scent of pine blowing in from the hills. He sat in the shade of a white shed and ate a cold tortilla with beans.

A cow across the tracks sniffed at one of the rosy fruits on a prickly pear. Javier wrinkled his nose, remembering the time his own curiosity led him to grab one of the fruits, his amazement at its bright gooey innards turning to alarm when he felt the dozens of tiny amber needles in his fingers. The cow sauntered off.

He noticed two young men farther down the tracks, sitting with their shirts around their necks. He wondered if their plans were the same.

The locomotive blew shrilly in the distance. When the northbound train screeched to a stop, Javier slung on his backpack and started to walk down the length of the train. This one only had twenty or so cars, and many of them were tankers with no space to ride. He finally spotted a couple of boxcars farther back, but they already had people hunkered down on top.

Javier kept walking south, seeing car after car with no space for him to climb aboard. He saw the young men from the tracks climb up on a ladder. The first tried to persuade the people up there to make room while the other hung on to the ladder. Javier thought he could piggyback with them.

"Disculpe." Javier tried to squeeze onto the ladder, his feet barely off the ground.

The guy scowled. "No," he said, and when Javier didn't stop, he stomped his hand, making Javier let go and land back on the ground.

Javier got flustered and his breaths shortened. He felt like he might cry, but he choked back the tears. Just as he was about to give up, he saw an opening on the second to last car. He ran over and climbed up the ladder. There were two teenagers on top, a boy and a girl, both lean and stern beyond their years. They looked him up and down for a measured moment and then went back to their conversation. He crossed his legs and put his backpack in his lap. He made sure his canteen and the picture were still inside.

Soon the horn blew and the train picked up steam. Javier looked out across the brush and the ocotillo. The year had started off dry, but they had some good rain the last few weeks. The cactus was full of rich red fruit. It would have made his mother happy. The thought hit him that he was abandoning their crops in good wet soil. Guilt tugged at his heart. He wondered what would become of it all. The rules were strict with ejidos. The plots couldn't be sold, only passed down, and they had to stay in use. If not, the land would go to the other ejidatarios. Javier wondered about the animals. He'd miss the goats. Would his uncle tend to them or sell them off? Would he even care?

Doubt rushed into Javier's head. He wanted to get off the train and go back. He crawled to the edge and looked straight down at the pale rocks zooming by. It was too late. He sat back down and gripped his backpack. Then he remembered something that brought him some peace—the last conversation he and his mother had about the farm, a week before her diagnosis.

She told him that he shouldn't ever get too sentimental about it. That if he had a better opportunity he should take it, so long as it made him happy. The farm and all their memories there would always be a part of him, even if he lived the rest of his life in a big city. The memory made the tears well up, but it strengthened his will. He had made his choice. He had to go on.

The train rolled, and Javier passed the time by locating an object in the distance, a boulder or a plastic bag on the edge of the tracks, and staring at it while it came closer and closer and eventually disappeared. He did this for a while, keeping his eyes occupied while his mind ran through scenarios about his arrival into the USA. He imagined standing on the very front of the train, above the engineer, with his feet planted firmly and his fists on his hips in a hero's pose. The wind tussling his hair, and the other migrants huddled behind him, whispering things like "He's so brave" and "Can you believe this is his first time?"

He imagined standing tall while the train crossed over the border, la migra looking into his brown eyes and then letting him pass because of the determination they saw in them. A grin spread across Javier's face while he dreamed these things, about everything going right. He continued to stare down at the tracks until a voice snapped him out of it.

"Aguas!" someone shouted from ahead.

Javier's head jerked, just in time to see a tree branch, longer than the car was wide and only clearing the top by a couple of feet, zooming toward him. He pushed off the metal surface hard with his hands and knees, sending him backward and spiraling over onto his belly. He flattened himself as much as he could, squeezing his face and his chest and his shins so close to the car's slanted roof that he thought he might break through. He felt it whoosh over him, from toe to head. He raised his head a few inches and saw that the limb had gone on past. Javier looked the other direction, to make sure it hadn't called in any reinforcements, and saw that it was clear.

He pushed himself up and realized that he was not alone. Everyone else did the same, cautiously rose, looked wide-eyed at their surroundings, checked to make sure friends weren't hurt. There was still the endless galumph of the train, but the humans were quiet, which suggested no one had been struck. They were lucky this time.

The teenagers behind him, who had previously done their best to avoid even looking in Javier's direction, now stared at him. He stared back. Javier had originally wanted to be left alone, to simply bide his time until he could leave the train with all its desperate passengers behind. Now it struck him that they were all in the same boat, and each would have to do some rowing.

"Cómo estás, chavo?" the girl asked.

"Bien," Javier replied. "Y tú?"

2015

Everyone sat at the long dining table. Jeff's girlfriend, Victoria, told a story about an elderly patient at the hospital where she worked. The man had dementia and was convinced he was on vacation on the Gulf Coast. He'd throw his gown in the wastebasket and walk down the hall naked, asking which way to the beach.

"I gave up trying to convince him he's not there," Victoria said. "So now I just tell him I'm a lifeguard and the beach is shut down due to shark attacks. He always tries to push back on that, but I tell him it will be open tomorrow for sure. Now go back to your room, Mr. McAllister."

Victoria's cousin Mari cackled and sipped her beer.

"Always tomorrow," Victoria said with weariness in her eyes.

Squat's current fling, high-spirited redhead Sarah, sat on his lap. She took the plastic cup from his hand, gulped, and handed it back. She had brought her friends Talia and Bonnie. The women were more than welcome after so many days of just them on the bus. When Sarah introduced her friends, she had put extra emphasis on the presentation of

Bonnie, a pretty woman in her forties, to Javier. He knew matchmaking when he saw it.

"So when are you going to play for us?" Talia asked. Dark satiny curls came down the shoulders of her shimmery black and gold top, and her red lips parted to show a set of perfect teeth.

"We're not," Dave said without making eye contact.

"Yeah, we're on vacation." Squat scrunched his nose. "That's kind of like inviting a psychologist to a party and then lying on the couch and making him ask you questions about your parents."

Sarah turned around and pinched the inside of his arm. He yowled.

"Be nice," she said. "And you should really learn to spell psychologist before you compare yourself to one."

"I know how to spell it," Squat said.

"Just one song," Talia said, holding up her index finger.

"I don't think she's gonna drop this," Bonnie said.

Talia shook her head and smiled. Bonnie shrugged and met Javier's eyes.

"Aw, why not," Jeff said. "Guys, quit acting like you don't want to jam."

Talia pumped her fist and grinned. Jeff grinned back, not picking up on Victoria's sideways glance.

"Later though. We have to get warmed up." Dave drained his can.

"Deal," Talia said.

They killed the partial of whiskey they'd found in the cabinet. Jeff poured the last few drops into his glass. They waited for Marck to break up enough weed to fill a blunt. Dave snatched Jeff's glasses and did his spot-on impression of Wendell Henderson. He was the exuberant, five-foot-nothing owner of the Stardust Saloon, and the first person to give the band a break, booking them for regular weekend gigs at his small bar near Texas Tech. Dave pursed his lips out and gave that unimpressed look over the rim of Jeff's chunky glasses.

"Y'all better play s'good it draws people in off the *street*," Dave said. Between Texas twang and the graceful singsong tone of his voice, his vowels seemed to bend and float and go on forever, just like Wendell's. "Cause, boys, I just checked, and ain't *nobody* out there. Poor Maria ain't even got nobody to flirt with at the bawr."

Sarah's coarse laugh was contagious. Jokes seemed funnier when she cracked up. Javier loosened up and hit the blunt a couple of times when it looped around to him. He knew it would be a long while before he'd have the chance again. He'd need to be razor-edged the rest of the way, but for now the steady mellow of the sativa crept in his skull and he settled into his seat.

"Hey, where's your liquor stash?" Talia asked.

"Stash? That was it," Squat said. All eyes darted toward him. "But, uh, I know a place we can get more."

The crack and hiss of the last beer can filled the room.

"Let's," Jeff said.

Squat roped Javier into riding along for the eight-mile drive to the nearest hooch market. The county had gone wet a few years back, but you still couldn't buy hard liquor in city limits. That's where Los Ybanez came in. The little community, populated by eighteen people, grew to about fifty on any given Saturday night, along with eleven dogs and a half-dozen chickens. If a person parked on the shoulder of Highway 87, they could look down the dirt road to the liquor store and see a line of white headlights coming and a line of red brake lights going, both extending back as far as the eye could see, until the dust kicked up by their tires engulfed them.

Around the drive-thru store were houses with unfenced yards, holes in their screen doors, mailboxes covered in bird droppings. To describe the community as a shell of itself would be to miss the fact that it was a shell to begin with, just like the leaning wooden frame of an abandoned construction project down the path. Forgotten but still standing, still hanging on.

They bought fifths of tequila and bourbon and a thirty-pack. Squat cranked up the radio and Tom Petty's "American Girl" ricocheted around the cab and into the breezy cool dark. They drove off, spinning the tires as the truck turned onto the caliche road.

"To the long road ahead." Squat raised his glass.

They drank their tequila down and the band took up their instruments. They found a plywood box for Marck to sit on and pound out a rhythm with his hands. He winked at Mari, and her eyes gleamed over the rim of her cup.

"Any requests?" Squat said, settling the guitar in his lap.

They looked at Talia, but she just shrugged. "Surprise me."

"What about 'Down by the Playa Lake'?" Victoria asked.

Jeff furrowed his brow. "That's more of a personal song, babe. Too introspective. We need party music," he said, raising his palms. Talia lifted her cup and wooed. Victoria crossed her arms and leaned back.

It was never just one song. They covered Dr. Dog and then Merle Haggard before moving on to Squat's favorite band: Los Lobos. They melded around Jeff and Marck's groove and made each song their own. As much as they wanted to sound like other bands when they started out, they found it was impossible. Back then it was a talent gap. They had to improvise and compromise to get the songs where they could handle them. Then it became the challenge of seeing how far they could stretch a song. Sometimes the result was awful and sometimes it was magic. Squat shot off a star-bright solo at the end of "El Canelo" that got the girls cheering. Webb even. Bonnie put her fingers in her mouth and whistled. She grinned and so did Javier.

Not long after the instruments were packed up, the party fizzled out. Victoria had a shift at the hospital the next morning, so she and her cousin headed back. Mari gave Marck her number on the way out. Jeff and Victoria made out on the porch, and he swaggered back in a while later.

Sarah asked if she and Talia and Bonnie could crash, and no one batted an eye. More drinks were made, but the mood had changed. Like a good joke with bad timing, the alcohol did its usual work but felt unwieldy in their bones. It was late. Blue-tinted LED bulbs filled in the blank spaces in ways the stray rays of sunlight hadn't. They exposed and highlighted things like the dark pouches under Javier's eyes, standing out against his brown skin. Like the small shiny spots up on Dave's scalp, the ones that suggested his flowing locks would give way to a vast hairless gap in the next decade or so. Like the weird patterns reflected on the empty silver beer cans piled up around them. They pulsed from light to dark continuously as the fan's blades cut through the blue light again and again.

They nursed their last round and then retired for the night. Squat, with his arm around Sarah's waist, pointed out where all the blankets, beds, and couches were and told them goodnight. Webb said he'd be on the bus if anybody needed him. Marck made a cot on the couch. Dave and Talia laughed and talked in low tones by the fridge and then went into the second bedroom with a couple of margaritas on the rocks.

Javier sipped his last beer and Bonnie came and sat across from him. Her expression didn't give away much, but her blue eyes were lively. Her skin was smooth except for a few creases on her forehead that told Javier some vague story about attrition and hard-boiled men.

"How do you put up with them all day?" she said.

Javier held up his beer and she laughed. "Nah, they're good guys. Damn fine musicians. They're just young . . . and stupid."

"Doesn't seem like that long ago I was their age. I was as dumb as them," she took a drink and gave Javier a mischievous look. "I just didn't know it yet."

She spoke without urgency. Her voice had less of the local nasally twang and more East Texas drawl. It didn't surprise Javier when she told him she lived in Nacogdoches until she was eight. Her father had moved the family to Andrews because of an oil field job when she was sixteen, and she'd been in the area ever since.

"You miss Nac?" Javier asked.

"Not really," she said. "But I don't think I'd miss here either."

Javier nodded. "I try to tell people about the dust storms and they just don't get it. It's hard to picture an enormous wall of dirt rolling in and blocking out the sun until you're here."

"Y'all have it figured out," Bonnie said. "Staying on the road."

Javier shrugged. "Everything gets old if you do it enough. Even change."

"Yeah," she said. "I guess it does."

Javier glanced at the clock and wondered where the time had gone. Squat ambled through in his boxers for a glass of water. Though obviously drunk, he set the overturned bottles upright and pulled Marck's blanket back over him before touching the portrait of his abuelos and heading back to bed.

Javier yawned.

"Sleepy?" Bonnie said.

"A little," Javier said.

"I think there's a free bedroom."

Javier felt his mouth open.

"Don't get too excited," she said. "I'm past one-night stands. At least on weeknights. I bet there's room for both of us in that bed though."

"You could be right." Javier set his empty can down and grinned.

———————

A six-beat birdsong woke Javier. He turned his head, and the fat gray dove perched outside the window bent its neck and stared back. Sunlight sifted through the thin curtains, but he didn't feel rested. He'd drunk more the last couple of nights than in the last few weeks combined, and alcohol only granted the illusion of sleep.

Javier rolled onto his back. The comforter was folded back on the other side, the nightstand empty where Bonnie's purse had been. Javier rubbed his eyes and sat up, questioning for a split second if he'd dreamed it all. But he pieced together the night.

They had talked for a while, lying on their sides and making eyes at each other. Javier remembered talking about his mother, something he didn't do with many people, and—did he start crying? He couldn't remember. They'd brought the bourbon into the bedroom and it got kind of blurry at that point. He did remember her kiss, soft and warm, and the glow he felt when their skin touched. He had brushed against that old-time thrill, but moments like that were bound to end too fast. A foundry fire destined to cool and harden into a moment they couldn't carry with them. She left without telling him bye.

He sat up, and it felt like a leather strap had been cinched around his head. He clamped his eyes shut until it eased up. His worries had been out of mind for a bit, the hose kinked, but now they burst out. *What if they got pulled for extra screening at the border? What if they ran into the cartel in Juárez? What if the band decided they were done? What if*

43

everyone found out how clueless he really was?

He shook his head hard, like he could scramble the negative thoughts back into brain dust. He stared at the midnight blue comforter stitched with golden cowboys and horses. He had to get it together. They were headed for the farthest reaches of Texas and into Mexico. The borderlands, where conflict was certain.

On the far nightstand was a notepad with a feed store's name and address at the top. Javier held the handwritten message up to his face and squinted. *Tried to wake you, but you were OUT. It was great meeting you. Call me next time you're in town.* Her phone number was underneath, all ten digits. He smiled to himself and carefully placed the note in his wallet. The worries weren't gone, but they had been swept into the back corner for the time being.

He lingered under the hot water in the shower, put on fresh clothes, and then dug his second phone out. He swept back the damp hair that clung to his forehead and punched their contact's number in, the one who was setting up the deal in Juárez. It rang and rang and eventually said the number didn't have voicemail set up. Then a burst of laughter came from outside. Javier eased the screen door behind him and took a seat in the circle.

"You know damn well that's not how it's pronounced," Jeff said.

"Salmon," Dave said, emphasizing the L.

"The L's silent," Marck said with a cloud of smoke.

"Everyone I know pronounces it that way," Dave said.

"Well you run around with some dull people," Jeff said, taking the joint.

"Tell me about it," Dave said. He continued, "Okay, tell me this. What do you call the bacteria that gets you sick if you eat undercooked chicken?"

"Salmonella," Squat said.

"A-ha," Dave shouted and pointed at him. "Why pronounce the L there and drop it for sa-mon?"

They stared at him blankly. They had this argument often. This one, or one like it. Javier leaned into his lawn chair and linked his fingers behind his head. They were burning daylight, but he was the one who had overslept. The band had already seen the girls off, eaten breakfast, and sparked a joint—their last until after the El Paso show, they assured him—by the time he was up and ready. Webb flipped on the radio and tuned it past a country song about drinking on the beach and an erectile dysfunction commercial, stopping when a flustered man's Texan growl filled the porch. There was no way his face wasn't diaper-rash red, ranting about the government.

"Not this guy," Jeff said. "Webb, you're better than this."

"I know he's a kook," Webb said. "But he's gotten some stuff right, *big stuff* that the mainstream media still don't acknowledge."

The husky voice went on about the globalists' mind control techniques, how they keep the working class distracted and self-destructive, the middle class comfortable and complacent. He talked enough for three men, stacking seemingly unrelated topics like a layer cake made out of pumpernickel, chocolate, and sardines. He floated off on a tangent about technology and how the Silicon Valley techies had sold out the human race to interdimensional aliens in exchange for their algorithms. He said that fluoride in the water was child's play now. These people, by way of alien rendezvous, were reprogramming humanity through radio waves in attention-sucking devices. They were leading us to extinction.

"I can't listen to this right now." Squat shook his head. "We need music."

He handed off the joint and tuned the radio to KPET. An old Waylon Jennings song was playing. He sank back into his chair, but his hard-set brow and cavernous brown eyes showed he was already stuck in a thought.

"He wasn't exactly wrong," Dave said. Jeff crossed his arms and waited for the explanation. "I mean, yeah, the alien thing is batshit, but the indifference that society drills into people? That's as real as anything. Billionaires and politicians don't want more people involved in the process. They want us distracted. They love how much we stare into our phones. And look where it takes us: we feel empty, consume, self-promote, rinse, and repeat."

Marck nodded. "Social media. That's as shallow as it gets."

"Yeah," Dave said. "I keep saying I'm gonna delete all that shit off my phone. It's fake people selling fake images."

"Well they're not all fake," Jeff said. "A lot of it starts with genuine feeling. The problem is the way it's commodified. Here's my hot take on the time change. Twenty-four likes. Here's a picture of my kid eating watermelon. Eighty-three likes."

"Here's a tribute to my grandpa who doesn't even have an account," Dave said. "But I'm going to post his picture and talk to him like he does. A hundred and twenty-one likes."

"I never understood that." Webb shook his head.

"We all bash it, but we fall back into the pattern. Scrolling and liking and streaming like it means something. Like it's anything other than a pacifier for our minds," Dave said.

"It does mean something. It gives us a voice to shout back at this interstate wreck of a world we live in. It connects us," Jeff said. "Think about our music. None of the traditional labels want any part of us. If we didn't put our demo online, only our moms would have heard it."

"Your mom for sure." Dave bumped his eyebrows. "She likes my range."

"Eat a dick."

"Mmhmm."

"Technology isn't all bad," Marck chimed in. "I just don't think we have the self-control to handle it. And the people making it know that."

Squat leaned in. His eyes had gone glassy, but he was paying very close attention. Javier refused the joint when Dave tried to hand it to him and crossed his shin over his knee.

"We can use that stuff as a tool or as a drug," Javier said. "I used to crave beer so bad after days nothing went right. Now it's the urge to check my phone, and it's always right here with me. I think about chunking it out the window sometimes, but then I'd be even more out of the loop than I am now."

"Drugs, tools, whatever. We need to put them down and smell the damn flowers every once in a while," Webb said. He eyed the joint the way a dog looks at a jar of cooling bacon grease when Dave passed it across him.

"I don't think it's an either-or deal," Jeff said. "You can be present *with* technology. Our problem is we're half in the real world and half in our phones, not really experiencing either one. Maybe the future is total immersion in the tech. Look up transhumanism. What they're doing will blow your mind."

"Don't bogart that." Squat stuck out his hand, but Jeff didn't notice.

"Like dudes putting on wigs and wearing cocktail dresses?" Webb said. "That's been fairly common since the Clinton administration."

Jeff ignored him and said, "What's it matter if our reality is natural or artificial?" He used the joint for emphasis. Squat tried to follow it with his hand. "I mean what's natural anyway? When a cub comes out deformed, the mama bear eats it. A male dolphin will kill some female's calf just so he can knock her up himself. That's as natural as it gets, man. How can a virtual reality be any worse than that?"

Squat finally got ahold of Jeff's wrist and took what was left of the joint with his other hand. Dave looked like he was trying to work through something in his head.

"Nah, man. Being alive, breathing salt off the ocean, getting your heart broke, touching boobs, that's what it's all about." Dave held up his hands to illustrate. "You can't just upload a human's mind into an android and say it's still that person. You just copied some data. That's a clone. Your soul can't be broken down into zeroes and ones."

"Well that's if you believe in a soul," Marck said.

Jeff pointed at him in agreement.

"How can you not believe you have a soul?" Webb said. "Were you not hugged as a child?"

"Alright, alright," Jeff said. "Let's not go down this road again. The point I was trying to make is that technology is going to keep advancing, getting more immersive, whether we want it to or not. We might as well embrace it."

"I have more faith in people," Dave said. "It feels wrong to assume the next generation is going to be even more sucked into the trap. Some will, sure. But we survive, man. We evolve. Who's to say they won't catch on to those tricks tech companies got us hooked with? They'll see our old asses with our noses in our outdated phones, taking filtered selfies at the nursing home, and go: *Whoa, I don't want to live like that.*"

"Yeah, because they'll have their own better technology by then," Marck said. "By the time there's brain implants, how do you take a step back?"

"Total immersion." Jeff nodded.

"The government ain't putting no chip in my head. I can tell you that right now," Webb said.

"Cheer up," Jeff said. "We'll be dead by then anyway. We might not even make it to the next iPhone at the rate we're at."

The silence was heavy now. Squat mashed the roach into the dirt. Javier glanced at his watch.

"We should head out."

They loaded their stuff, and Squat locked up the house. The others waited around outside, looking out at the caprock and breathing in the unusually cool morning air. The sky was easy blue, the sun rays golden through feathery clouds. They'd run out of jokes and philosophy. Though Javier didn't want to bring it up, it felt like they were thinking the same thing: that this might be their last bit of peace for a while.

The bus struggled up the caprock. Mesas and buttes and mesquite-dotted pastures leveled off into a world of disorienting flatness. After the stand of white wind turbines along the cap, only highline wires and the occasional house and barn broke up the selfsame expanse. Every reach of the eye showed miles and miles of cotton fields. It all used to be grassland, Javier had recently read, the buffalo hunting grounds of the Comanche. People who weren't used to the landscape often lost their way, scorched or frozen to death if they wandered from the trail. The land was all cultivated and tamed now, perfect row after row of knee-high plants, but the sea of green highlighted the vastness of the place just the same.

Squat noodled on his guitar and ended up staring at his finger-prints for a long while. Marck napped. Dave and Jeff tried to write a new song but got stuck on the first verse and picked up their phones instead. Javier picked up *Empire of the Summer Moon*, a book about Quanah Parker and the Comanche, but he kept forgetting what he read, his mind wandering off and then coming back to the same sentence again and again.

They were all a little spacey, whether they had smoked or not. Reality was settling back in. They were not in the clear, not by a long shot. In fact, they were heading toward the trembling darkness on the horizon. The funnel cloud of fear they had been able to put out of their minds for a couple of days descended once again.

Chapter 4

1984

IT HAD BEEN DARK FOR WHAT SEEMED LIKE A WHOLE DAY by the time the train arrived at the depot on the edge of Monterrey. Javier knew that falling asleep could kill him, but knowing didn't take away the temptation. He had to keep pinching his arm and fixing his posture, squinting at the fuzzy outlines of mountains just a shade darker than the sky. He had barely been able to see the people on the next car. He could only make out their hunched outlines when they moved.

Javier was glad to see the pale-yellow light in the distance when they neared the city. He got his second wind then, watching the outskirts of walled-in warehouses and overpasses with colorful graffiti. As soon as the train stopped, people dismounted and scurried to find places to wait until another northbound train departed.

Javier stood on the gravel near the tracks and tugged on the neck of his shirt. Monterrey's night air hung warm and thick. It wasn't long before he could feel sweat soaking his shirt beneath the backpack. He walked across the tracks, hopping rusty couplings and looking both ways before crossing an empty track. Streams of people up ahead, a few he recognized from the train, headed to what looked like a food vendor. When he got closer he saw that it was a booth serving free meals. They had a banner next to the booth with an outline of Our Lady of Guadalupe and some words underneath:

Así como yo los he amado, también ustedes deben amarse los unos a los otros.

It was something Jesus said. His mother used the verse to explain why it was important to help out those who were worse off. Javier asked a woman headed that way who the people were, and she explained that they were a volunteer group from the church who helped migrants on their journey to the United States. They didn't physically help anyone cross the border, but they would show up at crossroads and depots to provide food and basic medical care.

Javier approached the booth, set up beside an old Ford truck, and waited for the line to burn down. He received two corn tortillas and a cup of stew, which he took to an empty boxcar with an open door. He sat with his legs dangling off the side. The stew intensified the muggy climate. It made his skin flush with warmth from each sip. He wished he had something cold to drink, but his hunger wouldn't let him put it down. About the time he finished, the teenage couple from the train came and asked if they could sit with him. They sat in silence for a while. Javier tipped the cup up to get the last of the stew into his belly.

He looked around, noticed that they were alone. There had been other riders nearby, but they had finished their food and gone back to find the herd. There were two lights in the distance that seemed to be getting closer. Just as he was about to ask the teenagers if they were seeing the lights, he turned to find a pocketknife inches from his throat, part darkened by the shadows, part glinting in the moonlight. Javier leaned away, but the blade followed him, nearing his soft skin.

"Alto. Ahorita," the young man said, squeezing the bone handle in his right hand.

Javier froze. The young woman picked up his backpack and rifled through it. She took the remaining snacks and the canteen of water and put them in her drawstring bag. She took out the carefully folded clothes, a red shirt and a pair of jeans, and studied them for a moment before shoving them back into Javier's backpack. Javier prayed silently that she would not find the picture. She zipped up the main compartment and held the backpack with both hands. She looked at the smaller front pouch and then at Javier.

He tried not to tip her off, but his face betrayed him. He felt his eyebrows squeeze in, like they wanted to attack each other across the bridge of his nose. She stared at him and unzipped the front compartment. Javier opened his mouth to yell, but he felt the blade, now touching his neck. The young woman's hand went inside and came back to the surface with the picture of him and his mother framed in gold, his good luck charm.

The woman looked at it and then at Javier with something like sympathy. She stared at the picture of mother and child for a long moment and swallowed. The blade wasn't touching Javier's neck anymore. She began to undo the clasps on the back of the frame, but the sudden noise of metal on metal filled the car. They jerked their heads toward the door, but nothing had changed. It must have come from the next car down. The woman shoved the frame, picture and all, into her bag and slung it over her shoulder. The man collapsed the pocketknife and slid it into his jeans.

"Regresa a casa, chamaco."

Without another look in Javier's direction, they jumped down from the car and disappeared into the shadows. He sat there a minute, trying to will his heart to stop beating so fast. Fright had passed and anger hadn't yet arrived. He only knew the blank rushing sensation of shock. He felt the sudden need to distance himself from the spot he was sitting on. He put his arms through his almost-empty backpack and stepped to the edge of the car's open door. A bright light shone on him and made him cover his face.

"Alto," a man said.

Javier was sick of people telling him to stop. Where was he going to go? The man brought his flashlight down a bit, out of Javier's eyes, and he could see that the man was a federal, dressed in the navy-blue suit and hat. He asked Javier to step down and then asked about his purpose on the train. Javier was too tired for far-fetched explanations, so he just replied, "Me voy a los Estados Unidos."

The officer then asked if he had any money on him. Javier told him that he did not, but the man looked through his backpack anyway. He looked disappointed, a little bored, when he found only the shirt and pants. He handed it all back to Javier, and just stood for a minute, frowning with his meaty hands on his hips. Javier looked straight ahead, not really believing that all of what he had experienced, was experiencing that night, was real. He zoned in and out as the man plainly told him that they were taking him in, that he would be sent back home in the morning, asking if he was sure he didn't have any money.

2015

Billowing clouds burned off into a bright expanse. The furrows and pivots of the high plains turned into barbed wire and creosote bush. Faded blue mountains awaited them like apparitions over the horizon. They stopped in Alpine for a bite. The guys were craving Whataburger but—realizing they were somehow still in Texas and yet 140 miles from the nearest one—settled for Dairy Queen. Javier and Webb walked in and ordered a mess of burgers, steak fingers, cokes, and flipped ice cream. Waiting by the condiments, Webb obviously had something on his mind.

"Do you know I've been fired thirteen times?" he finally said.

Javier looked at him and parted his lips. Webb continued, "Most of those weren't in the music business. The first time I got fired I was seventeen, working in a wrecking yard. The boss had just bought an old LeSabre, but I didn't know that. It was parked near the compacter, so I loaded it in, thought it was one of the nicest junkers I'd seen. That one hurt."

"Number eleven, your order is ready," a young man with smudged glasses and a red polo two sizes too large called out.

"Another time I was selling pot to the college kids at Tech. The fella who brought me in told me the frat crowd was full of easy marks, just looking to spend daddy's money. Well it turned out they were sharper than he gave them credit for. I'd show up to a party to sell a few dime bags and they'd end up convincing me to fire them up, telling me how cool I was, having their girlfriends flirt with me. Wasn't until I got home that I realize all the weed was gone and I had no money to show for it. I got my ass whupped good for that one."

"Number twelve, your order is ready."

Javier and Webb collected the brown paper sacks so greasy they were see-through.

"Where are you going with this?" Javier asked.

"Well, you worked with me before, when I roadied for that tay-hano group of yours."

Javier nodded, still not sure what Webb was getting at.

"Why'd you pick me for this? I mean, I hate to be the one to break it to you, but I'm a loser," Webb said.

Javier grabbed a fistful of ketchup packets and dropped them into the bag. He rolled the top down and looked Webb in the eye.

"You may not have the greatest resume," Javier said.

Webb nodded in agreement.

"Or be the most tech-savvy."

He pursed his lips and nodded some more.

"Or the brightest."

Webb stopped nodding. His face screwed into a frown.

"You don't have the most street smarts either—"

Javier paused and topped off his drink from the fountain.

"But you know what you do have?"

"No?" Webb said.

"Loyalty," Javier said. "You put the team before yourself."

He stood face-to-face with Webb and placed his free hand on his shoulder.

"Those things are replaceable. I can get them from other people," Javier said. "What you have, in this business, I can't."

Webb grinned the whole way back to the bus. While they ate, Javier felt his second phone vibrate. He wiped the grease off his hands, saw it was a Chihuahua number, and stepped outside. They had just done business on word of mouth so far, using some of Javier's connections, but for the deal in Juárez he was using a middleman. Someone to find the customers, make sure they had the money, and deliver them.

"Bueno."

"Javier?"

"Yeah."

"You know who this is?"

He did, and hearing his voice put him on edge. His name was Ricky Madrid. A contact in Lubbock had put Javier onto him. He warned Javier that while Ricky was relatively stable, as far as coyotes go, he still had ties to the cartels. People who tried to navigate the Juárez underworld without those connections didn't last.

While the violence in other parts of Mexico had begun to taper off, Juárez was still raging. Javier's contact had first met Ricky years ago, when Ricky led him across the Chihuahuan Desert on foot. Ricky had a partner back then. The partner got himself busted by la migra, allegedly. But there were other rumors, and Ricky knew the desert's secret places like the back of his hand. Javier was warned to keep his eyes open.

"I have four ready to go," Ricky said. "But are you sure you don't want more? If you have an RV, you could fit a dozen no problem."

"Maybe, but it's the ones crammed in like sardines that get caught."

"Ah, a cautious man. I can respect that."

"You sure they can pay?" Javier said. "I don't want any sob stories or to hear about some rich relative in the US I can track down for the money. Cash up front or no ride."

"Relax. They're good for the money. I checked," Ricky said.

He and Javier worked out the details of when and where they would meet in Juárez the next night. Ricky would receive 10 percent of the cash for his troubles. The line went quiet for a moment and Javier assumed he had hung up until Ricky spoke again.

"Don't step on any toes in the ciudad. I can't do business with dead men."

He knew Ricky was messing with him, but it wasn't much of a joke. Getting your throat cut was a rather nice way of ending your life by cartel standards. At least there'd be a funeral your family could attend, might even get an open casket with the right postmortem cosmetics. The people who were decapitated, mutilated, hung from highway overpasses with Old Testament messages of vengeance carved into their corpses, they weren't so lucky.

Chapter 5

1984

THE DRIVER OF THE WHITE VAN PUT ON HIS RIGHT TURN signal. He drove at ten and two, taking a hand off occasionally to rustle for another piece of candy that smelled of tamarind and chile. The radio stayed off, and the full-blast A/C drowned out his labored nasal breathing. His close-set eyes would rise up and check on the kids in the rearview mirror, and then he'd pop another candy in his mouth.

What happened in Monterrey was about as normal as a traffic stop. The ones the federales could corner were shaken down. Some haggled to an acceptable sum of pesos and were allowed to go on their way. The ones who couldn't or wouldn't pay, they'd get hauled in. If the police thought you were holding out on them, you might be robbed of what you had and stomped on for the inconvenience. Because Javier was a child, and had nothing worth taking, he was sent back home.

Though he'd been the only child on the train, there were two others in the van: Jaime, a squirrelly fifteen-year-old, and Nina, calmer at nine than most adults in her situation, were on the second row of gray vinyl seats. Javier was alone on the third. He got cold enough that he pulled his arms inside his shirt and leaned his head against the warm glass. He saw a scraggly fawn-colored mutt by the road, loping in the grass in the same direction as the van. She had no collar and had missed a few meals. Her hips were gathered and the bones stood up like knobs above her back. Her withered teats sagged, and her rib bones were visible through the hide, like ripples on a murky pond. The dog turned her head toward them for a moment and looked on cautiously, but the van charged ahead, and she disappeared behind the hill.

Something about the dog's movements reminded Javier of a white boxer he once had. It showed up on their farm full-grown, so they had no idea how old it actually was. His father had called it Blanco, and that stuck. The dog followed Javier everywhere. When he ran to the goat pens, the dog ran with him. When he ate homegrown watermelon on the back porch, the dog did the same, pink juice sloshing out of its stubby black snout.

One day they had been out romping through the waist-high sorghum, waiting on Mariana to get home, and Javier went inside for a drink of water. He got sidetracked with a drawing he'd been working on earlier, and about the time he got the shape of the horse's head the way he wanted it, a high yelp electrified his bones.

Javier ran outside. Dust swirled in a big column down the road. He ran, panicked, into the dust. He couldn't see, but listened for Blanco, for another yelp or some panting. He heard nothing and looked down the road toward the vehicle. He could tell it was a blue truck, but the dust it kicked up obscured any other details. The dirt scattered itself back over the road, and Javier found him. Blanco was on the far side of the dirt road with a pool of blood near his muzzle. Javier slid on his knees and tried to wake him up. Bleary eyed, Javier looked down the road, but the truck was long gone. They had to have known they hit something. They had to know.

Javier remembered it all too clearly while watching the passing countryside out of the tempered glass. He felt a lot like that now, like his dreams had been wrecked, like happiness was a thing that could be taken back at any moment.

The authorities arranged for Javier to be sent back to his uncle Ramiro, who would meet the van at a rest stop north of the ejido. He knew his uncle would forgive him, but there would be no debate about moving to Aguascalientes with them now. He opened his backpack. The gold-framed picture of his mother was in the hands of thieves. They could have at least left him the photograph. They wouldn't be able to sell that.

A green roadside sign announced that San Rodrigo was sixty kilometers off, which meant they were less than an hour away. Javier had the thought to dart out at the first stop they made but realized the doors were locked from the inside. Even if the man left them alone, they'd still be trapped. He wondered if they transported murderers in vehicles as secure as this one.

Moving in with his uncle began to feel like fate. He lost the will to escape. He pulled his knees up and rested his head on his forearms and tried to go to a happier place. One where his mother was still alive, and the world was bright and warm. He tried his best to recall every detail of one perfect morning on the farm. Sunlight and song, fresh scents from the garden, even the work put him at ease. He felt cozy and safe, like he could curl up and retreat from the hurt. It still made him sad, but it was more bearable, the kind of sad you could live in. The more he thought about this place, fantasizing that Mariana had never died and he was still happy on the farm, the more it pulled him in.

The van jerked toward the exit. The driver had only spoken a few words and didn't appear to be on the verge of bursting with conversation now. He put a hand on his temple, rubbing it in small circles. When they pulled off the highway, Javier lifted his head. They pulled up to a small filling station. It was the one his uncle was supposed to meet them at. He looked for his dark green car but didn't see it anywhere.

Part of Javier wanted to stay curled up in the back row, but another part, rising from its sleep, unearthed a rare piece of advice from his father. It went something like: *The call of the easy path is strong, but the more you take it the weaker you become.*

It didn't mean much at the time, but now he felt the power behind the words. He didn't want to take the easy path. With renewed energy he looked around the van, searching for opportunities. The driver, who hadn't even told his name to the children when he loaded them up, pulled his wallet from the center console. He glanced back at them, giving each a stern stare.

He put his hand up, like you tell a dog to stay and rolled all four of the windows down about a hand's width before taking the key from the ignition and locking them inside.

Javier leaned forward in his seat, his elbows pressing into his thighs, forgetting all about his safe place. He watched the driver disappear through the glass door. Only one other car was parked nearby, and it sat empty. The gaps in the windows let in much-needed fresh air and warmth. Javier's mind focused while he looked for weak spots. His only desire now was to lead a jailbreak. He looked at Nina and Jaime, who didn't seem to share his thoughts.

He hopped over their row and into the driver's seat, punched the unlock button, and tugged on the handle. No luck. He tried to roll down the electric windows further, but that didn't work either. He searched for something to shatter the window with. Under the seat he found a two-piece tire iron and a small jack. He took half of the tire iron and reared back to smash the side window. Nina gasped, and he stopped. He looked back and saw how frightened she was. Jaime grinned and crept to the edge of his seat.

"Dale," he said, eager for what came next.

Javier couldn't take his eyes off Nina. Her hands grasped her sleeves and her eyes were like black marbles. He ignored Jaime's encouragement and set the tire iron on the center console. There had to be a better way. Breaking the window would be loud enough to bring the driver waddling back to the car anyway. He racked his brain for a way to get the window down. He pulled down on the window as hard as he could. It gave a little.

An idea hit Javier like a gunpowder blast. He took the collapsed jack and put it in the gap, the window fitting perfectly into the little groove in its base. Javier inserted the rod and began to crank. The jack expanded upward, connecting with the top of the window's frame, smushing the rubber seal and then tightening against the steel. Javier held the jack firmly in place with one hand and continued cranking it up with the other.

With the next crank, the window went down a couple of centimeters.

Javier's face lit up. He kept cranking, forcing the window down. Then there was a snap and the window fell down into the door panel. He motioned for the other two to go on through, and Jaime didn't have to be told twice. He squirmed over Javier, kneeing him in the chin on the way out. He hopped onto the asphalt and ran, no time for gratitude or strategy.

Javier looked at Nina and tried to take her hand, but she pulled it back. Javier glanced back at the filling station. He couldn't see the driver inside. Nina looked up at him with big wet eyes that made his throat feel tight. He couldn't understand why, so he demanded an answer.

She told him that all she wanted was to go back to her grandmother in Fresnillo and that she didn't want to run again. She ran from home and boarded a train with an older cousin, but it didn't work like she had dreamed. They got separated. It was awful. She told Javier in between quiet sobs that she believed God would bring her and her mother together in los Estados Unidos someday. Javier gave her a hug and told her she would have that reunion, don't worry.

He slung on his backpack and saw the driver paying out at the register. He crawled through the open window. When he looked back, Nina's face was up close to the tinted glass. He worried that the fat man, without anyone else around to absorb his anger, would blame her for their escape. The filling station's door swung open, and the man fumbled around with an armful of soda and junk food while putting his wallet back into his pants. Javier took a deep quivering breath, waved to Nina, and slipped into a row of dense brush near the access road.

He jogged south, deciding to make a quick stop back home. He'd need more supplies before his next try. He hoped that when his uncle got to the filling station and saw he wasn't there, home wouldn't be the first place they thought to look. He was a runaway, after all.

2015

Marfa was flat and spare, save for the little blue shapes of the Davis Mountains twenty-five miles east. Maybe it was the isolation or maybe it had something to do with the James Dean film shot there or the mystery lights on the edge of town, but Marfa was *out there*, spacey and enigmatic even by West Texas standards.

An artist from New York City bought land and made grand installations of concrete and steel. Minimalism. Artsy people told their artsy friends, and over the years they brought pop-up galleries and vegan restaurants to town. You were just as likely to see rich people in hip clothes and big sunglasses as a cowboy hat and a pair of boots. Celebrities were known to fly in to tour the collections and sample the avant-garde food trucks.

On the main drag, after passing the simple storefronts of places like Ranch Candy and the Museum of Electronic Wonders & Late Night Grilled Cheese Parlour, Webb braked for a slow-moving tow truck with a woolly man on its cross-shaped wheel lift. His skinny arms were stretched across the cross bar, chained snugly around the wrists. Javier first thought the man was being tortured, but when they got closer he could read the cardboard sign up top.

JESUS DIED FOR YOUR SINS
YOU ARE LOVED!

Javier didn't know what possessed a man to chain himself to a steel wheel lift in the middle of summer. Guerilla marketing for a new church, atonement for some sin of the flesh, sleeping with the tow truck driver's wife perhaps, or maybe he was just another Texas-variety maniac. Webb honked and the splayed-out man waved his pinned down hand as much as he could, shouting "Jesus loves you!" as they passed.

"Wow." Jeff shook his head in amazement. "This town is what you would get if you put Post and Austin in a blender."

"No, no, no. It's more like if some purple-haired Brooklyn barista hooked up with a Sam Elliott character. Their baby would grow up to be Marfa, the cowgirl who quotes the Book of John and hosts peyote retreats on her ranch," Dave said.

"I'd pay to see that movie," Squat said.

"This place is weird," Webb said.

"You say it like it's a bad thing," Jeff said. "We're weird."

Webb thought about this a moment. "Yeah, I s'pose we are."

When the band pulled into the Broom Closet's lot at six, the sun was still cooking. Dave, Jeff, and Squat walked toward the back door, all three wearing dark sunglasses and carrying their instruments in textured black cases.

Marck rolled out of the bunk and yawned. He pulled his headphones down around his neck and called out for the guys but got no response. He split the mini blinds and saw them going into the bar. No one had woken him up. He let the blinds pop back into place. He was sick of being left out or just plain forgotten.

He knew why it happened. Squat, Dave, and Jeff had grown up together. They shared roots. It made him feel like the guy still crashing high school parties long after he graduated. They couldn't just dump him though. He knew their secrets. If it came to it, he figured he could leverage what he knew for a decent payout. But he didn't like thinking that way.

This was his eighth band. He lived to drum, and after two ugly divorces he'd learned that life on the road was the only one he was cut out for. But something always kept him from sticking with a band. If he didn't quit, he'd self-destruct and force their hand. He never dwelled too long on why. He knew a deep discomfort took hold when he stayed somewhere too long, and that had always been enough of a reason to go. He wanted to see this one through though. He knew his bandmates were too idealistic when it came to their pipe dream of an album, but they had a shot at something special even if they only pulled half of it off.

The young trio had shuffled through three drummers by the time they hired him on. Not only did he have to audition with them, he had a whole series of interviews with Javier. Strange conversations. Javier would pepper vague questions about keeping secrets and unjust laws in with the usual background and compatibility stuff. Marck supposed he gave the right answers, because Javier told him all about their operation during their fourth conversation, what the position *really entailed*.

Between bites of pizza, in a dimly lit booth on the back wall, Javier had asked if he still wanted in. If he were still married, if any of the cash or notoriety or goodwill remained from his brief successes in the past decade, he probably would have said no. But, as it stood, it was just too much to pass up. Maybe Javier already knew that, could smell the desperation wafting off him when he walked in the door. Marck agreed to a cut of the cash and a small stake in the album if it made money, but that was no sure thing.

Marck enjoyed working with the band, but in quieter moments he felt a windstorm coming. One that Squat, Dave, and Jeff might lock arms and weather together but would carry him far away. Adrift again. He heard the faint whistle, felt the ripple at the hem of his shirt from time to time, and it scared him.

His heart rate began to climb. He could still hear the music from the headphones and feel its rumble on his neck. He rubbed his forehead and trudged over to his bag. He dug in its hidden pouch and emerged with an orange prescription bottle. He shook out a handful of pills—a multi-colored assortment of uppers and downers—separated two with the Ks punched out of them into his eager hand and then tossed them into his mouth. He worked his tongue around to get enough saliva and tried to swallow, but they stuck in his throat.

Gagging, he rummaged the bags and stacks of junk for a water. He felt the cool glass of a bourbon bottle under a pile of used clothes. There were a couple of drinks left. He tilted his head back and plugged it into his mouth. His Adam's apple bobbed up and down as the amber liquor dropped level by level until none remained. He set the bottle down on the counter with a clack that reverberated through the bus. He caught a loose stream of whiskey on his chin with the back of his hand and felt his eyes water and burn.

He sat down on the bunk and felt a slight rush of blood to his head, knowing a calm euphoria would soon be on its way. He knew how to get to that place. It was the staying there that caused problems. The drugs were always on call, as long as he had cash. They never conspired to abandon him, as long as he had cash. And right now—he had cash. He stared into the stitching of his sneakers for what felt like a slice of eternity.

Javier felt a tap on his shoulder and turned around to face Bill Moore. He was heavier, clean-shaven now, which exposed creases like old leather and a second chin that had been concealed. Bill stuck out his hand and they shook. Beards work wonders, Javier thought, unconsciously touching the stubble on his own face after releasing Bill's hand. Before Javier could get too judgmental, he remembered what he saw when he looked in a mirror nowadays. They were the same age, after all.

"How are you, Javier?" Bill said.

"I'm good. How's the family?"

"Well, since Linda's been gone, the girls don't come home as much. Sterling's at school in Austin, comes out for the holidays, and Sierra is still gunning for roles in Holly-weird."

"Two talented girls. You must be proud," Javier said.

"Oh, yeah," Bill said. "Both of them are hard workers and have these clear goals. I had no idea what I wanted to do when I was their age. Hell, I still don't."

"Me neither," Javier said with a gentle laugh. "I burned through enough dreams, you'd think I have it figured out by now. But nope."

"Tell me about it," Bill said. They got quiet, settling into the friendly silence.

Javier had gotten to know Bill when he was managing Los Sombras. Bill ran a honky-tonk in Odessa until a few years back, booking mostly local acts and past-the-date country musicians. Johnny Paycheck and Gary Stewart played his bar in their later scattered years. He'd started booking Tejano acts to fill the spaces when the crowds thinned and the demographics shifted. He was ahead of the curve in that way, though he lacked the killer instinct of great businessmen. He just wanted to make a decent living and create a space where people could unwind and have a good time. That's why Javier liked him. He was honest and treated the acts well, fading country stars or otherwise.

He ended up in Marfa because of his nephew, a hipster type who convinced him it was *the* place to open a new bar, that Bill's rustic sensibilities and diverse musical tastes were just the thing this town would eat up.

"So how you holding up?" Javier asked.

"I'm alright. Summer's kept us busy." Bill paused and adjusted his wedding band. "It gets lonely here. I catch myself wanting to move back to Odessa, but there's not much left for me there."

Javier hadn't known Bill to be a fortunate man, but he was always resilient and hopeful. His bar could burn down without an insurance policy in place and he'd still be picking up pieces and saying it could be salvaged. Now a sad submission hung in Bill's expression, and Javier had to look away. He stared at the exposed ductwork overhead, not knowing what to say. Finally, "What's Sterling studying?"

"Communications," Bill said. He seemed relieved that Javier had broken the tension with a harmless question and dove into the response. He talked about her classes and her part-time job at the college radio station. Then he talked about his other daughter, her acting classes, her nonspeaking role in that Russell Crowe flick last year. It was inevitable, though, that as Bill bounced from one story about his family to another that he ended up back at his dead wife.

"I miss Linda so much. My plans fell through so many times, but she always talked me into chasing the next one. She was the only one who really believed in me," he said with glazed eyes.

"She was an amazing woman."

"Yeah, she was," Bill said, and then after a long pause, "Well I've bent your ear long enough. Where are y'all headed after this?"

"We have a show in El Paso in a couple days. Well actually, there's a show in Juárez first. Tomorrow night."

"Juárez?" Bill blurted, like the word was a poisonous thing he had to get out of his mouth quickly.

"Yeah, I booked us at a little venue over there."

"You that desperate for gigs?"

"Nah, it's a good opportunity. Not many American bands play over there anymore."

"Even I can solve that mystery." He cocked an eyebrow. "You be careful down there."

"Don't worry," Javier said, slapping Bill's shoulder. "If you stay out of the places you don't belong, the odds are in your favor."

Javier looked at him again and saw his eyes glaze over. Bill sniffed hard and blinked a few times. "Well I better let you go," he said. "Go check out the bar. Drinks for you and the band are on the house. We have over a dozen regional and artisanal beers. My nephew says I should point that out more."

Javier looked him in the eye. "It's good to see you."

Dave introduced the band as Joaquin and the Machine. Squat picked out the opening line on "Tumble On" and they all melded in the rhythm. Dave leaned the mike over with both hands as if dipping a dance partner. His dark hair whipped back and forth over his shoulders while he moved to the beat. He took a step back, then lunged at the mike stand and crooned with his eyes fixed on the back wall:

Maybe I'll find something better
But baby, the odds are slim
I'll tumble on down the road
High on what could have been

Their opener got the place buzzing. The scattered wooden pool tables had filled up, and other patrons stood near the stage with drinks and cigarettes, nodding to the beat. Javier felt someone grab his elbow. When he turned and saw it wasn't Webb or Bill, or anyone else he knew, he reflexively snarled.

"Pardon me," the silk-shirted man said over the music.

Javier looked down at the man's hand and then met his eyes. The man let go.

"You're with the band," the man said, nodding toward the stage. "Right?"

"Yeah." Javier tried to place the guy but drew a blank.

"I saw you together earlier," the man said. "My name is Warren Dedmon. I'm in the music business myself."

Javier nodded, still suspicious.

"Can we talk outside?" Warren asked. "It will only take a moment."

They stood by the front door, facing the gravel lot full of single-cab trucks with gun racks, electric cars with Sierra Club decals, and everything in between. A man with a long graying mustache and tight jeans tipped his hat and sauntered into the bar.

"I'm a little more familiar with you than I let on," Warren said. "I know who you are, Javier. And I know all about the band."

Javier felt the squeeze inside his chest. Was he Border Patrol? ICE?

"And let me say, I'm a fan. That is actually why I came out here tonight. I intended to catch you in El Paso later this week, but I thought it might be easier to get a word in here."

Javier cocked his head. The man's face was taut and suggested youth, but his posture said otherwise. His accent hadn't come from anywhere around here. His thick eyebrows bounced when he talked.

"I want to work with your band," he said. "I'm an agent."

Javier's jaw tightened.

"They are generating quite the buzz in the region. But they need help to get to the next level."

"You don't think I can handle it?"

"No." He put his hands up. "Never said such a thing. Managers and agents serve different roles. You are an expert in your field, no doubt, building an audience, somehow developing a reputation without even a real band name. It's . . . impressive. But do you have the connections to expand? Do you know promoters from here to Los Angeles? Do you know the clubs it makes the most sense for your band to agree to a fifty-fifty split in? Can you provide them with opportunities to open for established acts in bigger venues? Do you have plans for merchandise and branding? Because I can offer all of those things."

"What do you want from me?" Javier said.

"I want to talk to them," Warren said. "I can convince them that they need an agent. I promise you, with my resources, we'll all be richer for it."

Javier still couldn't get a feel for the guy. "What about their band names? How do you feel about that?"

"Ah, it doesn't matter how I feel," he said.

"It will to them."

The man stopped and pulled his lips tight. He touched the five o'clock shadow on his chin with his fingertips.

"That is a problem for later. Right now, I would just like to expand their scope. Can you get me a sit-down after the show?"

"Now's not a good time," Javier said.

"I drove all the way from Santa Fe. Can you get me ten minutes?"

Javier shook his head. "Afraid not."

Warren frowned. His eyes moved back and forth along the gravel.

"What do you think they would say, if they found out their manager was not acting in their best interest?"

Javier shrugged. "Don't know."

"No," he said. "You don't. This is a business where opportunities are rare, and if they knew you tried to pass on one without consulting them—I'd hate to be you."

Javier was losing his patience. He stepped closer to Warren.

"You don't even know what you're asking for," he said. "You want what's best for them? Then leave."

Warren lowered his head but shot Javier a dark look over the top of his glasses.

"Have it your way, friend." He walked into the night.

The rumble from the show faded out and people made their way to their cars. Javier stepped out of the floodlights' glow. The scant lights from nearby houses and businesses didn't take much away from the dome of stars above. Thousands of pinpricks in the black western sky, once filling him with a sense of wonder, now only made clear that light-years separated him from who he once was. He wondered if the man was right, if he'd ruined a shot at success for the band that didn't risk prison time.

When he went back inside, the place was almost emptied out. He side-stepped a man setting chairs upside down on the tables. He found the band and his expression flattened. Warren was with them at the bar. Javier prepared for a confrontation, watching the effete man make some point, his slender hands graceful as a conductor's. Jeff laughed at his joke.

"Oh hey, Javier, this is Warren," Dave said. "He's a fan."

"Yeah, we met," Javier said.

"He's buying our drinks." Marck held up a highball glass full of red liquid and ice.

"That's great," Javier said.

"I was just telling the band," Warren said, looking right at him, "that

69

I know promoters out west who would be willing to book them—if they would be interested in something like that."

His sly grin showed how much he was enjoying turning the tables on Javier. Marck sipped through his straw until it gurgled. He set it down and motioned for another one.

"Have any of you been to Tucson?"

They shook their heads.

"Because I think it's a place your music would play amazingly well. I know a young woman who runs a hip beer garden there. I'm sure she would love to book you boys for a run of summer concerts."

"Really?" Squat finished his drink. He signaled to the bartender, who poured him another whiskey sour.

"Your manager and I were talking earlier about how much you would benefit from an agent. How that could help you get over the hump. You know, bands that don't get that push at the right time, even if they are talented, they can atrophy and die. Isn't that right, Javier?" Javier just gave a half-grin.

"Wow, that's crazy." Jeff slid his glass forward. He scrunched his nose and nodded when the bartender asked if he'd like another. She reached on her tippy toes for the bourbon on the top shelf.

"I've been an agent for years, actually," Warren said.

"No way," Dave said.

"Yes," Warren said. "And I would like very much to propel you to the next level."

Marck finished his drink. The others downed theirs not long after. They looked at each other and grinned. Javier was on edge. He wondered if this was it. If this was where the band decided to oust him and go straight.

"You never told us who else you represent," Marck said.

"Oh, some truly great artists and bands, I assure you," Warren said.

"Yeah, but like, who?" Marck asked.

"Florence Higginbotham, Pete Adebayo and the Death Spirals, the Dotted Maps. Oh, I could go on and on. I am currently in negotiations with a cousin of Beyoncé. She sings *and* raps. A wonderful girl."

Marck side-eyed the others.

"Well you've given us a lot to think about," Dave said. "Thank you very much for the drinks, Mr. Dedmon."

"My pleasure," he said. "Can I leave you my card?"

"You sure can," Jeff said. He took it, flat black with gold letters heralding the Dedmon Agency, between his fingers.

"It was great to meet you gentlemen." He gave cards to Dave and Squat as well. "I look forward to your call."

Jeff waved until he walked out the door and then crumpled up the business card and dropped it into his ice.

Dave mocked the man's dry tone. "*I have many connections in the Western United States.*"

"Who is Florence Higginbotham?" Marck asked. "Sounds like some roaring twenties shit right there."

"She's bringing ragtime back, bro," Squat said.

They laughed. Javier tilted his head.

"So you don't want those gigs he was talking about?"

"If they were real," Dave said.

"Do you know how many guys like that have come up to us?" Jeff said.

Javier shook his head.

"A few," Jeff said. "They try to convince us that the one or two bar owners they're friends with can boost our career. All so they can get a big piece of the pie once we get somewhere."

"That guy was full of shit. We could tell," Squat said.

"So why'd you go along with it?" Javier asked.

"He offered to buy our drinks," Dave said.

"We had to act interested with that on the table," Marck said.

Javier shook his head. "The owner of this place is a friend of mine, remember? He was going to comp your drinks anyway."

"Oh," Jeff said, raising his eyebrows and staring at the soggy black wad of paper in his glass. "Poor dude."

The tension had built up and now all Javier could do to release it was laugh. The band joined him, smacking the table and wiping their eyes. He laughed until his belly hurt, thinking about how smug Warren had been. They finished the round and left a big tip at the bar. Javier chuckled to himself, realizing just under the surface that it could always go the other way.

Chapter 6

1984

JAVIER MADE IT HOME AFTER DARK. It was a clear summer night, and the countryside was still. The crescent moon hung like a glowing toenail over the mountains. He stared in wonder at the night sky, a multicolored dome of deep blues, purples, and maroons dusted with countless stars.

His home sat on the east end of the ejido, farther off the main dirt road than the others. His abuelo had worked for the original owner, who over the years came out less and less from his other home in Monterrey. By the time the government took part of the land and split it between his abuelo and all the other petitioners, his abuelo was old and had a bad heart. After Javier's father and mother married, they moved in to help tend to his failing health and his crops. He died a few months before Javier was born, and then Javier's father did what he swore he never would. He gave up his dream of migrating to the US, learning a trade that would pay. He began to work the small patch of dirt that he had cussed all his life.

Though the other ejidatarios offered to help, his father renovated the shack himself. He was a contradiction in that way. He chose to make a life on communal land—land he could use as long as he wished yet would never own—but was still fierce with his privacy and independence. His mother never said so, but Javier figured that spirit was what led him to finally leave.

Javier took another step down the driveway and stopped. The breeze felt good on his skin. Near the front porch was a large ponderosa pine. One of its limbs dug into the roof's edge. Creamy tan paint had peeled off in patches, showing the original white coat. The roof leaked and the foundation was no good. His father had put in a lot of work, but that could only do so much to cover the house's nature. Though it hadn't changed, the house looked small and battered to him now. It had never felt that way growing up, when it was just home.

There was no light in the windows, and no cars were in the driveway, which gave Javier hope that his uncle was elsewhere, still looking for him. The doors were locked, so he got the spare key from the toolbox in the leaning shed. The electricity had been shut off. He flicked all the switches, but the house stayed dark. His eyes adjusted enough to navigate, but the details hid in shadows.

Javier ran his hand over the countertop, tipping over a pepper shaker and then a potted succulent, until he got ahold of the old flashlight. He searched the house with it, not quite knowing what for. He'd returned on a gut feeling, knowing he could at least grab some of his mother's canned fruits and vegetables for the journey. He couldn't find a replacement for the canteen that was stolen, but he did find a jug that could hold even more water. He also took the pocketknife from his father's old nightstand and stuck it in his jeans. Feeling its weight there comforted him.

He hunted in cupboards, drawers, and couch cushions. Nothing. He sat on the couch and shone his light on the small bookshelf. Illiteracy was common in the area, but his mother was a good reader. She could even read some English, what her father had picked up in Texas and taught her. They had no TV, so his mother used to read by a 40-watt bulb after supper. Then she'd read aloud to him before bed. Javier scanned the books and landed on the leather-bound Bible. Javier felt a kick in his chest when he noticed it. "Mira. Biblia. Javi."

The last words his mother spoke to him rattled around in his brain. He took the Bible in his lap and opened it. Behind the first page he found his birth certificate. He kept flipping, into Lamentations and Philemon. He didn't know if he would recognize whatever it was when he saw it. He handled the pages rougher the further he went, looking for another tucked-away document or an underlined passage or even a note in the margins. He ripped a page in Acts and then had to slow down. He passed through Revelation, realizing that his mother hadn't been in her right mind those last few days. She'd thought his father was in the hallway and kept telling the nurse to let him in. Telling him to look in the Bible was probably just another misfire of her exhausted mind. Then Javier pulled back the second-to-last page and found an envelope taped to it. He held his breath, carefully peeling it from the thin paper.

Inside was a stack of pesos. He flipped through them and felt the smooth inky goatees on Francisco Madero. It didn't seem real. He stared, soaking in that strange feeling, like his head had been filled with helium and floated above the rest of him. He noticed a scrap of paper peeking out of the envelope.

His heart thumped when he recognized his mother's handwriting and began to read. It explained that her time as his mother was coming to an end, but she knew he would turn out to be a good man. She asked him to forgive his father even if he never saw him again. She told him that she prayed that the US would offer better opportunities than she was able to give. She hoped that the money would help him get there, someday. For now, she told him he would be in good hands with her brother Ramiro and his family.

In the hospital she was too sick to talk, much less to come home and hide the money. He figured that she must have done it when she was first diagnosed. And where had it come from? Sometimes in the winter, when the food they'd canned was running low, she'd barely eat so he had enough. The only thing Javier could think of was the sale of the goat meat, about the only thing they raised that brought in cash rather than bartered goods. Now he had more money than he'd ever seen.

She ended the note by writing that she would always love him and that he shouldn't miss her because she would always be a part of him. She would breach heaven and earth to send love to her baby. Javier cried a long while there on the floor. He laid the flashlight down to wipe his nose and eyes. Though her note mentioned going with his uncle, his mind went back to those conversations they had in the garden, talking about freedom across the border. He hoped she wouldn't be disappointed, but someday couldn't wait.

2015

They looked at El Paso through squinted eyelids. A row of unconvincing palm trees lined the boulevard. These were mostly brown up top and didn't tower over the traffic like the ones in California or even South Texas. They had yet to put on waxy green leaves. Shocks of pale gold stuck up like cowlicks. Boards were strapped to the trunks to support them. They passed a beige shopping center with a dark red roof, and all Javier could think of was sand and dried blood.

The greenest thing on that road was the country club. Javier couldn't help noticing that golf courses, even in the desert, were green like nothing else. No matter how severe a drought or the water restrictions placed on a city, it would still have a lush golf course, all of it looking fleeting and bizarre against the harsh desert scrubland.

Squat plucked at his guitar and they chatted over its melody. Dave had a rhyming dictionary pulled up on his phone because they were trying to find a better end to a couplet than "the wrong kind of quiet." They leaned over Dave's shoulder pointing out other options.

"Something about a riot," Marck said.

"Yeah, that could work," Jeff said.

The road ahead looked like it ran into the brown slopes of the Franklin Mountains. Their folds were the only places the oppressive sun couldn't seem to reach. They passed a little restaurant with a single-cab pickup out front. The sign had a huge cartoon of a happy burrito on it.

The burrito was slender and white, winking and giving a thumbs up. The top of it was overflowing with what Javier assumed to be the meat and beans. Squat stretched his elbows above his head and yawned. He noticed the sign and cocked his head to the side like a curious pup.

"Why is that giant tampon smiling?"

"I think it's a burrito," Javier replied.

"I'm not comfortable with it having a face, either way," Dave added.

They went around back to the dumpster and purged the bus of anything that could bring unwanted attention: the THC gummy bears, the half-full liquor bottles, even the bananas on the counter had to go. Jeff ran a handheld vacuum over the couch, and Dave wiped down the surfaces with disinfectant. The others straightened up the bunks and checked the cabinets for anything they might have forgotten.

"Isn't it more suspicious for a band to be tidy though?" Squat asked. "I mean, if some uptight cops walk into Willie Nelson's tour bus and it's all shiny and smells like air freshener, they're searching the shit out of that thing, right?"

They argued the merits of "cleanliness is next to godliness" on the way to the border but fell silent when a sign announced the exit for Juárez. Its bold white letters and green background put a hex on their nerves. The bus soon slowed to a crawl, engulfed in a sea of vehicles. A lit-up sign showed a thirty-minute wait for the Ysleta Port of Entry. The road ahead bottlenecked before the checkpoint.

Webb realized they had to get over three whole lanes. He did so with the grace of a thick girl squeezing into her tightest jeans, cars honking for what sounded like miles. When they finally rolled up to the checkpoint, an agent in a dark uniform approached. Javier hoped they had cleaned the bus out well enough not to tip them off. His muscles tensed when he saw the officer—a stout man with a thick mustache—approach the side door. He put his hands on his hips, framing the gun in his side holster. He stood there looking in at them and chomping his gum. Javier was about to open the door for him when the man motioned for them to pull up.

Going into Mexico? No big deal. Move along.

Javier looked in the big side mirror and saw the backside of the officer heading toward the next vehicle in line. The bus pulled up to the final inspection booth, where they presented their passport cards. The woman in the booth had a tight ponytail and long fingers. She asked if they had anything to declare, then grinned and hit the button that raised the striped crossing gate.

"Buen viaje," she said.

They went between two rows of orange barrels and curved onto a new street. BIENVENIDOS A CIUDAD JUÁREZ, MÉXICO had been painted on the vertical face of an overpass in blocky white letters. A navy-blue truck with Policía Federal on the side was camped under it. Though he was unsure if it was relief from passing the checkpoint or a magnetism emanating from his homeland, Javier's mood improved the second the bus's last axle crossed the Mexico line.

Javier had spent enough time in Ciudad Juárez to know which neighborhoods to stay out of, especially at night. There were certain areas, like the Anapra barrio right up next to the razor wire border fence, that an outsider didn't go to unless they were looking for trouble. The city wasn't quite the war zone it had been a few years back—the one that made Americanos shudder when the word *Juárez* rolled off a tongue—but it was still a dangerous place.

The murder rates dipped a bit when the major cartels' grip on the area loosened. But they were still around, and in the gaps they'd left, ambitious local gangs like Barrio Azteca thrived. While the fear had lifted a bit and more people walked the streets again, it only took a second for a sense of dread to float in on the dry air.

Javier was the only one of the bunch who had been there before, and he could tell by their silence the others were scared of what they might run into. They loosened up some once they realized the highway was surrounded with fast-food restaurants and motels and people going about their days.

"They got Carl's Junior?" Marck said.

"What," Squat said. "You thought it was going to be all taquerías and tequila bars?"

Marck shrugged. "Guess you can get a lousy burger anywhere."

Webb veered right and the chain stores disappeared. The bus sidled down a narrow street with scattered cars parked on each side. The storefronts and apartments had seen better days. Tents set up in abandoned lots sold discounted strollers and blankets with Cowboys and Lakers logos. Many of the buildings had been left to the heat and the wind. Thin white paint hung off a cinder block building, yellowed and tattered enough to resemble an ancient scroll.

Another navy blue Policía Federal truck appeared out of the heat waves, and Webb pulled aside to let them by. An agent, dressed in all black with a mask over his mouth, stood in the bed with an AR-15 resting against the crossbar. Things like that wouldn't let you forget the city's reputation.

"What are those for? Breast cancer?" Jeff asked, pointing at a cluster of pink crosses around the base of a stunted tree.

"No," Javier strained to say. "They're for women who were murdered."

Jeff's eyes widened, the crossing taking on a different shape in his eyes. Juárez had also been known as "The City Where Women Disappear." Females of all ages were kidnapped and murdered at an alarming rate. Pink crosses were planted around the city, in places where they'd gone missing or where their bodies were eventually found. Investigations were uncommon and convictions rarer still.

Concrete barriers blocked off certain streets, and the graffiti declared the turf for Barrio Azteca. Still, people went on with their lives. They passed through the faded neighborhood and made it to the city center. Traffic was steady, and pedestrians with grocery bags and backpacks dotted the sidewalks. But there was something off. It wasn't some fashionably sterile American commercial district. These people weren't fearless. They carried on in spite of fear.

"Pull over here." Javier tapped Webb on the shoulder.

The familiar market was a welcome sight. Javier got off and waded through the vendors and produce stands while the others looked on from the bus's windows. He bought a stack of handmade tortillas and a cup of fresh salsa. A woman with her gray hair up in a bun counted his change. Then without seeing, Javier knew something was up. A chill had gone over the crowd. He turned. Two scowling men walked through, and people parted like the Red Sea. They were both young and lean, tattoos creeping out from beneath their shirts.

The woman ducked her head. Most of the others did too. Javier squinted, trying to gauge things. Both of them locked onto him. Their stares were like shrapnel blasts. Javier swallowed his pride and looked away. They passed on, going in the side door of a shop.

Javier asked the woman who those two were. She just shook her head and handed him his change. He was about to walk away when she said that they were dangerous men. They worked for Andrés Santiago, a local trafficker with a sadistic streak a mile wide. Javier had heard that name before, from connections back in Texas. Someone to avoid.

Javier nodded and thanked her.

"Cuídate," she said.

"Igualmente señora."

Javier returned to the bus with the food. The tortillas were still hot, wrapped in brown paper.

"Tortillas?" Dave said. "You know they sell those at every grocery store in Texas? I'm pretty sure they get their license revoked if they run out."

Nonetheless, the bandmates were hungry and tore into the package. While they dunked the warm tortillas in the salsa, oohing and aahing over the rich taste, Javier's mind went elsewhere. Those were kids that had passed him by in the market, but they had the battle-hardened eyes of soldiers. He debated whether to tell the others what he had heard, but decided against it. There was enough to worry about without some boogeyman named Andrés Santiago.

Chapter 7

1984

COYOTES NEVER MADE IT OUT TO JAVIER'S EJIDO. NOT many people were there, and those who were couldn't come close to the smugglers' prices, even considering the work they might be forced into to cover the difference. But Saltillo was just a half-day's walk away. It was the opposite direction from where he wanted to go, but it was a big city that had what he needed next.

His mother worked there for a while, until she got sick. Javier had been with her to the city to get supplies. He had seen the coyotes there before. A group of them hung out by the tire store on Calle Cuarta. They would be out front with a box truck, smoking cigarettes and letting the customers come to them. Their reputation was all the advertising they needed.

When Javier first asked his mother about the men—who stood out as both rough and flashy—she told him they were smugglers, men who made promises they wouldn't keep, men to stay away from. Javier believed her, but his curiosity grew and grew. He heard other stories about them in school, how they could get anybody across for the right price.

Cash in hand, he turned and walked back into the night, moonlit enough to save his flashlight batteries. The southwest wind felt crisp and energizing in his nostrils. He only stopped to swig at his water or piss behind some brush. He was so focused that the walk flew by. He made it to the edge of Saltillo by morning, when slender cobalt clouds streaked in front of the tangerine dawn.

He passed a block of houses that needed attention. Patches of gray decayed wood showed through their sun-faded colors. A bearded old man sat in a brittle plastic chair on the porch with a mug to his lips and a radio beside his feet. Its trebly cumbia warbled into the street. Javier nodded at the man, but he only stared back with tired eyes over the rim of his cup.

He approached the blue building on Calle Cuarta, unsure what to ask for or how or from whom. He cupped his hands on the window, but couldn't see anybody inside. Just an uncluttered desk, a wooden chair, and a bunch of empty space. He turned to leave, disappointed, and ran right into a man's chest. Javier looked up into man's hard, unblinking eyes. He recognized the man as one of them. This was his shot. Javier pulled his shoulders back and tried to sound unafraid.

"Quiero cruzar al Norte," he announced like he imagined an adult wanting passage would.

The man scowled. "Necesitas dinero para eso."

Javier reached into his backpack and pulled out the bundle of bills. He'd set a little back in case of emergency, but he offered the coyote almost everything his mother had left him. He held the bundle out to the man, who just stared at him for a moment. Then the man took it and counted it a 500-peso note at a time. He held the cash in his palm and looked Javier over. He asked Javier where he got it from, and Javier said from working. The man liked that. His laugh was rough as sandpaper.

"Okay," he said.

He put the roll of cash in his front shirt pocket and buttoned it. A salesman's smile flashed across his face. He told Javier that his timing was perfect. Their truck was headed for Houston later that very morning. Javier suppressed the urge to jump for joy in front of the man, just pursing his lips and nodding instead. He broke into a grin when the man walked away.

Javier refilled his water jug and then sat under a spindly tree with his backpack cinched up, watching the crowd grow. Some flocked together. Some stood alone. It was mostly men in their prime working years, unable to cross legally for work. The women stood out like cactus blooms in the brush. An old woman draped in a tangerine rebozo coughed into a balled-up rag in her bony fist. A young mother had a boy with her who couldn't have been more than four. His head nearly came to her waist, and she nervously stroked his hair with enough force that it raised his eyebrows with each pass.

Riding the trains to the United States hadn't worked, but Javier moved on, just like his mother showed him. When something bad happened, like when his dog got run over or his father took off, she consoled him for a while, but when he came to that line between grief and self-pity, which she always seemed to detect, she would ask him what sort of person he wanted to be. Did he want to be the person who sulked because of what he lacked, or did he want to be the person who made the best of what he had? Javier picked the second option more often than not, but he found it difficult, especially the last few days. He was full of hope and energy, though, and after spending almost all the money for passage on this renegade truck, he had to be all in. This had to work.

The sun rose, chopping up the clouds and brightening the parking lot. The people all began to look around at each other, acknowledging others outside of their little huddles at last. There were some brief pleasantries, some head nods across the way. Then the clouds all but vanished and the temperature rose like a sleeping giant.

Three men in clean beige uniforms arrived and raised the back door of a box truck. The inside was dim and empty, scarred metal floor and tie-downs dangling from steel tracks. Javier hadn't known what to expect, but this still didn't fit. One of the coyotes, who didn't look much older than sixteen, motioned them over. Person by person the coyotes checked their list to see who had paid what. Once he got in the truck, Javier took a space against the wall, close to the door. He tucked his knees up into his chest while the cargo area got more and more crowded.

Javier tried to count the people but had a hard time seeing them all from his spot on the floor. He figured there had to be at least twenty in the truck. The lead coyote appeared at the opening and everyone got quiet. Javier waited for the man to make a speech or give them some tips or explain the timeframe in which it would all happen. He only told them not to sit on the air holes—there were a dozen or so of them in the floor—and slid the door down with a long rumble. Then it was dark in the truck except for the bits of faint light that poked through the fist-sized holes. The engine started and the air brakes spit and hissed like mad cats. The truck lurched into gear and it already felt warm and musty inside. In the metal box, the normal whir of rubber on asphalt was amplified so that it sounded like a plane forever taking off underneath them.

Javier held his hand out in front of his face. He could see its shape but not any of the lines or finer details. He stared a while longer and his eyes adapted to the darkness. He glanced at the young mother and her son seated a few people over. The child's head lay against her shoulder. Her lips were moving, but he could barely hear her over the roar of the road. It seemed like she was singing some lullaby made of love and necessity. The boy drifted in and out of sleep while she sang.

2015

There was a slow drip of regulars into Dos Cuernos Cantina. When the band took the stage at nine, a dozen or so patrons were scattered between the bar and the pool tables at the back. Half of the bar had a scuffed wood floor for dancing, and three curious people had that space to themselves. The band played second fiddle to eight-ball, but that didn't stop them from swaggering out to their instruments.

Squat slung his Strat over his shoulder and plucked each string to make sure they were still in tune. The D was a bit flat, and he raised it by ear. He watched Dave—who had made a habit of waiting until the others got to their instruments before coming out on the stage—saunter out and flash a peace sign to their three fans. Crickets would have been a welcome addition. Every so often a beer bottle would clank against the others in the bin by the bar. Dave took his guitar pick from between his teeth and stepped up to the microphone.

"We are Josey and the Sentient Burritos, and we brought some tunes from Texas. How are y'all doing tonight?"

Nobody paid him much attention. Someone broke a new game with a loud crack. Squat thought he figured out the problem, so he leaned into Dave's microphone and spoke in hesitant Spanish.

"Hola, Ciudad Juárez. Somos José y los Burritos, uh, Vivos. Cómo andamos?"

The three on the dance floor did little shrugs. Squat had imagined the crowd would come to life after being addressed in their native tongue. No one cared. Dave waved the others in and called an audible. Instead of the planned opener they would play an old corrido bound to connect with the audience. It didn't. When their instruments burst into sound, a round-faced man looked at them over his pool cue as if they were to blame for his botched shot.

They often played for half-interested audiences who got more interested the more they drank. One time a couple of good ol' boys had wanted to see how well the band could maintain their focus with beer bottles whizzing over their heads and busting on the brick backdrop. Not very well, they found out, after they did the chorus of "You Don't Know How It Feels" three times in a row like a broken record. They stayed up there until they finished the set though. People usually came around. In fact, Squat saw a couple of new faces.

Scanning the crowd, he wiggled his fingers while Marck counted the next one in. He froze when he saw the woman standing by the support beam. She nodded to the music and watched the stage with a composed expression. She had radiant brown eyes, wavy hair tied back in a ponytail, curvy hips that her faded jeans clung to for dear life. Marck's drums had kicked in, but Squat wasn't sure how long ago. He had the feeling he was being stared at. Jeff slapped his bass like it had insulted his mother.

His bandmates continued glaring at him, and Squat realized they were in a holding pattern, keeping the same repetitive rhythm from the intro and waiting for him to come roaring in with the lead. It took a fraction of a second to regain his bearings and explode into a barrage of notes. He worked his way up the neck while the fingers on his left hand furiously pressed the frets. He slid back to the lower frets and evened it out, hitting his rhythm when he played the first repeating riff. His thick hands made their way around the instrument with ease, like they'd been designed for each other.

His thoughts faded while he played. Guitar had always done that for him. It allowed him to shut out the doubts, the ones that bothered him most when he was quiet and alone. The ones that told him he was stupid and undeserving and wouldn't leave him alone until he was back around other people. When he felt that way as a kid, he'd pick a fight with his big sister Anna. And though she'd usually put him in his place one way or another, Squat didn't mind. It was better than solitude. She was the one who got him into playing guitar, maybe just so he'd leave her alone.

Squat played the song pretty much like he always did, but his scattered embellishments ensured that he never played a song the same way twice. He revved into a frenetic pace and then began to wind down when the chorus approached. He hit the riff and leaned in to sing with Dave:

> *It's High Lifes for the low lifes*
> *Bartender this one's on me*
> *Not much round here goes right*
> *We just wanna feel free*

He stepped away and played a rowdy fill. The second verse started, and he casually glanced at the woman. She swayed, shifting her weight between her muscular thighs. Squat felt a strong urge to be between them. Then he realized—those eyes, sweet and intense as dark honey—she was looking right at him. She gently bit her bottom lip and then let it slide out from between her teeth, glistening. Squat dug in and let his guitar howl.

Dave sang the bridge without apprehension, excited by the hurdle ahead. The song required him to go up one-and-a-half octaves on the drop of a dime. He crooned the low tonic note, not taking it for granted. With a single-pointed focus, he worked through the chorus and nailed the falsetto part. He let the last note ring, raising his arms into the air like two vipers.

When he started singing in public, he'd tense up every time a challenging part came his way. He was brave enough to raise his voice, but never relaxed enough to excel. The notes would come out pitchy and strained. He was so afraid of screwing up that he guaranteed it to happen. The first time he'd been picked for a solo, in Mrs. Folkner's seventh-grade choir group, he took one look at the audience and ran offstage to puke. She had to get Alvin "Mr. Perfect" Cooley to replace him, and he didn't miss a note.

But Mrs. Folkner had seen something in Dave. She already knew he had the talent. In her carpet-walled studio in the back of the middle school he learned to resonate through his chest and to drop his larynx to hit the high notes. Even the ones that seemed unreachable after his voice changed. No, ability wasn't the problem. She told him the next time he felt himself tensing up, he just needed to think: What's the worst that can happen? Botching the solo? Big deal. Even professionals do that. Failure would happen, make no mistake, but it couldn't control him unless he let it. It was nice of her to say, but it didn't click.

She picked him for another solo at the Thanksgiving concert, and it loomed over him like a lightning storm. Every time he unzipped his binder and the sheet music peeked out, it felt like someone wringing out his stomach with both hands. The day came and the bright cafeteria filled up with family members who finished their heat-and-serve turkey and dressing and picked at remnants of pumpkin pie with white sporks while the kids took the stage. Mrs. Folkner pressed play and counted them in with her fingers: one, two, three. Dave stood stiff as a board.

The first and second verses zoomed by, and his solo came hurtling into view. He stopped singing with the other kids. He could feel his heartbeat all the way into his arms. He closed his eyes and Mrs. Folkner's words entered into his mind. *What's the worst that can happen?* He opened his eyes and saw his family. His mom and his dad were enjoying themselves. They smiled with interest into the bleachers. His baby brother sat in his mom's lap, playing with the amber leaf hanging from her necklace.

Other parents looked on, though some seemed more interested in their desserts. Younger brothers and sisters carved designs into their foam cups and shot ice pellets through their straws at each other until they were taken away. Dave had been worried they'd all judge him, but he saw that the stakes weren't that high. The girl beside him sang loud and off-pitch. It wasn't a big deal. That thought filled his mind and put him at ease. He opened his mouth and let the music fly like he was alone in the shower.

It became as natural as taking the mike off the stand. The more he did it, the more confidence and enjoyment came. When they started the band in high school, he was the no-doubt-about-it front man. On stage he could share parts of himself that he couldn't show any other way. He never even considered giving up on their music. He couldn't see himself doing anything else.

Dave howled and the speakers reverberated through Dos Cuernos. He jumped in place and his dark mane rose and fell with the beat. He slicked it back, out of his face, and anchored himself for the next verse. Something was wrong, but he couldn't put a finger on it. His usual energy was dulled, and it bugged him. His thoughts clouded the moment and he botched the delivery of the high notes in the chorus for the first time in a long time. He watched the crowd. Worse than laughter, there was no sign that they even noticed. At least mockery would've provided some energy to feed off.

He backed off so Squat could step to center stage and play a lick. He realized that he didn't want to be up there. He wanted to be alone. Since flight wasn't an option, he tried to manufacture some excitement. He danced around the stage while Squat played, really hamming it up. He took his shirt off and slung it. A woman stepped to the side and let the black garment sail onto the concrete beside her. He swore he heard a yawn over the booming guitars and drums.

———————

The song was in four-four time. Marck let the backbeat hang and stayed loose with the sticks. The lightness started in his chest and spread outward. His head and arms felt weightless, full of effervescent fizz. The whole bit was effortless now. It was like his muscles and connective tissue and nerves had grafted to the music, and now they were one.

Though he never looked up from the drum set, he could feel the adulation and gratitude of the audience hit him in waves. He felt the trifecta of body, soul, and rhythm in perfect balance. His ego was dissolving into eternity like a sand hill in the wind. Before he was lost to the stream, his last thought went something like: *Man, this shit is something else.*

They had been hanging out on the bus, playing cards, when Marck got that awful feeling in his stomach. The source of it was always muddled: anxiety over the smuggling, nagging loneliness, the disappointment of a wasted decade, spicy food. Take your pick. He just knew that he needed something to level him out before he snapped. He resented his bandmates' snootiness when it came to these matters. It was all good man, so long as it was *their* drugs. Booze was fine in their book. Weed was even better. But everything else was frowned upon—aside from the occasional "psychedelic tool" like the DMT they got from some redneck philosopher named Big Jack who synthesized it in his storm cellar.

When Marck first joined, he splurged on some good blow and tossed it on the table after band practice, thinking they would be thrilled. He ended up getting a ten-minute lecture from the pretty one and the brainy one about how they had worked too hard to turn into some caricature of a coked-up rock band, and did he know where that really came from? How many poor people had been murdered just so he could feel on top of the world for an hour and then be left impotent? And blah blah blah, while they smoked their legal-in-Colorado weed, financed by some corporate conglomerate that also dealt in kid-friendly vape flavors and slave labor.

Marck had popped a painkiller from his hidden bottle, but it just hadn't done the trick. So he snuck off and walked the streets of Juárez until he found a smoke shop a few blocks away. He sized up the clerk: mid-thirties, longish hair, tattoo of a grim reaper peeking out from the sleeve of his Metallica T-shirt. It was worth a shot. Marck asked in broken Spanglish if the man knew where he could get drugs. When the man replied that he should start at a pharmacy, Marck knew he had to rethink his approach.

He made sure no one else was around and said, "Illegal drogas."

The clerk did the sizing up now. The silence made Marck nervous, but then the clerk said, "Qué clase de drogas?" Marck knew qué was what and drogas were what he needed. He tried to think back to high school Spanish, but that was well over a decade ago and he'd barely paid attention.

"Bueno drogas," he replied and pointed at the ground. "Sedatives."

After staring at him with suspicion, the clerk motioned for Marck to follow him to the back. He made him wait by a stack of cardboard boxes and returned with a baggie of what Marck first assumed to be cocaine. The clerk held up the bag of white crystalline powder, and Marck saw that it was too grainy and lustrous to be coke.

"Ketamina. Veinte dólares americanos." He held up all his fingers and then blinked them again to indicate the amount, which Marck was thankful for. They made their exchange and Marck took off. He'd never tried ketamine before, but he was up for something new. A mental change of scenery would do him good. He did a few bumps in the bathroom before they took the stage.

He banged his drums and the drugs superseded his thoughts of isolation and abandonment. His desires and fears faded off into the distance. Marck perceived himself hitting impossible sequences of beats with precision and fervor. It was all about the music, and the music was good.

That's what he felt. However, the further into the set the more his style resembled an old man tentatively typing with his index fingers. He hit the snare, hit the hi-hat, hovered his sticks in the air for a few seconds, and then made another thwack. The ketamine obstructed the part of his brain that dealt with autonomous movement, his precious muscle memory. The part that governed elation and confidence, however, ran so fast it dragged the rest of his gray matter behind.

Marck continued on with his disjointed rhythm, taking his bandmates frustrated backward glances as acknowledgments of his virtuosity. The feeling in his chest had bloomed into a full-bodied weightlessness. His arms felt like autumn leaves in an updraft, though somehow they still snaked back down to the drumheads. His peripherals went dark and all he could see were the magnified drums. He continued the beat and leaned back on his throne, King of Percussion.

He mashed the bass pedal and hit a cymbal while the song drew to a close. He smacked the snare with his palm and everything around him fell away into the darkness. The stage was gone and he floated in space. Voices echoed through the expanse, and though he couldn't hear any words, their low tones put him at ease. He let go.

———————

The song mercifully ended. Jeff turned around when he heard a thud that couldn't have come from a drum. He put his bass down and rushed over to Marck. He lay on his back and kept touching his palms together and grinning with his eyes closed. Squat knelt next to him and tried to get him to come to.

"Marck, you alright? You bopped your head pretty good," Squat said.

Marck ran his tongue along his bottom lip. Dave stood over him, and Jeff put his hands on his hips.

"What did you take?" Dave said.

There was no answer, so Dave patted his chest. Marck opened his eyes a little and moved his lips and teeth in abnormal patterns, like he was kissing imaginary lips.

"Watt deed ju tack," he said.

"The fuck?" Dave said.

"Zee folk," Marck said.

"Man, he's gone." Jeff shook his head. "It's like a chimp trying to impersonate human speech."

"Where'd he get drugs? Javier made us ditch everything," Squat said.

Jeff shrugged impatiently. The whole tour had felt like one mishap after another. Instead of containing the mistakes, quarantining the operation until they could get on track, they just kept rolling downhill. A loaded drummer was just what they needed now.

They decided Squat and Dave would carry Marck backstage while Jeff stayed back and did some crowd work. Squat and Dave each hoisted one of Marck's limp arms over their shoulders. Jeff stepped up to the microphone with no idea of what to do or say.

"They'll be right back," Jeff said. "Our drummer isn't feeling well."

Those near the stage blinked at him. The area with the pool tables was booming. Jeff grabbed a handful of his hair and held it. He didn't want to sing anything a cappella and knew a bass solo wasn't that exciting out of context. He stood there until he thought of an idea and leaned into the microphone.

"I just want to say, the bravery of the people of Juárez—all the stuff you guys go through with the cartels, the constant threats of violence—is really an inspiration to me as an artist." He put a hand over his heart. "Gracias por su espíritu."

They hadn't been into the music, and they definitely weren't fazed by his flattery. Jeff went back to his bass and pretended to adjust the controls. Dave walked up and put his forearm on Jeff's shoulder. He leaned in and whispered, "Special K."

"What?"

"You know, ketamine, horse tranquilizer. That's what Marck is on. We got that out of him at least. Webb's going to keep an eye on him."

Jeff knew of ketamine but had never seen anybody on it, much less drum on it.

"The good news is that it's short-lived. From what we looked up, he should be good by the time the show's over." Dave then pulled the drumsticks from his back pocket. "In the meantime, I'm taking over for him."

Dave was competent on drums. He had filled in for a couple of their earlier sessions between drummers.

"I thought you couldn't drum and sing at the same time," Jeff said.

"I can't." Dave headed for the set. "You are."

Jeff couldn't believe it. Dave rarely gave up lead singing duties. Jeff had been pushing Dave to split the singing, so that he could at least do the songs he'd written, but Dave hadn't budged. Yet there he went.

Jeff was a bit anxious when he took center stage. The mike stand was cold on his fingertips. When it came to getting noticed, he usually settled for table scraps after the charismatic Dave and exuberant Squat finished up. He forgot about the crowd's indifference. In his mind all eyes were on him. He glanced at the set list taped to the floor. He adjusted the strap on his shoulder and ran his hand up to the microphone. Before he could get too worked up he heard four sharp whacks from the drumsticks and the song began. After a slight hesitation, he jumped in:

> *I can still see you shining in your Saturday best*
> *At the dance hall off 349*
> *We scuffed our love into that old wood floor*
> *Before we knew hard times*

He sang Dave's faded love song in a raspier tone than the lead singer. Jeff didn't like the tune much, thought the lyrics needed work, but he sang it like he meant it:

> *Waiting on the rhythm*
> *To return to you and me*
> *We still play the old songs*
> *But we're in different keys*

It was after ten now, and more entered the cantina for prime time. Some folks in the back seemed to be paying attention, or at least faced the stage while they drank. Jeff got a better reaction than Dave had. A low bar to clear, but it still should have produced a rush of pride. But at each lull he got that heavy feeling. It kept growing and reminding him of all the things could go wrong. *What if we get caught? My life would be over before it ever got started.*

Squat revved up on guitar, combining rhythm and lead and shaking his pelvis. Dave's tongue stuck out, concentrating on the drums. Somewhere backstage Marck was probably laughing at the sound it made when he smacked his belly button with his fingers. They didn't seem worried in the least, which worried Jeff more. When he next became conscious of his singing, they were halfway through the closer. No encore.

Chapter 8

1984

THEY WERE OUT OF THE SUN, BUT THAT DIDN'T MEAN MUCH. The inside of the box truck held onto the July heat like a cast iron skillet. The air hung dank and thick inside. A shadowy man stood up and faced the far wall. Javier heard what he was doing before the smell confirmed it. The coyotes hadn't even left a bucket to do their business in, but the hole in the floor at least allowed it to escape.

Javier pulled his shirt over his nose to stifle the festering odor. With some willpower, he redirected his thoughts to something more pleasing: baseball. When he grew up he wanted to be a combination of Fernando Valenzuela and Nolan Ryan. Back home, when the weather was just right, their radio picked up Astros games from Houston. The commentary was in English and he couldn't make out all the words, but he soon learned the important ones: double play, strikeout, home run.

The truck drifted onto the rumble strip at the edge of the highway, and it rattled the floor underneath them. Javier felt the vibrations all the way up into his teeth. Sweat rolled down his face and made his shirt cling to his skin. He smacked his lips and tried to wet them with his tongue, which felt like a dried-out sponge. He reached into his bag, took a swig from the jug, and fought back the urge to chug the whole thing. He swished the water through his teeth and wiggled his tongue around in it before swallowing. He sloshed the jug and figured he had half left. It was still a long way to Texas.

The trip was supposed to take seven hours. Though it was only a few hours to the border, they were being taken an extra three hundred miles to Houston. There were more jobs in that area, they were assured, and less of la migra than in Laredo or San Antonio. Javier thought that was considerate.

He couldn't tell how much time had passed, but he figured they still had another three or four hours to go. The loud vibrations of the road and the quieter vibrations of voices were interrupted by coughs and the occasional wallop of a pothole. The woman with the young boy rocked him back and forth in her lap. His eyes were closed and she brushed the dark bangs from his forehead as he slept. Javier listened for her song but couldn't hear it above the roar.

It was dark and sultry and deafening. The smell of body odor and piss was overwhelming. Wisps of exhaust fumes mingled in and made him queasy. He didn't know much about hell, but from what he had learned at church, this fit the description even better than fire and brimstone. He had another strong urge to run but nowhere to go. He leaned his head against the wall and closed his eyes, straining to conjure up better thoughts.

Since he was left-handed, and all the tattered gloves at his small country school were for right-handers, he played the one position you could usually get by without one: pitcher. He wore one of his father's old leather work gloves to at least have something to dull the sting of the ball when the catcher threw it back.

He got to where he could make even the bigger kids whiff with ease. They had no equipment, no opponents, no field besides the neighboring pasture they used for recreation. Javier dreamed about playing real ball in Houston, pitching off an actual mound, playing on grass that was soft and deep green instead of patchy and pale.

Eventually, Javier found himself in and out of a light sleep. When he woke, he realized his backpack wasn't there anymore. He sucked air in a panic and his eyes darted around, trying to locate it. Javier looked for the fat bearded man who had kept trying to get the people near him to share their canteens. But then Javier's hand brushed against the fabric, and he realized his backpack had just fallen from his lap. He felt ashamed for immediately assuming the man stole it.

His eyes felt puffy and he was more sapped than before his sultry nap. He didn't know how long he'd been out for, but it couldn't have been long. Not much had changed. Some slept. Others wore grim faces, blinking into the dark. He looked for the mother and child. The kid was still asleep in her lap. Javier wished he could be like the boy and sleep through the whole ordeal.

He located the fat bearded man leaning on the truck's rolling door and studied him for a moment. His cheeks jiggled from the bumpy highway and a receding sweat ring adorned his T-shirt. Javier was a little intimidated by him earlier, but now he just seemed sad. Javier pulled the jug from his bag and extended it toward the man, but he didn't look up.

"Oye," Javier said.

The man's head pointed toward the floor. Javier crawled over and extended the jug so that it was almost under the man's nose, but he still didn't budge. No whistling came from his nose like it had before. The truck hit another bump, and the man's head popped up and rolled over his shoulder. Javier cautiously tapped the man's shoulder and half-expected him to spring to life and grab him.

"Está bien?"

No response. He leaned in and felt cold sweat on the man's shirt when he touched it. No heartbeat. Javier wiped the sweat on his jeans. The smells once again overpowered him. He stood up and tried to decide what to do.

"Este hombre está muerto!" he shouted.

Heads turned. He repeated himself. The man was dead. A man with thin hair slicked back with sweat scrambled to the dead man and checked for a pulse as well. He slapped his cheek and told him to stay with him, but he was already gone. Javier's thoughts raced. Someone had to do something. He didn't know what that thing would be, but they were adults and they should know. When no one else moved, he did, toward the front, stepping over the people and bags and the pool by the piss hole. He made it to the front and began to bang on the metal with his fist.

"Ayuda! ¡Necesitamos ayuda!"

Someone hissed at him to sit down.

Javier kicked it a couple of times for good measure. The coyotes didn't hear or didn't want to let on that they did. The truck never even slowed down. Javier couldn't catch his breath. A warm fog had settled into his lungs that made breathing a chore. It was so hot. The sweat was pouring out of him now. He slid to the floor and realized he'd left his bag on the far end, across the mass of warm bodies. He felt the truck spin, spiraling into a sluggish heavy feeling, until a scream jolted him to attention. It was the mother.

"Mijo!" she cried.

Javier sprang to his feet. A rush of dizziness made him pause, but another howl from the woman sent him stepping over people in her direction. He stumbled over a knee, and a shoulder helped him regain his balance. When he got there the woman had the child on his stomach in her lap, patting him on the back while he wheezed. A man with long hair tied back in a thick ponytail kneeled in front of the mother. She said her son had a lung condition that Javier had never heard of. The long-haired man asked if he had a medication, and she said yes, but they'd run out. The man said they needed to get the boy to a hospital. He and two others headed to the front to try to get the coyotes' attention. He told Javier to try to keep the mother calm.

The woman had stopped yelling and now whimpered while stroking the boy's scalp. The others made it to the front and made as much noise as possible. They yelled and banged and kicked and whistled and cursed, but got the same response Javier had. They kept on though. The boy's breaths got faster and shallower. The woman said Hail Mary after Hail Mary and in a rapid and trembling voice. Javier didn't know how to keep her calm. He didn't know how to keep himself calm. The boy was on his back now. His eyes were open, but they fluttered white, trying to roll backward. The breaths weakened.

"No," she said. "Ay Dios."

The woman pressed the boy's face into her breast. Then there was no noise but the roar in Javier's ears. The woman's open mouth and quivering jaw made no noise. The people at the front who punched the walls with bloody knuckles made no noise. There was only the rushing blood in his eardrums. He sat with his shins pulled up close, and his mind tried to shield itself from another death, blotting out everything but survival.

Three people were dead by the time they made it to the abandoned parking lot on the edge of Houston. The fat man, the small boy, and the old lady. Javier never learned any of their names. No one was sure how long the old woman had been gone. She was silent and motionless in the corner when they departed and just stayed that way.

When they finally rolled the door open, almost nine hours after their departure, people fell out gasping and retching. Dry heaves. No one had enough fluid to vomit properly. Javier watched a coyote dump the old woman on the asphalt, like she was a sack of dirty rags. It took all three coyotes to lift the fat man, one at the legs and one under each arm.

The sun was so bright that it wasn't even dark when Javier closed his eyes—more like blood orange. The earth spun faster, like he was on a nightmarish merry-go-round. Murmurs nearby sounded alien and hostile. Javier dropped to his knees on the pockmarked asphalt, and the spinning and noise began to recede.

Though it was still hot outside, the breeze on his cheeks was heaven-sent. The moisture in the corners of his eyes puttered a little way down his cheeks. The fresh air was the best thing he'd felt since leaving Mexico that morning. As long as he stayed there with his eyes closed, maybe he would be okay. Maybe it would all just go away. He swallowed and felt a sandpapery sting. Tears welled up and he wiped them away.

He opened his eyes and saw that the mother of the young boy had torn the sleeve of her blouse. She shrieked at the coyotes, a sound only a mother can make, and held the boy in her arms, limp as string. The coyotes seemed scared she'd do something rash, but the fight had left her. She looked right past them, like they were harmless strays. Her baby was gone and she had nothing more to defend.

The coyotes pulled the last of the migrants from the truck. A couple of them couldn't stand on their own. When the coyotes let go, their legs crumpled under them. The mother's back was turned to Javier. He watched her shoulders rise and fall, rise and fall, trembling with sorrow. The others lay sprawled and wheezing in the summer heat, like the dead and wounded in some one-sided battle history couldn't be bothered with remembering. Before getting in the truck, the leader turned and faced the migrants one last time.

"Welcome to America."

2015

The owner had called it a VIP dressing room, but that was like labeling a sandwich cooler in a truck stop a gourmet dining experience. The walls were white cinder block, yellowed from grunge and the poor incandescent lighting. Wooden benches sat along the broad sides, and the concrete floor had a rusty drain in the center. A mirror the size of a cereal box, scratched with initials and curse words, was pinned above the porcelain sink.

Javier stared across the room at Marck, who lay with his knees bent and a forearm over his eyes. His upper half was still, but his knees spread wide and knocked together like a bored child's. He'd stopped babbling, which was nice. Javier leaned on the wall with his arms crossed over his gut. The low vibrations from the amplifiers and drums made a faint pulsing drone through the cinder block. When they stopped for good, Javier glanced at his watch. Right on time. One thing had gone according to plan.

He lost his temper when he found out Marck had snorted ketamine before the show—*again with this stupid drummer!*—but he had time to calm down. Marck removed his forearm and turned his head to Javier. At least he had the decency to pick a short-lasting drug.

"Where'd Webb go?"

"To help the guys load up," Javier said. "How you feeling?"

"All right."

Javier gently shook his head. "You *were* all right. Now you gotta deal with me."

Marck pushed himself upright.

"Where'd you buy it?"

Marck rubbed his eyes in circles with the heels of his palms.

"Place up the road," he said.

"Was that all of it?" Javier said.

Marck patted his jeans and felt the bag was gone. He nodded.

"I'm not your priest. I'm not your dad," Javier said. "What you do in your free time is your business. But now you made it everybody's problem. You know they have dogs at the checkpoints—"

"I was going to ditch it before we headed out," Marck said. "I'm not stupid."

"It doesn't take a smart man to know snorting horse tranquilizers before a set is a bad idea," Javier said.

Marck crossed his arms too. "So am I out or what?"

"Is that what you want?"

Marck didn't answer.

Javier looked in the dead center of his eyes and said, "Until we all decide we're done, no one walks away."

Marck watched him carefully, his mouth open a bit.

"We're all sticking our necks out," Javier said. "Right now, yours is out there the farthest. You know what can happen then, especially here in Juárez?" Javier waited for an answer that didn't come and then ran his thumb across his throat. Marck nodded.

"You have to make better decisions, Marck. Whether you realize it or not, those knuckleheads out there look up to you. They may not even like you, I don't know, but they respect your experience, your years on the road."

"Yep," Marck said quietly. "I understand." His eyes got a far-off look. They sat in silence until the rest of the band came through the door. They entered without the usual hooting and hollering that followed a show.

"Equipment loaded?" Javier asked. Dave and Jeff nodded.

"Where's Squat?"

"I don't know. He said he forgot something," Jeff said.

Javier's phone buzzed with a message from Ricky.

"Our guy's almost here."

"Sure you don't want some backup?" Dave asked.

"I'm sure," Javier said. "Just help Marck back to the bus."

Ricky and the migrants were on their way. In the meantime, Javier went to collect the payment for the band's performance. The door to the bar owner's office was half open, but Javier knocked anyway. The owner's shiny loafers were on his desk, one on top of the other, his face over a touchscreen tablet. Blue light glared on his reading glasses. Though Javier stood only a couple of feet from the desk, the man made no acknowledgment of him. Making the slightest of movements, the man laid the tablet down and slid his eyes up to meet Javier's. He stared with tight lips and a flat, annoyed expression. Javier held up eight fingers. One for each hundred in pesos they were owed for the show. The owner stared at him above the rim of his glasses. Javier wiggled his fingers for emphasis.

"Ochocientos," he said.

It was what they had agreed on beforehand. Forty bucks in the US. It was nothing compared to what they'd get from smuggling later on, but Javier could not make himself just let it go. It was the principle of it. The owner went back to his tablet. He swiped to the left, pressed in the center, and held it out to Javier.

A video played what looked like security footage, black-and-white in an empty corridor. Marck came into the frame and dropped his pants. He had his junk between his hands and pivoted back and forth on his heels like a sprinkler. The urine ran down the wall in streaks like paint put on too thick. The video cut off.

The owner held up eight fingers the same way Javier had. Then he put the first hand down and lowered the index and ring finger on the other. He rotated the lone finger to face Javier. The man opened a desk drawer. Javier tensed up and imagined a loaded 9mm.

But the man procured a checkbook and pen instead. He wrote in a swift yet controlled manner. The sound of the perforation tearing echoed in the quiet room. The owner slid the check toward Javier. He expected it to be a mean joke, that the amount would read zero dollars and zero cents. The check appeared real though, and the amount was the eight hundred they had agreed upon. Signed and everything. The only thing out of the ordinary was the memo box, which announced, in plain Spanish, that they were never welcome back at Dos Cuernos Cantina. Javier nodded and departed with the money that wouldn't even fill their tank halfway.

Before Javier could think on what had happened, a set of headlights flashed twice in the dark lot. The driver-side door of an old Dodge van creaked open. Javier had no doubt the man with the cowboy hat and a cigarette between his lips was Ricky. He flicked the butt and ground it under his pointed-toe ostrich boot. He had that lean cowboy walk, looking a little bit like swagger and a little bit like his underwear had ridden up on him. He shook Javier's hand.

"Ricky Madrid."

"Javier Espinoza."

Ricky turned so that he and Javier both faced the van. "I didn't believe it when George told me. A rock and roll band. Está extraño, güey. I've seen a lot, but—" Ricky chuckled and played air guitar. "How long you been at it?"

Javier considered lying but said, "Three months."

Ricky's face contorted like he'd tasted something bitter. He fished out a soft pack and a lighter from his shirt pocket. He held it out to Javier, who declined. Ricky nodded like he had something to say, but didn't speak until he got the cigarette lit and took a drag.

"You ever think about running drugs?" Ricky punctuated the sentence by waving the cigarette. "Meth, heroin, pinche fentanyl for all those fucked-up güeros. That's where the real money is."

Javier's jaw tightened. He shook his head.

"Eh, maybe that's smart. Moving the weight the cartels would ask you to, it's at least ten years if you get caught. I mean, if you lost that big of a shipment, you'd get your throat slit before it went to trial. Pero, in a perfect world, you're still looking at ten to fifteen years."

"Mmhmm," Javier said, wanting the subject to change.

"Me? I'm all about the people," Ricky said. "Harder to hide, but I like the challenge."

He took off his hat and rubbed his forehead. The streaks of gray in his parted hair belied his young rebel smile and the swagger in his movements. Ricky motioned for Javier to follow him to the van and opened the door to let him look inside. Javier casually brushed his elbow across Ricky's lower back when he leaned in, as if by accident, checking for a gun and feeling nothing but cotton and muscle.

The four migrants sat inside. Two sat close enough to each other that Javier could tell they were a couple. A young and sloe-eyed man put his arm around the woman when Javier peered in. It was dark, but moonlight saturated the interior and highlighted certain features: the tight lips on the young couple, the wild white eyebrows of the old man, and the plump cheeks of the middle-aged woman.

"Cómo están?" he asked.

"Bien," the old man said. The others nodded.

Javier turned away and asked, "Are they related?"

"No," Ricky spoke low. "That young couple came together, the rest I herded up myself. These aren't your average pollos. They have the right connections, family with money at least. The old man, though, he just pulled a fat wad of cash out of his sock and gave it to me." Ricky chuckled. "I have no idea what his deal is."

It wasn't what Javier had come to expect. A group of all men were most likely unrelated, heading north for work. The mixed groups they'd carried so far had been families. He wondered how Ricky found them.

"They need a professional to take them into Texas. But you'll do." Ricky nudged Javier in the ribs. "I collected before we came. Nobody's short."

Ricky took an envelope from the glove box. He opened it and began to count out bills on the hood. Javier tensed up but kept his eyes on Ricky, who smiled without looking up from the money.

"Relax," he said. "This ain't El Paso."

It wasn't the cops Javier was worried about. Ricky split it into four equal piles until nothing remained in his hand.

"This is to show I'm not cheating you. Four thousand per head, like we agreed on. Want to count it yourself?"

Javier shook his head. "I watched you."

"Alright then." Ricky picked up one of the stacks. "This covers my cut and the payment to El Jaleo."

"Whoa," Javier said. Ricky's 10 percent was expected. The other 15 percent wasn't. "What are you talking about?"

"El Jaleo, they run the coyotaje around here," Ricky said. When that didn't satisfy Javier, he went on. "They came up a couple years ago, after some of the bigger cartels splintered. It was chill for a minute, free market shit, you know? Then this guy Andrés Santiago started killing off coyotes who wouldn't come work for him. His gang runs drugs and pollos for the Juárez Cartel, so he has real power now. You either cut them in on your profits or—" Ricky put the two fingers clamped onto his cigarette to his temple. There was that name again: *Andrés*.

"We're the ones doing the work," Javier said.

"I know. You think I like it? I have to pay too. I used to work for myself, didn't owe nobody nothing. Now I can't find a peso on the sidewalk without them taking half," Ricky said.

"You lied," Javier said.

"This is the way it works down here. You're lucky it's just a quarter. The ones they've got their claws in, sometimes they only get to keep a couple thousand. And they're carrying way more people than you, getting busted all the damn time," Ricky said. He gathered the other three stacks, put them in the envelope, and handed it to Javier.

"I want what we agreed on."

"Well you're not getting it," Ricky said sternly. "If I were you I'd take my money, get across the border, and forget about Juárez. This ain't a city for fair trade. Try Monterrey. Shit, just stay in Texas. The music business has to be better than this."

Javier slid the envelope behind his jeans. Anger rose in his throat like gurgling motor oil. He was furious at the thought of getting ripped off. Ricky might have been telling the truth about this Andrés guy, or it might have just been a scare tactic. Either way, they had a deal and he'd just ripped it to shreds.

He eyed Ricky's handful of cash. Javier was almost certain he didn't have a gun on him, but there could be one in the van. If he let this guy push him around, it might become the new normal. What happened if they had to deal with him again? Javier's outrage blocked out the logic that, nine times out of ten, would have convinced him to just let it go. The odds weren't on his side, and this wasn't his home turf.

But something inside Javier's head gave way. He closed the distance between them, gripping Ricky's collar and sleeve. Javier got him off balance and swept Ricky's leg, knocking him on his back.

"Chingado!" Ricky shouted.

Javier took a step toward the money, which had landed on the ground. Ricky pushed up on his elbows, staring him down. Javier felt like he was on autopilot. A small part of him already screamed with regret, but the adrenaline kept on coursing and guiding the way. He knelt down to pick up the cash. Javier counted out twenty hundreds, the 10 percent they'd agreed to, and slapped it on the hood. Ricky didn't protest. He didn't lunge for a gun. He just slowly got up from the asphalt and brushed himself off with the stoic look of a man who'd played this game many times before.

"Ten percent," Javier said. "If that gets you into trouble, that's your problem. This is what we agreed on."

He opened the van's back door and told the migrants it was time to go. They'd seen what happened and scrambled out to follow his order. Javier's confidence surged. He'd backed Ricky down. The migrants trailed Javier, who glanced over his shoulder. Ricky stood by his little stack of cash on the hood like a spindly ocotillo cactus, somehow tall and crooked at the same time.

Ricky shook his head, a slow burn in his eyes.

"This could've been easy."

———

Javier and the migrants turned the corner as Squat stepped off the bus, almost running into each other. Squat flinched and blurted out, "I was just charging my phone."

Javier nodded warily. He ushered everyone inside and had them sit in the living area. He apologized for the trouble with Ricky, explaining that he and his men were not like him. They would not put greed over their welfare. He gave each of them half of their cash back, told them to hold onto it until they made it safely.

Then he explained how the run would work. He'd given the same speech to several groups over the last few months, attempting to smooth any fears or mistrust the migrants had. It was automatic at this point, passionless. It'd struck him as funny that these runs were about the only times he still spoke Spanish. In work, in life, it was almost all English. He didn't forget, but sometimes it felt strange coming off his tongue. It sounded like somebody else. Spanish was his first language, his only real language until he mastered English in his teens. Now it was relegated to convincing skittish migrants that they were in good hands, as far as rock bands moonlighting as coyotes go.

He told them where they'd be hidden. He demonstrated with two hard boot stomps the signal that meant they were almost to the inspection checkpoint, and the need for total silence. He repeated the vital information, including what would happen after they crossed the border. Javier explained that they had to remain in the cases until they made it to the storage unit in El Paso.

Everyone had to know their job, even if it was just to stay quiet and out of sight. These weren't all rookies though. The old man said he had snuck across the river more times than that boy had birthdays, motioning at Jeff. The man said he didn't need to be taught how to lie down and shut up. Javier told him if he understood so well, he could start now. The old man glared but kept quiet.

"Pues," Javier said. It was time.

Though it seemed like two whole days had passed since crossing into Mexico that morning, it was still Friday. The traffic had thinned. Neighborhoods that had bustled in the daylight looked like ghost towns after dark.

Webb drove and Javier stood on the recessed steps, looking out the cracked windshield. No one spoke. There was only the gentle whir of the pavement and the hiss of the brakes when they stopped. Javier clenched his jaw over and over again, like he tended to do when he got anxious. He hadn't expected to feel any different.

He glanced in the mirror. Squat rubbed his palms back and forth on the thighs of his jeans like something stubborn was stuck on his hands.

He cocked his head, listening for something, after the bus hit a pothole.

This port of entry was smaller than the one they took into Mexico that morning. There were only six lanes, and two of them were closed. The bus idled toward the bridge and stopped with ten sets of red brake lights in front of them. The flow was less steady at this hour.

Webb bared his teeth and yawned so big that he looked like a puppet. The yawn's magnetism pulled the others in one by one until Javier did the same. He didn't feel sleepy but still smacked his cheeks and reached for the tepid energy drink in the cup holder. They moved up in line by a car length.

An old man in a flowing beige shirt walked down the line of cars with sombreros hanging from stakes on the wooden pole over his shoulder. The vendors did most of their business during the day, at times when the gridlock gave them a captive audience. This man apparently hadn't made enough to call it a day yet. He walked the road saying "Sombrero eight dollar" to each vehicle he passed with a smile. Javier stared past him into the brake lights ahead. The man went to the next lane over and snaked back toward the checkpoint.

Javier felt a knot in his stomach. The kind that normally climbed up his ribs and settled behind his eyes. The bus filled the gap in the line, which moved like sap down a tree. Something about Squat bothered him. He kept cutting his eyes to the floor, shifting in his seat. They all knew he was bad at keeping secrets.

"Squat—"

"Yeah."

"Something wrong?"

"No. Why?"

"You're acting funny."

Squat crossed his legs and his arms in a poor attempt to look casual.

"Just nervous," he said. "This is risky."

That was true, but Javier knew that wasn't all that was bothering him. Then a detail from earlier in the evening returned. The attractive woman from the show, the one Squat had been making eyes at. He'd seen them flirting after the show but didn't read much into it. Squat wasn't telling him something.

"Squat, that woman you were talking to after the show—"

"Who?" Squat said, and when Javier just looked at him, "Oh, yeah. What about her?"

"What were you talking about?"

"Oh, you know. Music. And stuff. She was a fan."

"Yeah?" Javier said. He traced Squat's eyes to the little table between them and walked over to it. It was bolted down so it stayed in place on the road. If you removed that table and slid out the wood panel that its wide base straddled, it revealed a small crawlspace beneath the floor. For their first run, before the reinforced road cases, they'd used it as a hiding place for a few migrants. It was too hot and cramped to pack four people down there for a long journey, but for a single woman, at night, it could work just fine.

Javier put a hand on the table. Squat tried to play it cool, but he had an awful poker face, like a kid whose lie was almost out of rope. The other band members didn't seem to be picking up on any of it. Javier knelt by the A/C vent in the floor. He said, "Hello." There was no answer, but Squat's eyes looked like they were going to get as big as cue balls.

"Está bien?" Javier said. He waited. "Oye!"

"Estoy bien," a woman's muffled voice said.

Squat's eyes dropped. The other bandmates looked on in surprise.

"Whoa," Dave said.

"The hell Squat?" Jeff said.

"Look, hear me out." Squat put his palms up. "Her name's Isabel. She's a really nice girl. We got to talking after the show. She told me she's been trying to get into Texas to find her dad. She hasn't heard from him in months and she's worried something happened."

"What made you think you could sneak her on without telling any of us?" Jeff said, anger buzzing through his vocal cords.

"Squat," Javier said, frowning. "You should have told me."

"What would you have said?" Squat said. "Better to ask forgiveness."

"Well, you're not getting any," Jeff said. "You can keep up the good Samaritan act if you want, but I saw the way you were staring at her. It's not your conscience at work. It's your hard-on."

"Hey," Squat snapped. "That's not true."

"Whatever." Jeff looked out the window. "We have to ditch her. We can slip her out the door while the agents are busy. We pay her to take off and keep quiet."

"She doesn't want money," Squat said. "She wants to find her dad."

"I go to Texas," Isabel said beneath their feet.

"Great," Jeff said.

"What's one more?" Marck rolled a drumstick between his fingers. "If we don't, like, show mercy and compassion, what's the point in any of this? What is the meaning of life—if not to love?"

They all turned and looked, wondering whose words were coming out of Marck's mouth.

"Look." Jeff pointed at Marck and then at Squat. "You two are done making decisions. The adults will figure this out."

"What were you thinking?" Dave shook his head at Squat.

"She has to go," Jeff said. "Now."

Javier listened to them argue but kept his eyes ahead. There were seven vehicles between them and the checkpoint. The agents had stopped at the second one in line to speak with the driver.

"No time," Javier said. "We have a better chance if she stays put."

Javier surprised himself with how well he kept it together. After everything that had gone wrong, in the midst of chaos, his focus held strong. Marck and Squat's knuckleheaded decisions were troubling, but something allowed him to move past it. Getting across the border was the goal, and to do that they'd all have to adapt.

"This is insane. They'll find her," Jeff protested.

"You want to throw her out now?" Javier pointed through the windshield. "You might as well walk up to those agents and confess everything."

"Javier. I don't think this is—"

"She stays," Javier said.

The two agents, small figures from that far off, went inside a travel trailer up ahead. This was no place for indecision. He was angry and disappointed in Squat, but he'd deal with him later. Javier refocused, took stock of his surroundings. He put a hand on the table and felt the sturdiness of its base. At least Squat had done something right. Then something shiny caught his eye.

Headlights glowed white in the side mirror. Javier squinted. A black Ram with no plates pulled up in one of the closed lanes and then whipped in behind the bus. Its lights shut off and two masked men bailed out and hustled toward them. Ricky's pointy-toed boots were the first thing Javier recognized, and then the pistol in the other man's hand.

Chapter 9

1984

JAVIER HAD ALWAYS WANTED TO SEE THE OCEAN, AND when the coyotes announced Houston as the destination, it seemed like fate. He dreamed of going to the beach, maybe getting taken in by a nice lonely couple unable to have kids of their own. He'd be a fisherman, and she'd be a schoolteacher. Javier would go to school and get fluent in English. Maybe he'd get to see Nolan Ryan pitch in person.

But none of that fit what he was seeing. It didn't seem like he was anywhere near the ocean, or even a city for that matter. Everywhere he looked it was cracked asphalt and blocky warehouses and overgrown trees. He started walking. Though she was long gone, the wails of the childless mother still rang in his ears.

Eventually, a bit of the skyline appeared over the trees. It was far off but let him know he was going in the right direction. Javier still didn't know what came next. The air was muggy, and his heavy feet scraped the concrete. Some clouds came in and blocked the sun, and he thanked

God for them. But they got more aggressive, and a charcoal-colored front roiled in from the east. The thunder growled a stern warning.

Javier found a filling station and locked himself in the bathroom. He turned the cold-water knob on full blast and put his mouth under it. When he had his fill he took the jug from his pack and filled it as well. He wasn't going to take water for granted again.

Then he caught himself in the splattered mirror. His hair swirled in several directions and his bangs were mashed flat across his forehead. His shirt was drenched in sweat where it touched his skin. He peeled it off and splashed cool water on his face and under his arms. He stared into the mirror, unsure if he recognized the kid looking back at him. Someone banged on the door.

Javier jumped. "Un momento."

He used the bulky white hand dryer to dry his torso and shirt the best he could. The door banged again. Javier put the warm damp shirt back on, and in just a few seconds it undid all the good from the cool water. It clung to his skin and made him flush. His stomach was tight and unsettled. When he opened the door an older man stood with crossed arms. Thick hair covered his forearms and poked out of the top of his shirt. He had on a clean blue cap with *J&R Pipeline Supply* on the fat front panel.

"Take a damn bath in there? Who you think pays the water bill?" The man stuck his head inside the bathroom, checking the state of things. Javier lowered his head. The man grunted. He went back behind the counter and unfolded a newspaper.

The snack section, particularly the beef jerky, caught Javier's eye. He hadn't noticed his hunger on the truck, if only because his thirst was so much stronger. His stomach had settled, and his mouth watered while he eyed the spread. He picked up a big and unnaturally shiny plank of beef. He reached into his backpack and pulled out several rumpled pesos. There weren't many of them left.

In spite of his hunger, he decided that getting into the city had to come first. He had seen a bus stop down the road. He decided to see if he could catch one to the city center. Then he'd get food with what he had left over. He began to leave.

"Hold it right there," the man snapped. Javier did, confused. The man continued, "And where are you planning on going with that?"

The man's eyes fixed on the beef jerky, which Javier suddenly realized was still in his hand. Javier took a step away from the door and held it up.

"Perdón," he pleaded. "No quise—"

"No hablo Mexican," the man said. "Speak English, young man."

Javier knew enough to get by, but he drew a blank. His mind scrambled for the correct words, but it only came back with fragments and nonsense, so he said nothing. The man took this as a sign of defiance. His legs splayed out and he put his hands on his waist.

"Come with me. We're going to wait for the police in my office."

While Javier had a hard time forming his own English, he had no problem understanding that he wanted no part of this man's plan.

"I pay." Javier fumbled for the pesos in his backpack.

"Money with dead wetbacks on it ain't no good here. You have American dollars? Washingtons? Jacksons?" The man pronounced each syllable like Javier was hard of hearing. Javier shook his head.

"That's what I thought." The man stormed around the counter, and Javier chucked the beef stick at his face. He took off, out the door and down the street, with his stomach sloshing. He pumped his legs as hard as he could, but they gave out much quicker than he was used to. He doubled over and vomited thin sink water onto the asphalt. He could hear his heartbeat in his ears. He finally caught his wind and felt some relief when he looked around and saw no one coming after him.

He walked a little while, and the sky flashed in front of him. He couldn't see the actual lightning, but the clouds lit up like a flashlight through a cotton sheet. The air smelled different here, musty and steeped with exhaust fumes. There was no one around. Everyone had scurried for cover like the rabbits did back home when the coyotes' howls started to sound more like promises than threats.

The downpour drenched Javier before he could find shelter. It seemed like the whole ocean was being poured out. He found a concrete block building with an open bay and darted inside, watching the rain pound cars and pavement. He noticed his breath, loud and shallow, resonating in the absence of the battering rain.

The smell of metal shavings and grease floated up to his nostrils. A radio played a song full of bouncy accordion. Javier turned around and saw that he was in an auto body shop. Three Latinos were leaning on a car and watching him. Javier asked how far downtown was and they said about ten miles and pointed in the direction he'd been going. They told him he could stay until the rain let up.

They finished their Cokes and went back to working on an older Nova. He watched them cut away the driver-side fender and part of the front bumper. At first he stood back, but then he crept up closer to where they were working. He thought they might run him off, but they just went on with their work like nobody was watching over their shoulders.

"Oye." The heavier man motioned him over.

Javier was hesitant. The man got Javier to hold up on the bumper and take the pressure off while he leaned under the hood with his socket wrench. His plump cheeks had black smudges. He scrunched his lips, turning his coarse mustache into an upside-down U, while ratcheting the last bolt out.

Javier liked being helpful. Once the man got the rest of the bumper laid aside he walked away and came back with a foil package and a Coke. Javier's stomach rumbled. He felt like he could eat a whole cow. Inside were two cold tacos, refried beans wrapped in flour tortillas. They were delicious though. Javier tore into the food and drank the Coke too fast. He finished the first taco and roared out a burp. The men laughed and told him to slow down.

They asked him why he was headed into Houston. He lied and told them he had family there. They nodded. The one with the gray stubble said that a boy his age shouldn't be traveling alone. He told him he didn't know what foolish ideas he had in his little head, but that he should go back to where he belonged. Javier tucked his chin to his chest and belched into his fist. The man who'd given him the food laughed and said that was a good response.

He asked if Javier needed a ride. He was headed toward the city after they closed up and could take him as far as Brays Bayou. Javier didn't know what that meant but nodded and said that would be great. A half hour later they washed up in the shop sink that had probably once been white but now looked grayer than the sky outside. It had finally stopped raining.

The man loaded his toolbox into the trunk of his old sedan. The front seats had old oversized Oilers T-shirts stretched over them. The ashtray was full of pennies, and the interior smelled like burnt steel and garlic. Once they were on the road he finally introduced himself as Toño. He said he was from a little town between Monterrey and Reynosa. Javier told him where he was from. Toño asked how long he'd been in the US, and Javier said not long. Toño gave him a knowing glance and left it at that.

They made a little small talk about the rain—the hot sun peeked through, steaming off the damp concrete—but they mostly just listened to the radio. A polka-rhythm Ramón Ayala song came on and Toño whistled to it. Javier wished the ride wouldn't end. He felt safe watching the highway pass and the sunset fade into pale purple over a grove of oak trees. Being near Toño gave him a good feeling.

It wasn't until the deejay came on and announced they were tuned into the Gulf Coast's premier Tejano station that it hit Javier. He was in the United States. He'd known that since he escaped from the truck, but he hadn't felt it. Now it finally sank in. His mother didn't get to see it. Neither did Nina or that teenage couple from the train. He made it. He felt like he might cry, but he didn't want to appear weak in front of the kind stranger. He sniffed and held back the tears.

They crossed the bridge over Brays Bayou, and Toño pulled over at a bus stop. He asked Javier if he knew how to get to his family's place, and Javier said he did. Before he shut the door Toño offered him a piece of advice: Be aware of your surroundings, but don't live in fear. They'll get you or they won't.

Live your life, chavo.

2015

It might have been a mistake to haggle with Ricky over the amount, Javier realized, watching the two men come around the front of the bus. They didn't waste time, but they didn't seem afraid of being seen either.

Yellow light shone off the skull mask on Ricky's partner. His body was all lean muscle, his gait fluid and determined. He had a large tattoo of a bear paw on the side of his neck. The claws ended just short of his earlobe and jawline. It seemed to wave when he checked his surroundings. His handgun was drawn but hung low and discreet near his leg.

Javier's fresh confidence wilted. Breathing became a chore. He couldn't convert what he was seeing into words.

"Uppffh."

The bandmates looked on in confusion. Javier reached over and locked the door. Skullmask tugged on it and scowled. Ricky brushed him aside, pulled down his own mask, and tapped the glass with the muzzle of his gun. Webb's eyes were big, looking for an escape route in vain.

"Who is that?" Jeff said.

"He's our connection," Javier said. "The one I told you about."

"Why is he *here*?" Dave asked.

Ricky stood patiently, crossing his arms with his handgun resting on his bicep. They weren't going anywhere, Javier knew. He saw an agent in the distance, and somehow letting the armed men onto their bus felt like the wiser option. Javier unlocked the door, which Skullmask slung open. He stood at the front of the bus, keeping his 9mm close to his untucked black shirt, but his target was unmistakable. Javier tried to bring his focus away from the barrel's black eye, from the fact it could make meat scraps of his torso.

Ricky took his time stepping into the bus. He stood beside Skullmask with his hands on his hips, staring at the band members. They had all stood up as if it might help, eyes wide and mouths ajar.

"Sit."

The bandmates obliged, cramming onto the little couch so that their shoulders overlapped. Ricky's eyelids hung heavy over the whites, but his eyes were focused and devoid of emotion. The red truck ahead pulled up a space and left a gap between them. Javier felt the wicked density returning to his chest. Slowly—like someone was stacking a load on him brick by brick. Webb stared at the gap and then at the gun. His Adam's apple bobbed.

"Pull up." Ricky tilted his head that way.

Webb shifted. The bus lurched. He communicated he was sorry with a sideways glance. The bus crept up nearer to the truck and stopped. Skullmask leaned toward the windshield. His black lace-up boots creaked. A dog led an agent to the SUV idling just thirty yards away.

"Cameras will see your truck," Javier said.

"Good luck to them. No plates," Ricky said. "Now the money. Get it."

Javier wanted to do nothing less than turn the money back over to Ricky. Money they had earned, or were about to before he showed back up. His partner finally pulled down his mask, revealing chubby cheeks that didn't seem to match the rest of him, like his real face had yet to emerge from under a layer of baby fat. He looked nervous too. His grip on the gun tightened and loosened and repeated. He kept his finger outside the trigger guard, thankfully. His dark eyes seemed to look not at Javier but at something past him, maybe past the border entirely.

Javier knew he had no choice. Not complying would get them shot, busted, or both. He had no desire to test the mettle of men who had shown up armed to one of the most heavily policed places on the continent. Ricky's coiled stance seemed to herald foul deeds.

Javier went to the cabinet, opened the door, and removed the false back. He tossed the manila envelope to Ricky, who dropped it. He gave Javier a flat, annoyed look and picked it up. Ricky dumped the bills on the counter.

"Where's the rest?"

"I let them hold onto their other half until we're in El Paso," Javier said.

Ricky shook his head like that was a stupid thing to do. He counted bills, making a small stack off to the side. He held it up when he finished.

"Add this to what you gave me earlier and it makes 25 percent."

Ricky picked up five hundred more and held it up like the rest.

"This is my pickup fee. If you would like to avoid the pickup fee"— he paused and made eye contact with Javier—"don't be a pendejo and make us chase you down."

He folded the wad and stuffed it in his back pocket. He put the rest in the envelope. Javier studied him. Were they really not going to take all of it? Ricky must have seen as much on Javier's face because then he scowled.

"Look, I'm not a bad guy," Ricky said. "But you were going to put me in a bind. And that just can't happen."

"Why'd you let me leave with it?"

Ricky shrugged. "I wouldn't have gotten to see this look on your face."

He felt the envelope as if he were weighing it, as if its feeling lighter put the world back into balance. He tossed it to Javier, who clasped it against his chest.

"You got balls. I'll give you that. Now you know I do too. Don't forget it. Nando, vámonos." Ricky motioned to his partner. He paused at the steps. "But don't mistake a fistful of cojones for power. Andrés Santiago is a maniac. Especially when he thinks he's being cheated. He'd cut all of our throats and move right on with his life, never regret it for a second. People either help him grow his power or they're in the way. I just did you a big favor, cabrón."

Ricky went out the door. Nando lingered a second before putting his mask back on and following. The bus idled low. Javier tried to process all that had just happened. He saw the pickup's headlights and then its brake lights in the mirror while they turned around and drove out onto the one-way road. Their heart rates plateaued.

"What just happened?" Dave asked.

"We got jacked," Squat replied, staring straight ahead.

The red truck pulled up again. Webb followed right behind this time, hands gripping ten and two like an anxious student driver. Javier was jarred, but he wasn't angry. Ricky had surprised him twice. First by showing up here and then by not using his leverage to rob them blind.

Reading people, making quick judgments about their motives, was vital to his job. This time he'd failed. Ricky was neither the harmless hustler nor the cold-blooded gangster Javier had seen him as in flashes throughout the night. He wondered what he'd missed, halfway watching two agents and a dog approach the travel trailer ahead of the red truck. They shone their flashlights and went inside, unaware of what had just taken place with Ricky and the money.

"Shee-it," Dave said, his inner hick coming out and stretching it into two twangy syllables.

Jeff nodded in agreement. "What the hell was that about?"

"We had a disagreement about the split," Javier said.

"And you didn't think that was worth mentioning to us?" Jeff said.

The bandmates remained crammed on the couch until Marck pried himself out from between them. "Did you see that gun, man? I didn't sign up for this. No way." Marck's laidback attitude had abandoned him on the backside of the ketamine high. He rubbed his stubbly hair and paced the floor. "I don't like guns."

Javier saw the glazed eyes and shell-shocked expressions of the bandmates and knew they couldn't dwell on this. Not now.

"I take the blame on that one. You can rip me for it later," he said. "But there's no time to lose focus. See those agents? They'll be here on the bus in a minute, looking for anything suspicious."

"Great, yeah," Jeff said. "Everybody act like we weren't just held at gunpoint."

"Javier's right," Squat said. "We gotta keep it together. We don't have any other choice."

The others looked at him in solemn agreement.

Marck gripped his scalp with both hands. "My heart's beating so damn fast. I think I'm gonna have a heart attack."

"Marck, it's gonna be okay."

Marck's eyes flashed with fire. More fear than anger. Javier nodded and put his hand on his shoulder. Marck's look softened, and he wiped his nose with his forearm.

"I didn't have a good feeling to begin with," Marck said. "But now there's guns waving around—"

"The only thing that matters is not tipping off these agents right now. Everything else is later problems," Javier said. "Have a seat. Take a few deep breaths. Don't give them a reason to be suspicious, and maybe they won't invent one."

Marck sat down at the table, and then there was a knock at the door. Through the glass Javier saw a man with thin arching lips and wheat-colored hair gelled into a stiff cowlick. He opened the door and squared up to Javier immediately, blinking quicker than most.

"Documentation."

Javier handed it over. The agent flipped through the stack of passport cards, pausing on Javier's green card. Agents always got hung up on that. It might allow Javier to pass in and out of the country, but it didn't mean he was a citizen. Not even close, in their eyes.

"What's your purpose in the US?" he asked.

"Oh, we're Americans," Webb said. "Sir."

"Kill the engine."

Javier gave Webb a look that he hoped communicated he should shut up and let him do the talking. Webb faced forward and turned the key.

"We're a rock band," Javier said, enunciating carefully. "We do a lot of shows in the region. Had a gig in Juárez tonight and now we're coming home."

The agent leaned past him to look over the band members. Marck sat at the table, reading or pretending to read a magazine. The other three remained on the couch. Squat grinned and waved.

"This is the band," Javier said. "I'm their manager." He had grown accustomed to the stony demeanor of border agents, so the silence didn't bother him much. The agent's pale searching eyes were starting to though.

"Did you acquire any articles in Mexico that you need to declare?"

"Just some tortillas," Javier said.

The agent opened his mouth like he was about to say something but stopped.

"Anything I'm forgetting, guys?" Javier asked.

Jeff and Squat shook their heads.

"Nope," Dave said.

The agent nodded and said, "Would you all move to the front of the bus? I need to have a look around."

They moved to the front and crowded around Webb. Javier wondered where the man who had been with him had gone. He and the dog could already be searching the storage compartment underneath them, sniffing out the secrets they had worked so hard to conceal.

The agent searched through drawers and the closet in the sleeping area, rapping his knuckles and focusing on the sounds, looking for hidden compartments. The work had his full attention. His expression was flat, but his eyes were focused and bright. Every step he took reminded Javier of Isabel, how she was probably holding her breath and trying her best to be invisible with the agent walking right over her. A dog barked outside.

"So you're a band, huh?"

Javier nodded.

"What's your band's name? Sly and the Family Stallone?" the agent asked.

"No," Javier said. "That was the name of the band we bought the bus from."

"So what's your name?" he asked, turning toward the bandmates on the couch.

"Their name is—" Javier started.

"I asked *them*," the agent said. "They're the musicians, aren't they?"

Jeff said "Airbrake" at the same time Squat said "Whirlwinds."

"We're between names," Dave said.

The agent cocked his head. "Between names?"

"Bad dog," a hoarse voice shouted outside. The dog barked again and then fell silent.

The other agent came up the steps. The sturdy man held a dog on a leash that looked equal parts German shepherd and pit bull. The Frankenstein dog had the rabbit-like back legs of one breed and squatty muscular frame of the other. The agent stared at his partner and then the dog.

"What's wrong with Jada?" he asked.

"I don't know. She growled at me again when I tried to lead her," he said with a thin Mexican accent.

"Did you see the way she bared her teeth at that guy earlier? He almost pissed his pants in front of his wife and kids. I'm afraid she's going to bite someone, Luke."

The dog looked up and Dave backed away another half step, squeezing into Javier's side. Luke bent down and put his face near the dog's muzzle. She appeared calm and relaxed and began to pant when Luke scratched her behind the ears.

"Good girl," he said.

"Don't coddle her. That's the last thing she needs."

"She minds me, Gabriel. If you worked with her more—"

"Like I've got time to train this dog on top of everything else." He stared in the band's direction. His dark eyes zeroed in and his bottom teeth showed. He didn't say anything but his expression bent into a frown. His eyebrows bore down on his eyelids while he stared at them. Jeff met his eyes for a second but soon blinked and looked at his shoes. Squat smiled nervously and then let it fade when it was ignored. Dave brushed his hair behind his ears and bumped into Javier again. He hadn't taken his eyes off the dog.

"Double check the interior with her," Luke said.

Gabriel pulled on the leash and the dog barked twice and it filled the bus. They all jumped. Squat's eyes looked too big for their sockets. Gabriel stared at him for a moment, squinting. "C'mon, Jada." This time she followed.

"I'm going to need you all to step outside," Luke said.

He asked them to unlock and open the storage compartment. Javier tried to stay calm, to keep breathing. He opened the door in a slow controlled manner, hoping to show that he wasn't bothered by the agent's inquiry into that particular area. He shone his flashlight inside, between the cases and into the darkened corners. He examined boxes and instrument cases and rapped on all sides of the compartment like he had done inside.

"What's in the cases?"

"Those are our road cases. They've got pedals, cables, spare strings, heads, that sort of stuff," Javier said.

"Heads?" he asked.

"Amp heads," he blurted. "It's what you put on top of a cab. Drives the speaker."

He nodded. "There isn't enough space to raise the lids, so we'll have to bring them out."

"They're pretty heavy," Webb said.

"That's okay."

Javier's lips stretched into a smile. "Sure thing."

They helped the agent roll the boxes onto the pavement, careful not to jar anything inside. The bandmates kept shooting Javier worried glances, but he ignored them. They had been over this. All they could do was trust that everyone was well hidden.

The cases had the shape of Texas stenciled in silver. The agent opened both the cases, peering into one and then the other. The false bottoms were still in place and on top of them were tangles of equipment and cords. He picked up an effects pedal and a reverb stompbox, then stepped back. Javier knew the migrants must be freaking out, but the cases were as silent and still as you would expect of any inanimate object.

Gabriel followed the dog down the steps. The dog tried to turn left, but he held firm on its leash. The pit shepherd stiffened her legs and dug in. Gabriel tugged and she hunkered down lower. His thick arm jerked the leash and the dog relented. He joined his partner near the boxes and the dog sat. She appeared calm then, panting and looking at nothing in particular with lax eyes.

"All clear inside," Gabriel said.

"I need to look in that storage space." He crawled in with the flashlight.

Gabriel led Jada to the cases. She sniffed until a knock came from underneath the bus. The dog's ears perked up and she whipped her neck in that direction. When she was convinced that Luke was okay, she continued to sniff, more curiously than businesslike, the way most dogs smell a patch of grass that's been pissed on again and again. Gabriel watched the band, studying them like an equation that hadn't quite clicked.

"I've seen you guys," Gabriel said.

"Oh yeah?" Javier said evenly, trying to conceal his nerves.

Gabriel just nodded and narrowed his eyes.

"Jada pick up on anything?" Luke said, crawling out and brushing himself off.

"Nope," Gabriel said.

"Alright." Luke turned to face Javier. "Thank you for your cooperation. If you would—"

"Wait a minute," Gabriel said. He squeezed Jada's leash in one hand and brought the other up and pointed at the band with his meaty index finger.

"I *know* you fucking guys."

Javier hadn't thought the vise on his heart could get any tighter, but the agent proved him wrong. No one met the agent's stare. Squat shook his head. Jeff tucked his chin into his chest to hide his face. Gabriel kept the finger on them. His accusing look roused into a toothy grin.

"You're that band," he shouted.

Javier's eyes widened. He, along with the others, didn't know whether to feel relieved or more nervous.

"Y'all played that big Halloween party in Midland last year. You had the Alice Cooper makeup and highway patrol uniforms. I almost didn't recognize you." He grinned and stared. "What was your name then?"

"Cooper Troopers," Jeff said.

"That's right." Gabriel laughed. "You guys are crazy."

Javier sensed they were still in danger, but the vise had loosened a few turns. The band sensed this as well.

"I bet you had to be pretty stoned to think of that," Gabriel said.

A series of mumbles came from the bandmates.

"My daughter played me one of your songs," Gabriel said, his accent growing thicker the more excited he got. "At first I couldn't really get into it. All over the place, you know. But then I started really listening, hearing all the instruments do their thing, and I was like, whoa these dudes are badass. That conjunto you had backing you in Midland, where are those guys at?"

"Oh," Javier said. "I used to manage the bajo sexto player in another band. They happened to be in town and were willing to play for beer."

Gabriel considered this and then said, "Well that was a hell of a show. The way you blended all those instruments—that was sick, bro."

"Thanks," Jeff said.

Jada jerked on the leash. Gabriel grasped it with both hands and held on. The dog barked and gnashed her teeth, trying to pull him down the line. Even with all his weight, the dog hunkered down and steadily moved in the direction she wanted to go.

"Luke, I think she's on to something." Gabriel turned to Javier. "Think you can roll those cases back in yourselves?"

Javier and the others nodded in unison like bobbleheads.

Gabriel held firm on the now lunging Jada and said, "Be careful out there."

"Will do," Javier said.

"You too," Jeff added.

Gabriel let the dog pull him on, soon transitioning from walk to jog. Luke looked at the band and then at Jada on the trail.

"Load your equipment, pull up to the next checkpoint, and they'll process your documents," he said.

"Thank you, sir," Javier said. Squat tipped a nonexistent cowboy hat to the man.

Webb pulled up to the last booth. An old man with round glasses took their passport cards and papers. He flipped through them and pecked at a keyboard, cross-referencing their IDs with an international criminal database. The man glared at the screen and scratched a thin wisp of white hair. He punched a couple more buttons and then glared again, his squinting face illuminated by the computer. A chime went off and a green bar flashed on the screen. The man grinned and pressed the button to raise the boom gate.

"Welcome back to the United States," he said.

They drove through the last gate and back onto US soil. A floodlight shone on a raised Texas flag, and its lone star rolled in the night breeze. Javier knew the nerves of the migrants in hiding were singed like his. But they'd won this round. The border and its armed agents faded away, and El Paso shone hazy gold in front of them.

Chapter 10

1984

JAVIER LAY ON HIS BACK, ONE ARM BEHIND HIS HEAD, staring at industrial light fixtures that looked like upside-down mixing bowls. There were no windows, and the lights never shut off. If not for the large clock above the steel door it would have been impossible to tell one day from the next. Even with it, he was still unsure. It felt like Monday, which would mean it was his fourth day inside.

The detention center swirled old gymnasium, refugee camp, and prison into one tasteless dish. Javier overheard that it was the first of its kind, the ungodly byproduct of a contract between the US government and a for-profit corporation. He wasn't sure what that meant, but he didn't like the place one bit.

Chain-link dividers split them into four sections. The detainees wore no uniforms, which made it seem a little less like prison. Everyone wore their own clothes: all shades of blue jeans, T-shirts with American logos, worn-down sneakers. Breakfast was white bread with a pat of margarine and a bruised apple. Dinner wasn't much better. The grown men in the other sections didn't seem to get any more than the boys did. Word was that women were kept in a separate wing.

There were something like a hundred detainees in Javier's area and only two toilets. He had peed his pants waiting in line the second day. The urine stung his thigh, but it was the embarrassment that felt like it was going to kill him. A thin-mustached teenager noticed and snarled in disgust. Then he saw Javier's pained, flushed face and took him by the arm. He marched Javier to the front of the line and announced he was next. The kid up front tried to argue, but the teenager wasn't having it. When Javier tried to thank him he just said "por nada" and shoved him toward the empty toilet.

The facility had more people than beds. Those who were lucky slept in rows of steel-framed bunks with thin blue pads on them. Javier had spent his two nights on the concrete, curled up and shivering with his arms pulled into his shirt. He got a bunk after a quiet boy with close-set eyes was sent back to Tamaulipas. They told Javier he would be processed soon, but he learned that *soon* could mean weeks.

Javier traced the exposed ducts above, wondering if they could be used as escape tunnels. He laid his forearm over his eyes. What was the point? Even if he got out, they'd just catch him again. He hadn't been in the US for two whole days before he got picked up. Some migrants lived here years and years, worked jobs and raised families without being caught. And he didn't make it forty-eight hours. He felt sick and utterly alone.

Javier had slept in a park his first night in Houston, underneath a big twisting live oak. He ran out of food the next day. He didn't want to ask for a handout, but the hungrier he got, the less his pride seemed to matter. At a deli downtown, the lady working the register gave him a free meal, but by the time he was on the second half of his turkey sandwich a man in a suit walked in the door. Javier tensed up when he stopped at his booth.

The agent showed his badge and asked Javier where his parents were. Javier lied and said they were at home, a couple of blocks away. The cashier wouldn't make eye contact with him, and Javier knew she had called.

The officer asked for his address, and Javier blanked. He was broke and tired and lonely and sore. He didn't see the point in lying anymore.

The officer asked if he had any papers, and Javier shook his head. He noticed the man's blue eyes then, observant and weary. Before he called it in, the officer let Javier finish his meal and refill his drink. He gave Javier his card, introducing himself as Thomas Haskins, and said if he ever needed help to call. Javier wanted to rip it apart, show him what good his help could do, but he stuck it in his backpack instead. Then a woman with the INS came to take him away. That was it. So simple it almost seemed like fate. And he'd been in this cage ever since.

The kid on the lower bunk coughed again. He'd been at it all morning and most of last night. Sludgy rattling coughs that weren't going away anytime soon. Javier was ready to get it all over with and be sent home. It was his destiny, he supposed, to go back to Mexico. His uncle would still take him in. He'd have a real bed, even if he had to share it, and real food. But more than anything, he just wanted to see the sun and feel the breeze on his face again.

There was a thump at the heavy door. The ever-smirking guard turned his key and buzzed the door. Javier lazily rolled over to look, but it wasn't the dinner cart like he suspected. It was Lydia, the woman who had processed him the day he arrived. She stood tall in her navy pantsuit and heels, looking like a no-nonsense detective. She had her clipboard, which meant she was about to call another name.

"Casarez, Pablo," she said. A slick guy around sixteen hopped off his bunk. He wore a white undershirt and had a flannel draped over his neck. He stopped before the door and held his arms out and spread his legs so they could frisk him.

"Espinoza, Javier."

Javier's eyes darted toward her. There had to have been some kind of mistake. She looked up from the clipboard and scanned the room until her eyes landed on him. He looked around just to make sure he hadn't misheard, that she wasn't looking at the guy behind him.

"Javier Espinoza," she said, louder.

He leapt down and stood by the door the way the guy before him had. They were led down a white corridor and through a barred door.

Lydia took Pablo into her office and made Javier wait in a padded chair against the wall. A small eternity passed with Javier on edge, burning up to see what it was all about. Was he going to get an immigration hearing? He hadn't expected to get processed so soon. Most of the others had been in longer than him.

A guard led Pablo out of the room and down another hall. Lydia went around the corner and returned with a middle-aged couple, a long-necked Latina with big hair and a broad white man with a flattop. Javier looked past them, but they came alive when their eyes landed on him.

"Yes." The woman put a hand over her mouth. "That's him."

Then they were all over him. She wrapped him in a hug. He tousled Javier's hair.

"We were so worried," the woman said in a high voice.

"We just found out he was in here this morning," the man said to Lydia.

Javier had no idea who these people were. He hadn't called anyone. He didn't know anyone here. The man's heavy hand perched on his shoulder. The woman knelt down to his level. Her eyes were unflinching.

"Ready to get out of here? You'll be safe with us, Javier," she said. "God, you look so much like your mother."

Lydia studied them with a polite smile and nodded. "If you'll step into my office, we have some paperwork to fill out before I can release him to you."

"Sure," the woman said.

Javier was floored. The couple followed Lydia to the office, but the woman held back a step. She stared at Javier, tilted her chin, and winked. He dropped into his seat, losing touch with the detention center and the office workers buzzing around him. What rushed through him was part hope, part fear, part thrill but was failed by those words. The strange couple went into Lydia's office. They set off alarms in his head, but Javier was already imagining a brighter path. Sadder but wiser, he'd leave this place and never look back. He hadn't come this far to turn down a fresh start.

———

2015

The migrants were disheveled and eager to be on solid ground. The young couple, Eloy and Patricia, kissed and held each other. Eloy signed with a slight tremble in his hands. Patricia said, "Sí, mi cielo," and wouldn't let go of his cheeks.

The tension released after they'd held it in so long. Marck went up to the older woman Roberta and hugged her neck. She didn't seem thrilled at first but patted his back just the same. The old man stood with a wood cane that Javier didn't remember seeing earlier. He looked around and nodded, a faint smile possibly hiding among the deep creases of his face. Dave whooped and thrust a fist into the air. The migrants had no clue about the dustup with Ricky—it had probably only registered as murmurs and rumbles through the road cases—but being hauled out by those agents must have shaken them.

Squat led Isabel out of the bus. He fell all over himself around her, looking at her with equal parts awe and angst. He didn't get like that often. The hour or so spent in the hot crawlspace had left her flushed and with a lopsided hairdo, but her allure was still undeniable. Her head was high, her toned shoulders were back, and she wasn't afraid to make eye contact with any of them. Her brown eyes flashed when they caught the light. She looked down at Squat's hand, still on her arm, and he clumsily jerked it away.

"So this is her," Javier said. "The girl you risked everyone's freedom for."

Squat nodded. Isabel stuck close by him and eyed Jeff with distrust. He'd wanted to throw her out at the crossing. She wasn't going to forget it.

"You didn't think this through," Javier said. "You put us all in danger, her included."

Jeff crossed his arms and nodded in agreement.

"I like you, Squat," Javier said. "But if you ever pull anything like that again, I'm gonna leave you in Mexico with a headache that won't go away." Squat scratched the back of his head and nodded at the pavement.

The migrants handed over the rest of the cash Javier had allowed them to hold onto this far. Jeff helped him count and put the wads of cash into a drawstring backpack with a Friends of the Library logo. Jeff held the last bit, which belonged to the old man, out to Javier and made his eyes big. It was a grand short. And Javier was sure he hadn't miscounted in Juárez. Ricky definitely hadn't.

"Oye." Javier went over to the old man, not quite sure how to handle this yet. The old man stared back. One eye, clouded by a cataract, seemed to be looking in from some distant dreamworld. He said nothing.

"Viejo, dónde está el resto?" Javier asked.

The old man cocked the brow over his good eye. With a scratchy voice he told Javier he paid for professionals, not amateurs, to get him across the border and that he could have done better himself. Javier was worn thin at this point. On another day, he might have admired the crusty old man's audacity. But after the mess on the border, today was not that day.

Javier looked down, saw the slight bulge in the old man's boot. The old man squeezed his cane, his bony knuckles whitening.

"Grab his arms," Javier said to Squat, who was still at Isabel's side.

"What?"

"Do it now."

The old man swung the cane hard. Javier caught it under his armpit, but not before it thwacked him on the ribs. Squat rushed over and pulled the old man's arms back, holding them behind him like handcuffs. Javier wrenched the cane away. He wouldn't allow himself to touch his ribs where he'd been hit. No pain, no weakness. He just knelt in front of the old man, careful in case he decided to kick, reached into his damp sock, and pulled out the wad of cash. He was tired of people trying to take what was his.

He motioned for Squat to let go of the old man. Javier stood up and swung the cane at the old man's head, stopping an inch or two from his temple. Patricia cried out. The old man didn't even flinch though, just the hint of a grin again. Javier didn't have the stomach for anything more. He handed the cane back.

"Vete," he said, and the old man went.

With his duffel bag in one hand and his cane in the other, he walked off without another word. He had a bad hip and jolted each time he put weight on it. He paused at the corner and looked back, streetlight catching his one cloudy eye, and then he was gone.

The delight had drained from everyone's faces. Javier told the remaining migrants they were free to go but offered them a ride to Lubbock after the next night's concert. It would create some distance from the border and decrease the odds of being caught.

The dustup didn't scare them off. To Javier's surprise, they all stayed. Roberta said the further from the border the better. They picked up a few pizzas from an all-night place off Montana Avenue and found a little park with free RV camping. Huddled in the bus, comforted by the cabin lights and the scent of mozzarella grease, their nerves eased, and they began to talk. Javier asked them questions in Spanish and they answered, reservedly at first. The others joined in and Javier translated, sharing their stories with the fascinated bandmates. Even Jeff seemed to soften up.

Patricia made up for Eloy's silence. She wove a detailed story of their relationship, starting when they met in art school—she beamed mentioning the sketch of her that he gently slid across her desk—up to their first failed attempt to cross from Juárez. Their story only spanned six months, but she spoke like they'd been lovers for a lifetime. Eloy watched her lips and nodded. He was reserved, but the confidence was undeniable each time one of them met his placid eyes. Patricia said Eloy was an artist, a mixed media wizard. This perked up the bandmates' ears, learning a fellow creative was on the bus. They asked him questions, which Javier translated into Spanish and Patricia signed to him, and then a response went back down the chain. Patricia was going to help him get into art school in the US. She said everyone would know the name Eloy Arellano, just wait and see.

Roberta reminded Javier of one of his tías. She was quiet and watchful, carrying herself with a warm patience, the type of person who made you feel at ease. Violence had forced Roberta from her home in northern Honduras. It had been getting worse for years, but it didn't click for her until her fourteen-year-old nephew showed up with some older boys at the shop where she worked and shook down her boss. She kept trying to catch his eye. When she did he looked right through her, like he didn't recognize her. She remembered him, before the gang got their claws in him, as an introverted kid who was interested in boats and dreamed of becoming a sailor. His body turned up in a landfill a few weeks after that shakedown, and Roberta decided that was enough. She sold everything she had and left for Mexico, where she'd been for the last year, saving up for her passage. A brother in Oklahoma had loaned her what she lacked.

Isabel talked more about her father, Alfonso. She said he used to come across legally for work, spending most of the year on the South Plains. He had an under-the-table cash deal with a cotton gin in Brownfield, not even an hour's drive from the band's home. Alfonso worked as much as eighty hours a week during the fall, dead tired but grateful for all the pay he could send back home. He had been called up in May to help with repairs on the gin stand. It was supposed to be temporary, work a few weeks and then come back home until ginning season started up, but they never heard from him again.

Isabel said that her father had a pay-by-the-minute phone with notoriously bad service, and it was common to go a week or two without hearing from him. But two months had passed and a call still hadn't come. With her father gone, she juggled taking care of her teenage sister and disabled mother with part-time work, waiting for a check that never came. She asked around but heard no news. The not knowing was the worst part. Javier understood all too well what it was like to have a dad who never showed back up.

Isabel was adamant that her father would never abandon them, and that was why she had to go find him. Something must have happened. He must be in some kind of trouble.

Isabel said she took a bus to Juárez, where the border was even less inviting than she imagined. The coyotes wanted a lot of cash or things she had no intention of giving. She met a group of guys and they tried to hop a fence. They were caught and dumped back in Juárez, threatened with jail if they were caught again. She had no money, and each day grew more desperate. She had gone to the cantina looking for a job. She planned to earn a little cash until she could figure out her next move, but then she saw them and their big shining bus with Texas plates. She knew it must be fate.

"I will find him." She wiped away a tear.

Squat rubbed her back, and she leaned her forehead into his shoulder. It was quiet for a long while then, each person fading off into thoughts that couldn't be turned into easy conversation. Everyone was exhausted and started to settle in for the night. Isabel nuzzled up to Squat on the couch. The bandmates gave the bunks to the other migrants. Dave caught Javier in passing and said, "That was a shitshow earlier."

"Yeah. I know it was," Javier said.

"We aren't criminals, Javier. Not good ones anyway. We can't keep doing this."

Javier opened his mouth, trying to find the words, but Dave was gone before he could get any out.

Javier didn't sleep well. When he woke, he stepped off the bus and the wind brushed his face. For as hot and loud as yesterday had been, the morning was easy, cool, and quiet. The sky glowed orange underneath a stretch of wispy clouds and a stonewashed blue above it. The slow-moving traffic murmured along a boulevard where palm silhouettes jutted into the dawn. The streetlights had gone dark, but half the vehicles still had their headlights on. He watched them for a while in a satisfied daze. The early morning was serene in a way that Javier knew would not last. That broiling sun was about to come up, and they had another show to do.

The Saturday crowd was scarce for the local opener, Los Trabalenguas. Like everything else lately, the lineup had been subject to change. As recently as a week ago an indie band out of Denton was slated to open the show, but they ran their van into a ditch and had to stop the tour until they could get the axle fixed. The promoter, a young UTEP grad, told Javier not to worry. He would find a replacement that would put butts in seats.

The norteño group's accordion and bass lines bounced through the thin crowd. They were a tight group, looking slick in matching burgundy jackets. The front man stomped his foot while he sang and played the squeezebox. He had a soul patch and a pair of blackout shades. His silvery voice rang through the crowd. The band had chatted with them before sound check. Most of the group was in their early twenties like them. They agreed to come up and play a song or two together at the end of the night.

About the time Javier thought that their energy was being wasted, people started to stream into the venue. Between songs, the buzz of conversation grew louder. The bald spots near the stage filled in. Potential energy collected and hummed.

Javier hadn't taken the gig because he thought it would be a good payday. Even though the promoter claimed to be a fan, he only offered them a 25 percent split with no guarantee. They'd actually lose money if no one showed up. But they didn't need a big turnout, just enough to brace up their alibi.

The burly security guy let Javier through and he walked back to the bus. Jeff slugged at a tequila bottle and passed it to Dave. Los Trabalenguas had begun to cover "Friday I'm in Love" in Spanish. The bandmates belted out a verse along with them in English. Their voices were clear and on key, which was a good sign.

The migrants mostly observed. Patricia nodded her head and Eloy held her close around the waist. Roberta sat on the couch, sipping from a red cup and watching the bandmates with the curiosity of seeing a strange animal for the first time.

They'd purged the bus of all alcohol before crossing into Mexico, but it had come roaring back. Alongside the fifth of tequila sat a fifth of nice bourbon and a case of beer. Gifts from the promoter, Javier guessed. He plugged the tequila.

"Don't get too crazy," he said. "You go on in a half hour."

"We're celebrating. All these nice people"—Dave motioned with a beer—"are now Americans. Because of us. Is that cool or what?"

"For sure," Javier said. He looked around for Squat and Isabel and noticed the accordion door leading to the bunks was shut. Squat's low voice and then a giggle came from behind it. Javier felt restless all of a sudden. He stole a piece of Webb's nicotine gum.

"Have a good set," he said on the way out the door.

The place was rocking. The crowd—an actual crowd for the first time—cheered when the band took the stage. Javier couldn't believe the turnout, the energy. Dave said, "Good evening, El Paso. We're the Spirit Coyotes and we'd like to play some rock 'n roll music for y'all," and they erupted.

The first song was an upbeat number that had been in their repertoire for a long time. It got the crowd moving and engaged. After that, they played a new one, an eerie tune of Jeff's. It was sure to be on the album, when the time came.

Marck shone on drums. He sounded nothing like the sloppy drugged-out version of himself he'd been back in Juárez. He pounded out the rhythm and stomping backbeat like footsteps at a funeral march. Dave came in with:

> *You gotta go, you gotta go, you gotta go*
> *You gotta go, you gotta go, you gotta go*
> *Gotta get up outta here and leave this place*
> *You better flee, you better run, there'll be a chase*

Javier watched from the wings and Isabel came up beside him. He half-grinned at her and went back to watching the band. He felt better now. Dave sang lead and Jeff made a sinister-sounding *o-o-oh* into his microphone. Isabel leaned toward Javier's ear and said, "Thanks for letting me stay."

Her English was good, just heavily accented like his was when he first got to Texas. He had the hardest time pronouncing words with "sh" in them. There was no equivalent in Spanish. So he said things like "I spilled something on my chirt," and then "chut up" when kids teased him for it. He learned to make that hushing sound. Not before he got into a few fights, but eventually. His pronunciation was good enough now that he could blend in with the pochos, not even a trace of an accent if he really focused. Came in handy at the border. Many agents treated him with caution at first, especially when he handed over a green card instead of a US passport card. But they visibly calmed when he spoke, hearing he was a real American and not one of those wetbacks they were trained to detect.

"I didn't have a choice," he said.

"Yeah," Isabel said. "You did."

Marck and Jeff kept the groove dark and steady. Dave raised a hand to cover half of his face like a mask and sang:

> *You got a heavy metal foot*
> *And a half tank of gas*
> *Shadows all stare like faces*
> *On the overpass*

Javier crossed his arms, tapping his fingers on his elbows. The sun had gone down by the time the opening act finished, and now it was full dark. Javier could see quite a few stars above the lights' glare. He turned to say something to Isabel, but she had slipped away.

The band brought the song to a somber end. Waves of applause and woos broke the heavy silence. They had the biggest grins. It was a hard feeling to beat. While the bandmates paused to hydrate and retune, Javier's phone buzzed. It was Bonnie. When she'd left her number on the nightstand, he sent his in return.

This text from her said "???" with a link to a clip from the disastrous Juárez show. Somebody had shot video of Marck tumbling off his stool and then replayed it in slow motion while the concert noises faded out and "Falling Slowly" became the soundtrack. It had a ton of views.

Javier started to type a response but deleted it. He wouldn't mind talking to Bonnie again—she had a similar sense of humor and was easy on the eyes—but he didn't feel like he had the time now. And he didn't want to get her involved in all this.

Marck clacked his sticks together and thundered into the next one. He'd taken his shirt off, putting his collection of torso tattoos on display. A dark-haired woman, maybe an old flame, covered one pectoral while some intricate Japanese characters adorned the other. His stomach featured a zombie hand flashing a peace sign. He played like a madman, moving between the snare and toms, the crash and the ride, in a manic loop. The crowd ate it up.

Across the stage Javier saw that Webb now had the other migrants with him in the wings. Patricia and Eloy swayed and kissed. Webb pointed out something to Roberta, and she grinned and nodded. Isabel swept her hair behind her ear and bobbed her head. Squat looked back and smiled while he strummed.

Dave poured the rest of his water on his head. He pogoed behind the microphone, took off running, and slid on his knees, all without missing a note. They skidded into the out chorus, exhilarated and nearly spent.

"Goodnight, El Paso," Dave said to the raucous crowd.

They huddled offstage, sweaty and winded. Dave put his hands on his knees. Wet strands of dark hair dangled like tassels in front of his eyes. Marck still hadn't found his shirt. Bent over, his zombie hand disappeared into folds of thin skin. The audience was already chanting for one more song.

Los Trabalenguas walked up with their instruments in hand. They complimented the band on their set. Their bassist slapped Squat's shoulder and asked him how he felt.

"Like a Beatle."

They roared in laughter. The singer asked what they were going to play. After some back and forth they decided on a song that both groups were comfortable with. They prepped the accordion guy and the bajo sexto guy and the tololoche guy and then stormed the stage.

They had spent all night building and building, and their energetic cover of Juan Gabriel's "No Tengo Dinero" brought the house down. This crowd was the biggest yet, and they were all in on the band. Javier sensed it, something taking shape that would change everything. He thought about what Jeff had said, about them not being cut out for crime. But they were only getting started.

The band's playing style meshed perfectly with the rambunctious norteño outfit. There was pure joy on each of their faces while they played the last verse. The sound the band had been searching for reverberated into the starry El Paso night.

Part II

Pray that your flight may not be in winter . . .

MATTHEW 24:20

Chapter 11

1984

"WOULD YOU RATHER GO BACK IN THERE?" THE WOMAN said after Javier stopped on the sidewalk.

Disoriented, he followed them down the block into a nearly empty parking lot between a Methodist soup kitchen and a nightclub with unlit neon guitars fixed to the bricks. The man approached a town car, cream-colored and angular with a little grill that looked like a bunched-up mouth, clean except for the pale dried mud splattered around the fenders. He held the back door open.

Javier thought about bolting but didn't know where to bolt to. Wandering the streets of Houston hadn't worked out. At least this, whatever it was, put distance between him and the detention center. The man's golden mustache hung over his lip, and Javier couldn't tell if he was grinning when he motioned Javier inside. Javier paused another moment and then got in the car. He could always take off later.

They drove out of the city, trading the bustling loop and big buildings for a thin strip of asphalt with wild green growth looming over both shoulders. The woman twisted around to face Javier. She had one of those puffed-up hairstyles that seemed to be common in the USA. A mole dotted the skin under her left eye. She studied Javier, squinting like he was in fine print. He fidgeted in his seat and looked away, catching the man's slashing blue eyes in the rearview mirror.

"I guess he wants to know what this is all about." He pulled his sunglasses from the clip on the visor.

The woman, still facing him, said, "Javier, this is Drew. He's not quite as mean as he looks." He chewed his gum, and the shades blocked out his eyes. She went on. "And I'm your Aunt Yolanda, your tía on your mother's side, as far as the authorities know."

His mother had three siblings, two brothers and a sister who died of polio as a child. Yolanda gave him another one of those winks and faced forward. The cigarette lighter popped out and she touched it to her slim. Drew ran his tongue along the low-hanging mustache hairs and made a right turn at the junction. Javier waited for one of them to explain why they got him out, why they lied to the authorities, but neither spoke. Drew cracked the windows and popped an eight track in the deck. He cranked it up when the big drums and reverb took hold, twisting the A/C knob to match, like everybody did here. Javier didn't mind. If it got much more humid he'd need gills.

The traffic had thinned to almost nothing on the two-lane highway. Cloudbursts scattered across the sky, the little strip of it visible between the trees, like the cleanest explosions he'd ever seen. The grass in the ditch was waist high and the cattails barely moved in the sultry afternoon stillness. Everything was so green and lush. They pulled into a filling station and Drew went inside to pay.

"Dónde estamos?" Javier asked.

"You already showed your hand," Yolanda said, "No more Spanish. You're in America now. It'll serve you better to speak English whenever you can. All the boys speak it. You'll see."

Javier cocked his head to the side.

"They're good kids," she continued. "Some were locked up like you, others we found homeless and all alone. Our place is near Huntsville, about seventy miles north of Houston. You'll like it."

A loose hunk of panic tumbled through Javier. "How you know my name?"

"Your file was on the top of the stack." Yolanda tilted her head back and laughed. "The government is a lot less competent than people think. If you claim someone as family and promise to get them to their hearing, they want to believe it as much as anybody. They don't want to pay for your upkeep."

Drew finished pumping and got in.

"Why?" Javier asked.

"I can answer that," Drew said. "We have a nice deal for you, kid. Probably the kind you dreamed about when you left your little barefoot village."

Yolanda's eyebrows came down and she gave him a disapproving look, but he didn't seem to notice.

"What if I no want this?" Javier said.

"Then we take you back," Yolanda said. "There's no gun here. You can get out now if that's really what you want."

"What we're offering you"—Drew put his fist up and raised a finger with each benefit—"is a place to stay, plenty of food, a sense of purpose, and most importantly, your freedom."

The last word struck a chord. "What about the—" He struggled with the last word. He turned to Yolanda. "Cómo se dice la audiencia?"

"Your hearing," she said. "Don't worry about that. If you work with us, we'll get you papers."

He couldn't help getting a little excited. He still wasn't sure about the couple or the situation with the other boys, but the opportunity to live in the US long term drowned those thoughts out.

"No catch," Drew said. "You just have to be willing to work, get your hands dirty. Farmers in the area hire our crew. It's mostly hoeing this time of year. Some harvest work in the fall. Maintenance and tree trimming in the winter. We'll keep you busy."

"And you'll get a little spending money in your pocket," Yolanda said. "How does that sound?"

Javier nodded. Trading work for a life in the US was what he had hoped for. It sounded more than fair. The tires whirred over gravel and eased across a wash the rains had carved through the road. When they sped back up Javier could hear the globs of mud slinging off the tires and into the wheel well.

A toad-colored farmhouse in need of a new coat of paint sat at the end of the drive. The trees that hid their property from the main road were woolly, a few dead gray limbs jutting away from patches of healthy leaves. They pulled around back, under a corrugated lean-to that didn't match the modern car. Something about the place made him tense up, but then the doors flew open and he was following them up the back steps. Drew latched the screen door behind him. The kitchen smelled like tobacco and ammonia and something else he couldn't identify.

"This will be your new home," Drew said, standing close enough that his musky aftershave and dried sweat overwhelmed Javier, who took a step back. Drew's eyes traced the Formica countertop to the phone on the far wall with its long, coiled cord. Only muffled sunlight entered through the curtains and worked its way through the smoke of Yolanda's next cigarette. She flicked it over an ashtray surrounded by magazines and advertisements and pill bottles. A framed cross-stitch on the wall said HOME SWEET HOME.

"Well, not here exactly," Drew said. "You and the other boys stay in the bunkhouse. It's nice and cozy."

Through the hazy doorway Javier's eye caught a silhouette in the living room. He waited for the smoke to shift and saw the slender gray cat with green eyes. Its tail was long, almost impossibly long, along the top of the headrest and hanging almost to the seat. Its eyes locked onto him. They'd had a series of barn cats back home, but this one raised the hair on his neck.

"So, are you ready?" Yolanda put her hand on his shoulder.

Javier swung his head around. "Ready?"

"For work," she said. "We'd let you stay here, but we have some business to take care of. You'd be bored out of your mind. Don't worry, it'll be a short day. Ease you into it. Sound good?"

"Okey," Javier said, thinking that working outdoors was better than staying in this house.

"Wonderful," she said. "Drew, get him set up. He'll need a hoe and some gloves." She looked down at his ratty sneakers. "We'll get him boots next time we go into town."

Drew backed a single-cab pickup out of the barn and threw a long-handled hoe into the bed. Unlike the modern town car, the old truck lacked A/C and a working radio and had rust around the fenders. They bounced down the rutted road in silence, and Javier felt the heat returning to his skin. He tried to quiet his worries, telling himself this was a great opportunity. That it was just what he'd been hoping for.

2015

Webb hadn't minded referring to himself as a roadie or a driver, but he sure liked the way *production manager* sounded. The band had promised him that role once they signed their record deal. His job wouldn't change much, but it came with a raise and that fancy title, his prize for keeping his mouth shut about the work they'd done across the Rio Grande.

It was the kind of title his mama would have appreciated if her mind was still right. She always saw him in some tie-wearing gig, as if management was really a possibility for a dropout with his record. "But you got your diploma at seventeen, Christopher," she'd say. He'd correct her. "GED, Mama." They weren't the same, and any employer could tell you that. Many had.

The only people who still called him Christopher—after his mother forgot who that was—were the bill collectors. Ever since high school, he'd been known by his last name. He'd introduce himself as "Chris Webb," but people always lopped the first part off. He kept thinking of himself as Chris for a while and then one day he just accepted it. He was Webb.

Webb puffed on a bulky vape rig—a compromise he'd been able to reach with the band—and untangled the TS cables for Squat's pedals. He blew spearmint vapor from his nostrils and frowned. He hadn't felt this mixed-up in a while. Things had changed rapidly in the six months after the El Paso show. He hated to see Javier go. Truth be told, when the band had canned Javier, Webb suspected he was next. But here it was

December and he was still around. He got the feeling they were scared of him talking if they cut him loose. They didn't know him very well, if that was the case.

He picked up Squat's Strat and hit the pedal. He strummed a few power chords and adjusted the low end on the amp head. Before he came along the band used to do all this stuff themselves, but they got used to being the talent. He had to bitch and moan just to get them to help him lug the heavy stuff anymore.

Webb pulled off his jacket and tossed it on a stack. The Echo Park venue was standing room only, no bigger or nicer than places they'd gigged before, but the bandmates were all riled up because it was Los Angeles. *Big deal.*

It was his first time in the city. It hadn't exactly lived up to the hype. Sure, the palm trees and the mild baby-blue December afternoons were nice. There were a thousand things to do and see and eat. He could see the appeal, if you didn't have to weave through a horde of vehicles and bodies everywhere you went. They went to a coffee shop and waited in a line that went out the door. Webb felt like the oldest sardine in the net. All for a five-dollar cup of coffee that tasted like raisins and old pennies. Their bulky van was a tight squeeze on the freeway and in parking lots that catered to tiny hybrids. Places like that made him glad they weren't in the bus anymore.

Folks back home would tell horror stories of the stuff that went on in California. The ones who identified as men ate kale chips and got dodge-ball banned from schools. The ones who identified as women would press charges on you for holding a door open for them. There were others that identified as unicorns and ate glitter and oats out of shoeboxes.

Webb still caught his mama's voice bubbling up in his own thoughts. She was a good woman, generous with her time and possessions to anyone who was hard up. She was also a good Southern Baptist and thought the West Coast was a snake's den of heathenry. Webb believed in God and right and wrong, but he also figured people should live their lives how they wanted. He hadn't always seen it like that though.

Back in Slaton, where Webb grew up, there was only one guy who everybody knew was for-sure queer. The middle Hampton boy. "Ham."

They were in the same grade. He didn't have a car, or even a bike, so he walked everywhere. One day Webb threw a half-drunk chocolate malt at his head, goaded by two of his buddies, when they drove by in a sort-of-borrowed GTO. Ham got killed by a drunk driver a few years later, after Webb dropped out and headed for the Hub City. He did a lot of things wrong back in his younger years, but picking on that shy kid still bothered him.

That morning though, sauntering a few steps behind the bandmates through Griffith Park, Webb spotted a couple, men his age, holding hands and walking under the California live oaks. They were happy, laughing and pointing out birds. Warblers sang a golden melody from the limbs. It all made Webb hopeful for reasons he couldn't express. Mama wouldn't agree, but he figured that wasn't much different than the love Kenny Rogers sang about. He couldn't help but smile and enjoy the sunshine. Then the Greyhound the men had on a leash bunched herself up and left a big pile on the grass, and Webb came back down to earth a little bit. Still though.

"Hey," Jeff said.

Webb sucked in air, realizing how far he'd spaced out.

"Yeah?"

"You seen my fuzz pedal?"

Webb nodded to the opposite side of the stage.

"Thanks."

"You know, I've been thinking. If you crank up the gain even more you can get this nice sinister buzz on that opening for 'Yellow House Canyon—'"

But Jeff was already gone. Webb sat down at the edge of the stage and drew the sickly-sweet vapor into his lungs. People didn't listen to him. They told him to be quiet and haul the amps. Nobody cares what you think, cable monkey. Not for long, he thought. No one tells a production manager to shut up.

―――――――

Dave had once embraced the mystery of ideas. They came from no-where, stalks popping up where he didn't remember planting seed.

Lately though, he had been blocked. Apart from a couple of new songs he and Jeff cowrote—and Jeff did most of the work if he was being honest—he hadn't written anything usable in the last six months. The jolt of a unique idea had once come so naturally that he never even considered life could be any different. Now the rarer they were, the more reverence he paid them.

This had to be a good one. He wanted to write it down before it crumbled back into the earth. He'd lost too many good ones by shrugging and saying he'd remember them. He picked up a pen and paper. This was the song that would get him back on track. He could feel it.

Dave hummed the melody on repeat and scribbled a verse. He stretched his fingers out while reviewing what he wrote, made a couple of corrections, wrote the chord progression up top, and handed it to Squat.

"Tell me what you think," he said, staring a hole into the back of the paper while Squat mouthed the words.

Jeff had been on a roll, and it made him uneasy. Dave had penned all the songs starting out. He was a natural, churning out smooth love songs to impress girls and fuzzy abstract pieces to impress his stoner friends. Jeff was always editing and reediting, endless drafts, only to squeeze out an overwrought turd.

But, Dave had to admit, Jeff had raised the bar with his latest stuff. Simple songs of love and pain, meditations on purpose and place, character ballads that read like short stories, all set to sweet melodies. The first song or two filled Dave with pride and joy. Jeff had finally put it all together. But then he just kept going. Song after song. Dave had enough. It was time to remind him who the pack leader was.

"Well," Dave said after Squat lowered the paper from his face. "Do you like it?"

He squinted. "It's good."

"Dammit," Dave said. "You paused. C'mon, tell me what you really think."

"It is good. But it's pretty much a rehash."

"Of what?"

"'Still Here.'"

Dave's face contorted and gave away his frustration. "What do you mean?"

"They're both about missing a girl, they both use the desert as a symbol for loneliness." Squat motioned to the page. "It's basically the same chord progression, except for that E minor you threw in."

Dave snatched the paper back, crumpled it, and threw it over his shoulder.

"Whatever. I can come up with another one. *Easy.*"

"Sure, man," Squat said. He wouldn't look Dave in the eye.

"Jeff's having a nice run right now. Good for him. But it's all ebb and flow. I'll get back on top."

"Totally."

"I mean, that's how it was with Lennon and McCartney."

"Uh huh." Squat narrowed his eyes.

"I'm Paul, of course. Jeff's shit's good, but he takes himself way too serious. I'm not above writing silly love songs."

"So that makes me Ringo?"

"What? Sure," Dave said. "Don't you think he's getting a little uppity? We can't lose touch with the primal element, you know? Good music is supposed to vibrate your soul."

"But Ringo played drums." Squat looked out the door with glazed eyes. "I wanna be Hendrix."

Dave blinked at him.

"Wait. But I also wanna live past twenty-seven," Squat said. "So like Hendrix, but if somebody had rolled him over on his stomach that night. *Or Stevie.* Yeah, I'll be Stevie Ray Vaughan."

Dave dragged his palm across his bottom lip.

"I need some air," he said.

For all the hope and excitement in the air—for being back in the van, playing shows in new places—Dave feared things were beginning to fall apart. They had already sunk their earnings from smuggling into a small building back in Lubbock. It was going to host their own private studio, maybe a headquarters for their own recording label eventually. It was a sweet vintage brick building, on the century-old red brick streets of downtown, but problems kept popping up like zits on a teenage fry cook. First it was the leaky roof and then the wiring and then the cost of acoustic insulation. Then there were the utilities, the taxes, the 10 percent to the guy Javier found to wash their money, and before they knew it they were nearly broke and only had a half-finished shell of a studio to show for it.

Dave resented Jeff for holding out on the record deal they'd been offered. Everything had to be perfect with him. Every last detail or he wouldn't jump in, just like when they were kids. Dave would be doing gainers off the diving board, while Jeff would psych himself out trying to do a simple flip.

There came a point where you just had to take what was in front of you. Dave fixed his hat the way he liked it, cocked just a little to the right, and eyed the venue's back entrance. A scruffy bouncer leaned against the bricks with his arms folded. Most of them were muscle-bound, thick at least, but this guy's arms weren't much bigger than his own. The guy nodded at him, projecting quiet confidence and the kind of wiry strength that's easy to underestimate.

Dave tried to think of a song for the man. One of those world-weary characters Jeff was so intent on creating. He would keep it simple, call it "The Bouncer." A minor ballad. It'd be a first-person lament about this little guy from a factory town in Pennsylvania. His father knocks him around, the kids pick on him, and he learns that using his fists can ease his pain. Things go bad, maybe he finally snaps on the old man, maybe the cops are looking for him. He comes to LA to leave that life behind and pursue his dream of being an artist, but the only work he finds himself qualified for is backing down drunks at dive bars and strip clubs. He can't outrun himself. He feels the walls closing in.

Yeah, that could work. Energy surged through Dave, his mind buzzing like a transformer. He ran to the green room, got a pen, and started scribbling. He finally dropped it and shook out his cramping hand.

"That's stupid," he said, crumpling the sheet into a ball and tossing it with the others.

Squat stretched his arms overhead and yawned.

"Where's my pen?" Dave asked, bursting through the door.

Squat pointed to it on the counter. Dave found another scrap of paper and scribbled furiously. Squat went outside before he had to critique anything else. Dave couldn't accept that he and Jeff were both good songwriters. It had to be a competition, and he had to be better, but the added pressure wasn't doing him any favors.

The lukewarm wind ran across Squat's arms and ruffled his hair. It was strange to be able to wear short sleeves outdoors this close to Christmas. The others talked about Southern California weather like it was heaven, but Squat didn't care for it. Winters were for coats and chile verde stew, not warm sunshine. He got enough of that in the West Texas summers to last the whole year.

He figured it had something to do with that trip to the mountains when he was a boy. It was the only vacation his mom took his sister and him on. She came back to Lamesa excited and talking about change, back when they still believed her. She carried him and Anna to New Mexico, some village up in the Sacramento Mountains. It was New Year's Eve, but all the shops and light posts still had their Christmas lights and red bows up, like a snow globe in real life. They stayed up there for three days, eating pancake breakfasts and going to the bowling alley or the movies after the early sunset. Then she took them back and they didn't see her for another six months. After that, though, he had an ideal version of what winter should be, and Los Angeles wasn't it.

He gave the bouncer by the door a nod. "What's up, man?"

"Just guarding this door," the bouncer said.

"Anybody tried to bust through?"

"Nope. You want to try? I'm getting a little bored."

"Maybe later." Squat chuckled and stuck out his hand. "Squat Montoya."

"Mac Klein."

"Tell me Mac, what caliber of female clientele can we expect tonight?"

"Lot of pretty girls come here," Mac said. "What do you play?"

"Lead guitar."

"You'll do just fine." Mac made the A-okay sign. "If you said bass, that's another story."

"Nice." Squat gave a sly grin. "So how long you been in LA?"

"All my life, more or less. I grew up in Van Nuys."

Squat looked around and nodded. "I bet it was cool to grow up here."

"I guess." Mac shrugged. "Where are you from?"

"I was born in Lamesa, Texas. You probably never heard of it."

"Luh-meesa?" Mac shook his head. "All I know of Texas is the big cities, Dallas and Houston. Is it close to those?"

"Well, from Lamesa you can drive five hours east and be in Dallas, or drive five hours west and be in El Paso. And it's way closer to Mexico than it is to Houston."

"So middle of nowhere then."

Squat thought about it and replied, "It's somewhere to some people."

Mac chuckled. "Well LA is the center of the universe to too many people. I'm ready for a change. I hear Austin is cool."

Squat shrugged. "It's alright." They both watched a pigeon scurry down the sidewalk like it was late for a Pilates class.

"I better head in," Squat said. "Nice meeting you."

"Good luck tonight."

Squat made his way to the empty stage. He studied the motionless shadows on the seats and felt the loneliness creeping up his spine. He grabbed his phone to see if Isabel had responded. She hadn't. They'd seen each other a couple more times after the El Paso show. But then the band got busy with their music, and she headed back home after striking out on finding her father. She said she'd keep in touch, but he heard from her less and less. That could've been the end of it, but Squat did the thing he bragged he'd never do and caught feelings. He had texted to say that their tour was wrapping up, and that he'd like to come see her.

Now that they were playing to full houses, he was a lot more attractive to attractive women. Squat knew his sixteen-year-old self wouldn't be able to wrap his head around it, but sex had come to feel like a chore. Something he had to do to tread water. The thrill was gone. No matter who he was with, how steep her curves or enthusiastic her moans, Squat made believe it was Isabel.

The little things stayed in his mind, like how angry she got when somebody was being taken advantage of, or the way she said his name, "Skwat," or how her soft eyes focused on his fingers when he played, or how she let her bottom lip linger between his when they kissed. He couldn't shake that feeling, like an electrical current flowing through his body, energizing and terrorizing him all at once. It took all his willpower to keep from calling her every day.

Squat's phone buzzed and he snatched it from his pocket, thinking it might be her. He stared at the screen until his eyes unfocused and it became a blur. He blinked and read the notification again. A musician with a blue checkmark next to his name had reposted Squat about that night's show along with the line: "Looking forward to it." Squat took off running to find his buddies.

"Guys," he shouted. "You're not gonna believe this."

Jeff, Marck, and Squat sat in a booth at the back of Mescalito, a low-key hipster bar on Sunset Boulevard. The bar was cool and dark, and a chalk mural of lush palm trees fronting a dusky California sky stretched across the far wall. Jeff had been wearing the same unimpressed expression since they'd arrived. Dave couldn't get enough of the LA vibes, so Jeff hated the city on principle. Overpriced and overrated. Where's the *soul*? The truth was that so many people here shared his hip sensibilities that it started to make him feel a little irrelevant. So he made snap judgments about the Angelenos to help himself feel better. Like that guy over at the bar, the one with the pointy nose and fancy scarf and ironic Carhartt toboggan, who looked like he couldn't even change his own tire. *Fuuuck* that guy. Jeff took a sip of his craft cocktail, feeling slightly better.

Then Squat had run in just repeating "Tweedy" over and over until Marck snapped, "What the hell about him?"

"This show? He's coming to this show?" Jeff asked.

"Yeah," Squat said, holding up his phone and beaming. "He had to have seen one of our live videos."

"What if he asked us to open for him on his next tour?" Jeff said. "That'd be so awesome." He downed a shooter of mezcal and sucked a lime. What he'd give to bounce new songs off that guy. Now there was someone who had no use for genres.

"I don't see what the big deal is," Marck said. "Dude's been downhill since he left Uncle Tupelo."

"You don't know what you're talking about," Jeff said sharply. "He's an artist."

"If by artist you mean pretentious, sure," Marck said. "But a double amputee could count the number of great Wilco albums on his toes."

"Your taste is shit," Jeff said, slinking back into the low-slung booth.

He stared at the menu and spaced out, imagining the conversation he and Jeff Tweedy would have. Maybe they'd talk shop awhile, probably bond over their mutual appreciation for The Replacements. He would crack some sly joke and they'd both laugh and laugh. Jeff might insinuate that Jeff had the talent to leave his bandmates behind, but Jeff would say no on principle, and Jeff would respect Jeff even more for it.

"Sir?"

Squat's elbow in his ribs jolted Jeff out of his fantasy. "Oh, uh, it's between the tempeh nachos or the hummus and salsa shawarma."

The waitress adjusted her glasses and looked at Jeff's menu. "I'd go with the shawarma."

"That sounds great."

"What the hell kind of bar and grill doesn't serve real burgers?" Squat asked when she was out of sight.

Jeff tapped his temple with his finger. "A vegetarian grill, Squat."

"You're not a vegetarian," Squat said. "Why'd you pick this place?"

"I'm expanding my horizons."

"Well I'm not looking forward to the bill. Those beers were seven dollars a pop," Marck said.

"*You're* going to whine about beer money?" Jeff said. "The guy who hasn't had to pitch in a cent for our studio?"

"Not this again," Marck said.

"Hey man," Squat said. "No worries. We're about to sign a record deal. The cash is coming."

"Is it?" Marck snapped. "If Jeff drug his feet anymore he'd be a fucking zombie." He swallowed the dregs of his beer and pushed himself up from the table. "You songwriters can handle the tab."

"What's his problem?" Squat shrugged at his own question. "So you think Tweeds will hang after the show?"

"Huh?" Jeff said, distracted. "Yeah. I don't know."

His mind kept returning to the recording deal on the table. A mid-sized label had offered to put them in a nice studio for a couple of days, set them up with a top-notch sound engineer. The catch was that the label had final say on the track list, the mixing, the artwork, and even the album title. They would take an executive share of the profits as well. That was exactly what Jeff wanted to avoid, being beholden to somebody else's interests. It didn't seem fair to Jeff that they had risked so much just to hand their work over to strangers now. His bandmates were getting impatient though. He could only hold them off for so long.

Jeff ordered another mezcal. After all that had happened, he saw no rational way of turning the deal down, yet he was still reluctant to sign. The surge of discomfort sent his fingers scrambling. He checked the notifications on his phone, mindlessly scrolling through pictures of happy people and their dogs and workout routines and babies and craft beers, landing on one of the bandmates with their arms locked, standing triumphant and sweaty after the El Paso show back in June.

The show had been a hit, their biggest crowd to date. It had fronted the entertainment section of the *El Paso Times* with the title "Been through the Desert for a Band with No Name," accompanied by a glowing review from Angelica Cavasos, the city's top music critic. A couple of well-shot videos collected ten thousand views each over the next couple of weeks. Venues and promoters started calling. They rode the wave, booking a mini tour from Kansas City to Los Angeles. For once, the possibility of making money off their music seemed realistic.

Javier didn't take well to the change. He planned for more smuggling runs, into Sonora and Baja California this time. They could charge even more there, he assured. But after Juárez, they were done. They couldn't get past the showdown with Ricky, especially once they realized how easily it could have been avoided. They knew smuggling was dangerous, but it wasn't until their stomachs dropped at the first sight of the gun that they recognized how real the danger was.

Javier was persistent, trying to convince them to stick to their goal, that just a couple more good runs would put them over the top. It got to be too much. Jeff and Dave agreed on something for once, and they voted three to one to cut Javier loose. Squat was the only holdout, unless you count Webb, which they didn't. Javier took his bus back home and they hadn't heard from him since.

Jeff would never say it aloud, but he missed Javier sometimes. They ran up against a bar owner in Denton who stiffed them on their split. Jeff and Dave tried to reason with him. When that didn't work they tried to get tough, claiming they knew a lawyer. He told them it was cute that they knew a lawyer, but he had one on retainer. They ended up taking the L. Javier wouldn't have stood for it. He would step into these guys' offices and, without even voices getting raised, come out with the money. Every time.

It was hard to carry too much concern for Javier though, with so much energy tied up in worrying about his own emerging career. He always thought the feeling would be fuller, being this close to making it. There were gilded moments of hope. At times they seemed to tilt closer to certainty, but more often than not Jeff felt scared. Scared of losing something he had yet to grasp.

"You okay, Jeff?" Squat asked, his face big and concerned.

"Yeah."

"You've been different lately. Distant," Squat said. "I know you know this, but if you ever need to talk about stuff—"

Jeff nodded. "I know."

"Cool cool," Squat said.

He wasn't all right. He knew it and Squat knew it, but there wasn't much point in talking about it. He didn't even know how to put his feelings into words. Whenever he tried it came out wrong, unrecognizable to his own ears from what he actually felt inside.

Besides, once their album was out in the world, he'd feel better. He could finally listen to music again without comparing himself to those he admired. The nagging voices would shut up, and he could enjoy all this.

It struck him as undeniably twisted that he found it so hard to sign the recording contract. A label was offering to pay them to do what they loved: make music. And somehow that wasn't a no-brainer. He worried that they were being asked to sell off their ideals, just a few for now, in exchange for entrance into the music business. Sometimes that seemed like the honest-to-God truth, and other times it seemed like a scared man's cop-out.

The red sun floated just over the buildings when Marck left the bar. He squinted and brought a hand to his brow. The cool breeze teased at the hem of his shirt. He brushed across a palm tree whose trunk had been wrapped with silver tinsel and a strand of lights. He was feeling his alcohol. The tequila and light beer made for a rippling buzz, shushing the constant drone in his mind for a minute. He'd been trying to dial it back since the Juárez show. No more ketamine and fewer percs, but he still couldn't tolerate himself or his messed-up back for very long without chemical assistance.

He roamed the streets with his hands stuffed in his pockets. The haze from the evening commute and the sun's fiery glow made it look like the woolly hills in the distance were burning. People were out enjoying what was left of the day, dressed in everything from cut-off shorts and tank tops to jackets and scarves. A thin woman on a thin bicycle weaved through the crowd.

At the crosswalk the crowd parted for an old man in a ratty flannel coat with a cardboard sign. Marck caught the sweet scent of carnitas floating in from a taco truck across the street. He ate three tacos that left a trail of orange grease down his palm and took a deep hit of the Blue Diesel to help line him out before the show. He found his bandmates backstage. The green room still wasn't much to look at—gray walls, grayer carpet, a couple of black couches, a folding table with a few refreshments—but at least there was no fear of tetanus.

Marck grabbed a water from the cooler and sat between Jeff and Squat on the couch. They were still going on about that hack Tweedy, entertaining fantasies of him becoming their mentor. Even if this was all true and they did meet him, so what? That was no guarantee of success. When Marck was with the Mudslingers they got to hang out on the Stone Temple Pilots' tour bus after a show in Omaha. It was a kickass night: blow, gin, guitars, groupies. But did the Pilots ever give them a call about coming out on the next tour? Did they ever think twice about the southern rock band from Nebraska who graciously shared their cocaine? Not a chance.

His bandmates were young and naïve. He wanted them to get on with it and sign the record deal, but unlike them he knew that their problems wouldn't end there. Living gig to gig might seem like torture for a young band set on a breakthrough, but it was so much simpler than what was on the horizon. They had no idea. The record execs' *suggestions*, the subzero nights up north, the expectations for their follow-up album, the emptiness that came with getting just what they'd asked for.

He knew what he wanted, and it was a lot simpler: a regular cash flow. He could try to catch up on the whole dad thing, buy his girls the bikes they wanted for a start. He could get some of the debt collectors off his back. He could get more Percocet. Marck idly thought about this while Squat and Jeff kept going back and forth, debating which shitty album was the hack's finest.

He came out of his daze, noticing a woman in the door. The black-haired beauty leaned into the metal doorframe, looking both confident and a little lost. One by one they noticed her and dropped their conversation. She was utterly gorgeous. Her black dress, long-sleeved and short-hemmed, was snug in all the right places.

"Excuse me," she said. "I have a problem. Maybe you can help me."

"Yeah," Dave blurted. "For sure."

"What can we do for you?" Jeff asked.

She coyly clutched her bag and walked over to them. They barely blinked.

Squat popped up off the couch. "Have a seat."

"Ah, a gentleman," she said.

She ran her hands down her sides, smoothing her dress before she sat on the couch. Squat pulled up a folding chair. The woman turned and grinned at Marck. He felt his heart kick but caught himself before he melted. No, he wasn't going to fall for this again. Nobody was interested in the old drummer in the back.

"My name is Monica," she said, touching her neatly manicured nails to her collarbone. Marck liked the way she pronounced it, Moh-nee-cah. It was like taking an everyday name and giving it a lemon twist.

"Hi Monica, I'm Squat." Squat went around the circle introducing the others. She smiled at all of them, but Marck couldn't help feeling like it was just for him.

"So." Squat rested his chin on his fist, like that made him look distinguished. "What is it we can help you with?"

"Well, I want to show you something." She shifted her weight, brushing her oh-so-smooth thigh against Marck. He gulped and began to hang on her every word, ready to take up murder-for-hire or hot yoga or whatever it took to be with her.

Monica got her small clutch, unzipped it, and took out her phone. The bandmates all leaned in and stared as she carefully tapped it, her nails clicking on the screen. "Here we go," she said, bringing up a screen with a grainy image of a wooden desk and an empty leather chair.

Monica's thigh was still next to his. She had that exquisite youthful skin, shiny but not greasy, firm yet soft. A tinny voice cut through Marck's wandering thoughts.

"Oye."

There was someone in the leather chair now, but the details were hard to see. Monica handed the phone to Marck and got up. Their eyes stayed on her as she went over to the refreshment table and picked up a finger sandwich.

"Hola, mis coyotes!" the phone hollered.

Their eyes shot toward the screen. The picture had cleared up and now they could see Ricky, sitting up in the chair and tapping his cigarette over a fancy bronze ashtray. Why Ricky though? Marck looked to Monica for some kind of answer, but she didn't even notice, licking her fingers and then taking a beer from their cooler.

"What do you want?" Dave said.

"Just to see my buddies," Ricky said with a grin, pushing his black felt cowboy hat back.

"No. We can't be talking to you," Jeff said. "Not tonight. Tweedy's here."

"Like the bird?"

"We don't want any trouble," Dave said.

"Trouble found you in Juárez, kid."

"We're hanging up." Marck reached for the red End button.

"I wouldn't do that," Ricky said sharply.

Marck's finger hovered in the air. "Or what?"

The picture moved from Ricky's body to a shot of the ceiling. It wobbled as he messed with his phone. Marck felt Monica's phone buzz and a notification flashed on the screen.

"Check those out," Ricky said, once again centered in the frame.

Marck opened the message and scrolled through the pictures while his bandmates crowded near him to see. One picture showed Eloy and Patricia, the young couple from Juárez, climbing into one of their road cases. The next was a crisp picture of the bandmates and Javier standing behind the bus, their license plate in clear view.

"You know," Ricky said. "Johnny Cash cut that great album in San Quentin. Of course he was just visiting. But still—prison might push your music to its peak."

Marck gulped and the phone felt like a grenade in his hand. He couldn't go to prison.

"If you turned us in," Squat said. "You'd get busted too."

"You're right. I probably would. But shit, I have connections. I could live a decent life on the inside. Bodyguards, drugs, an untraceable phone for nude pics and watching Lakers games, you name it. What about you pretty boys?" Ricky leaned up close to the camera and licked his lips. "All that long luxurious hair—from the back, it could almost fool a man. Especially one doing life."

That sent a shiver down Marck's spine.

"Pero I don't think any of us want that. What's best for us is to make one last run, earn some good money, and ride off into the sunset."

"One last run?" Dave asked.

"Yep. I got a job for you," Ricky said. "Mario Ruiz. He's a politician from Chihuahua City. I've known him for a while. Real slimy dude, pocketed money from the state for years. The dude directed funds to the Sinaloa Cartel, helped with their narcotics distribution. Everybody got rich. Happy ending, right? Wrong. See, the Sinaloas are like the Roman Empire—don't give me that look, pendejos, I read books—they're too spread out and now these smaller, more mobile gangs started taking their home territories back. One of them is Andrés Santiago's gang, El Jaleo. They're connected to La Línea and the New Juárez Cartel. It's a complicated web, amigos."

Marck felt his hand starting to shake, so he clamped down on the phone.

"Entonces," Ricky continued. "Andrés tries to get Ruiz to come on board, but he says no, thinks the Sinaloas are too powerful to cross. So he hangs a price tag on Ruiz's head. And now the Sinaloas can't protect him anymore. They have bigger problems. Him and his family are in hiding. He got in contact with me, said he wants out of the country pronto, but he also knows Andrés is watching."

Marck sat there blinking at the screen. He forgot most of the names and connections before the story was done—man, he could not go to prison. What about his girls? Would he ever see them again?

"Why the hell do you want us?" Jeff said. "This sounds like a job for people with *way* more experience. Why can't *you* do it?"

"Ruiz wants somebody he can trust. And he doesn't trust the coyotes around here. He's made too many enemies to put his family in the back of some truck that might get parked in the desert and set on fire. And I would do it if I could. But my paperwork isn't in order, if you catch me. I told him I knew just the guys though."

"Why does he trust you?" Jeff asked.

Ricky shrugged. "I told you, it's complicated. So are you in or what?"

"How many people?" Dave said.

"Just four," Ricky said. "Ruiz, his fat wife, and his two brats. You're the perfect team for the job."

Marck had already made his mind up, and his bandmates' sullen expressions and glazed eyes said that prison wasn't even worth considering. This was their only move.

Dave shook his head but said, "Okay."

"Bueno," Ricky said. "Where's your fearless leader? You'll fill him in?"

"He's not here," Marck said.

"We fired him," Jeff added.

"You're joking, right?" Ricky's laugh was jangly and too high for his voice. "You really fired him? Well that's no good."

Ricky sat back in his chair and stroked his chin, thinking about it.

"Hire him back. I want the same crew as last time. And get yourself a burner phone. This may take a week or so to take shape, but if you get a call from a 432 area code, you answer it, I don't care if you're onstage or between the sheets. Entienden?"

He waited for each of them to respond.

"All right then."

The call ended and the phone went back to its main screen. Monica walked up and stuck out her hand. Marck had forgotten that she was there. She stared down at him flatly, all the flirt gone from her demeanor. She cleared her throat and he realized he still had a death grip on her phone. He handed it over and she promptly spun around and ninja-starred it into the concrete wall, smashing it to pieces.

"Thanks boys," she said. She grabbed two more beers from their cooler and left the room. The bandmates sat scrunched together on the couch, dazed.

"We're fucked," Marck said.

Chapter 12

1984

THE EAST TEXAS AIR HUNG ON JAVIER LIKE A WET WOOL blanket he couldn't kick off. It was hot and headed for blistering. Sweat rolled down his back, his body's futile attempt to cool him off. He gripped his hoe handle with both hands and leaned into it. The blade sank into the soil. Drew came by every couple of hours with water, and unless Javier's sense of time had failed, he was late. He stared across the cotton field at the dense green stalks in perfect rows—speckled with cream-colored blooms and a purple one every now and then—that sloped down to a draw full of tangled elm. He wiped his brow. The others' hoes made soft pocks behind him, scraping the dirt as they uprooted rogue cockleburs and ragweed. Six other boys—ranging from Elizondo, little Eli, at nine to Beto at seventeen—hacked at weeds the plows had missed.

It was Javier's third week, and the work had been constant. They were in the fields from dawn until dusk, with a couple of hours off when the heat peaked. Javier had been eager to work when he arrived—he wanted to prove his worth, and farm labor was nothing new—but it had begun to take a toll. He did his best to keep up with the older boys, but on those especially steamy afternoons he felt himself fading.

The boys worked in the fields Monday to Friday. Saturdays, Yolanda had them cleaning or doing laundry in the morning, but when they finished they had free time to play cards or kick a ball around. In the evening, Yolanda and Drew would let them gather around the living room TV to watch wrestling. The boys looked forward to it all week. Javier asked once if they ever got Astros games. Drew just snarled, "Why would anybody want to watch them?"

Sunday mornings they had English lessons. They were expected to speak it at all times, stammering and miming if they didn't know a word. Yolanda called it immersion. That was how she'd learned, she said, and they would all thank her someday. Javier still didn't understand why she felt the need to teach them if all they did was chop weeds.

Regardless, the dining room would turn into a classroom for a couple of hours with Yolanda chain-smoking and giving them phrases to repeat, and Drew misspelling words on the small chalkboard behind her. She had torn into him for forgetting the first R in *surprised*. "And English is your *first fucking* language," she said, shaking her head and drawing hard on her cigarette.

Drew was a coarse-grained East Texan, but Yolanda could cow him in a second. Nobody went against her. One look and any of them would freeze like a doe that had wandered into a mountain lion's pouncing range. There was no running, no talking your way out. All you could do was stay still and hope she moved on. She was shorter than most of the boys, with posture that suggested a hunchback down the line, but nobody doubted her power.

"Hey," Jesús snapped. Javier took his weight off his hoe. Jesús mimed chopping, and Javier got back to work. The two of them came upon a dense spot of blueweed. They chopped away at the horde of tiny pale plants that looked like they belonged at the bottom of the ocean. The bigger ones had gone to seed and their offspring poked from the dirt, dense as leg hair. It seemed like they'd never get through it all, but a couple of hours later they had them cleared out.

Javier spied Adrián hunched over and hacking away on the far end. A few days ago Drew had found his hoe on the ground next to all the others on the rack. Maybe it just fell off, or maybe Adrián had a careless moment, but that didn't matter. Drew had come into their bunkhouse holding a short-handled hoe. The blade was similar to the others, but the wooden handle wasn't even a forearm length. El cortito. Javier's mom had told him about them. How his abuelo, when he went into Texas as a bracero, had to use one in the fields. The landowners insisted on them because they forced the workers to stoop, keeping their eyes closer to the ground and all the tiny weeds up next to the stalks. Drew said long-handled hoes were a privilege, and Adrián had lost his for now. That was on Tuesday, and it was Friday now. Adrián's faraway figure rose up, bent backward with his fists in the small of his back, and then hunched again, all alone in the weediest part of the field.

The seven of them could get through a quarter section in a week or less, depending on how attentive a farmer it belonged to. They had just finished cleaning up a patch of soybeans for a drive-by farmer named Danny Ray Carroll. He showed up the first day in his three-quarter-ton truck and camped out on the turnrow, spitting out the window and blasting the A/C. After half an hour or so, he saw enough to trust the boys' work and rumbled away.

Javier went into another of his spells that afternoon, looking back into one of those crisp daydream windows that portaled him into a real school, making friends, striking out batters on a Little League team with sharp blue uniforms. Clouds rolled in and provided a welcome buffer from the hot sun. The afternoon moved fast. By the time Drew pulled up and yelled "quitting time," he couldn't pick out any one moment from the blur of the day's work. His mind and body were both busy but miles apart. It didn't used to be like that back home.

Bouncing along in the truck bed with the other boys, Javier gazed upon the thick rows littered with uprooted casualties and the huge portion of the field that remained woolly with weeds, all fanning past him in the fading dusk. He closed his eyes and imagined one of his mother's songs, feeling his heart break when he realized he could no longer recall the exact sound of her voice.

2015

The coffee maker gurgled and dripped behind him while Javier stared into the familiar blankness of the kitchen. The calendar displayed bright November foliage even though December was half over. The rust-spotted fridge held only beer and old takeout containers. The blinds accumulated dust so fast there was no point in cleaning them, and the slow wall clock reminded him he should be in bed instead of making another pot of coffee. His eye settled on the jagged hole in the wall, the one he had punched through after he was fired.

He'd kept it together in front of the band, like he always did. He tried to reason with them, but their somber tones revealed there was no convincing them to stay in the game anymore. So he shook their hands and wished them well. He kept the fury bundled up tight until he got home, and then he threw a full-bore punch, splintering the wood paneling all the way through. He kept intending to fix it, to hang a picture there at least, but hadn't found the energy.

Even putting a hole in the wall didn't make him less angry, not immediately. He paced the floor, rubbing his throbbing hand. They thought they could fire him and forget everything he did, forget the tiny dive bars they were relegated to before he came along. They'd be nowhere without him. Their music was awful, and they would soon be forgotten. But even at his angriest, those thoughts didn't ring true.

Javier calmed down and the blame turned back on him, like it always did. He kicked himself for pushing so hard, demanding they keep smuggling when the music had begun to sustain itself. Now it was too late. They were on the brink of legitimate success without him. It had been right under Javier's nose, but he ignored it. Because seeing them as a legitimate musical act meant recognizing just how fleeting his influence over them was. Now he was nothing but the captain of an empty bus.

They cashed out his cut, but it sat untouched in a safety deposit box downtown. He once kept a list of things he wanted to do, places to go, if he had the means. He wanted to buy a horse, a dun mare like his father once had. He wanted to go to Coyoacán for Día de Los Muertos. He wanted to sit right behind third base at an Astros game. Now that those things were possible, they lost their appeal. Just something else to chase, another thrill bound to fade.

In the months that had passed, Javier stayed in the same single-wide trailer on the edge of Lubbock and drove the same stepside pickup with the same burnt-up clutch. He got hired on with a framing crew as much to avoid being alone with himself all day as for the paycheck. The nights were hard enough. He stopped returning Bonnie's texts, and she stopped trying. He hadn't gone to shows, much less scouted for a new band to represent. He hadn't hit up his connections for any more smuggling opportunities or lifted a finger to help any of the migrants he once thought he cared about. The world ran on money, not morals.

After work he stayed up half the night, watching trash TV or scrolling through sensationalized news on his phone, feeling worthless and sapped. He ate a sad bachelor's diet, frozen TV dinners or gas station burritos most nights, and dulled the pangs of dissatisfaction with a steady supply of light beer and cigarettes. He was smoking full-time again after three years off. Javier had no anchor to keep him from tumbling each time the ferocious winds changed. There were moments he felt his old spark, that sense of purpose that once kept him going, but most nights that wasn't enough to get him off the couch.

Javier poured a cup of piñon coffee, lit a cigarette, and sat in the sagging lawn chair on his back porch. The yellow light threw his oversized shadow into the yard, bent it around a stack of railroad ties he'd intended to make something out of. The north wind sliced at his dry, cracked skin. West Texas Decembers were mild and sunny by Yankee standards, but the nights dipped below freezing without fail. And the gale-force winds had a way of making a forty-degree evening feel Arctic. It wasn't nearly so cold where Javier grew up. Still, he came outside most nights to sit a while, if for no other reason than to feel the chill and see something other than the glow of a screen.

The wind died down, became bearable. It hummed across the loose window screens. Javier could hear the low seashell roar of trucks on the

Clovis highway, an occasional shrill bark from the border collie down the road. It was cloudless, and the stars popped in the undeveloped blackness. He found Gemini and then Orion, moving on to other constellations, pointing and naming the way his mother taught him to, until landing on La Osa Menor and its tip, Polaris.

That one was his favorite growing up, its cosmic light shining the path to El Norte. Here he was, in the US for so many years, and what did he have to show for it? He was older now than his mother had been when she died. She had saved everything she made to give him the cash for his passage by then. What had he done for someone that amounted to even half of that? He sipped his coffee, his eyes settling on the red windmill lights in the distance, all appearing and disappearing in unison like a fleet of alien ships.

The train started out distant and faint, the blare of its horn unmistakable in the quiet winter night. The bursts grew louder, hit their peak, and receded into the black. Then, sure as clockwork, came the bark of a coyote. It always followed the train, its fading blasts giving way to a series of piercing yips.

Another coyote replied. Its voice was clear and bold in the southwest. After a back and forth they joined in together, casting their tremulous yips against the cold dark dome of stars. Just a couple of coyotes could create a wall of sound that stirred feelings of smallness in your heart. Even the border collie down the road didn't dare interrupt. Sometimes the coyotes sang all night in the hollow spaces blown out by those booming horns. Javier didn't know if they spoke of territory or prey or something else humans long ago ceased to comprehend, but he recognized the tune.

Javier woke around seven, feeling rested for a change. It was his day off, so instead of his usual packaged concha he decided to pick up some eggs and cook himself a real breakfast.

He hit the red light by the John Deere house. Pickups with grill guards and flatbeds filled the spaces out front. Men in faded Carhartt jackets bustled in and out of the door carrying stripper parts and five-gallon buckets of hydraulic oil. Everybody was trying to make their repairs while the dew was still on the cotton. It reminded Javier of the old days.

Though they were miles away, he could make out a couple of the downtown buildings on the horizon. It wasn't that Lubbock was that big or its buildings that tall. The land was just that flat. It was easier to hunt a buffalo than a hill in this area. You could watch your dog run away for three days. On a clear afternoon you might catch a glimpse of the back of your head. Javier had heard all the sayings by now.

He turned on the radio and caught the forecast: mild today, cold front blowing in tonight with chances of ice and snow, frigid the next couple of days, and then back in the fifties for the weekend. Sounded about right. He stopped at the store on Indiana for the eggs. At the counter he pointed to a pack of reds.

"That's my papaw's brand," the girl with straight bangs said.

"Oh yeah?" Javier said.

"Well it was—he's dead now," she said.

"I'm sorry."

"It wasn't lung cancer or nothing. Stroke. After Nana died he didn't have nobody to monitor him for the signs, like they say in those commercials. F.A.S.T. Face, uh, speech, time. I can't remember the A. Act? Either way, nobody was there to do anything. I wish I could've been, but I still got my little ones to take care of, you know?" The girl handed Javier his change. "Thank you and have a God-blessed day, sir."

"You too."

Instead of going straight back, he decided to go for a little drive. The nicotine helped take the wobbles out of his train of thought. He cracked the windows. The first hard freeze had come late this year, and the morning air was still steeped in frost and fresh death.

At the end of a block of unlit Christmas lights, dead Bermuda grass, and inflatable Santas, a grizzled meter reader with a toboggan almost covering his eyes, carrying a waist-high screwdriver like a cane, left the alley. He paused there, and Javier followed his gaze to the sorority sisters jogging by in a tight pack, cheery and red-faced, skin-tight leggings accentuating lively butts of various shapes and sizes. The meter reader watched them pass, let out a hazy breath, and headed for the next alley.

Javier's old truck creaked and rattled over the red brick in the Depot District. In the daytime, its deserted bars reminded him of seeing a woman who normally wore gobs of makeup and hairspray without any of it on. They were pale, unremarkable buildings in the morning sunlight. He drove by a fading mural of Buddy Holly, grinning behind those thick black frames. The band had only scratched the surface of his music when he first took them on. They had heard the big hits like "Peggy Sue" and had seen his name and likeness on street signs and buildings and art trails, but they never really knew what made him unique. Javier played them his last single before he died, the Latin-influenced "Heartbeat," and they loved it enough they started folding some Crickets deep cuts into their sets.

Javier couldn't keep his thoughts from returning to the band, driving by all the nightclubs he'd booked them at. He wondered if they still stayed in that cheap rent house on Second Street. When he left, they were still split about whether to stay in Lubbock or move on. Squat was the only one who expressed much fondness for the Hub City. He argued for the friendly locals and the magnificence of yoga pants season in a college town. Jeff was with him, but he mostly argued for the low cost of living because it meant they could afford more recording equipment. Marck thought Lubbock was the flattest, dullest place he'd ever seen. And he was from Nebraska. Dave had convinced himself that Austin was where a band had to go to make it. There was some truth to it. It was one of the best music scenes in the country. But that leap could be jarring. Like all the hotshot local quarterbacks who tried walking on at Texas Tech, only to realize that everyone around them had been stars in high school too.

The internet had made it so that living in an isolated place wasn't the creative desert it used to be. People from all over the world could watch and comment on your music video. They could stream your songs and put them on playlists to send to their friends. And the actual creating had never been a problem. West Texas was a place you had to make your own fun, and the bandmates were good at that.

Javier headed back home with the eggs next to him on the frayed bench seat. He tightened up when he saw an unmarked white van in front of his trailer. His driver-side door groaned shut, and he approached it. No one was inside. He eyed the sports drink bottles and toll road receipts on the dash and the black tree hanging from the rearview mirror.

He walked around back with his egg carton tucked under his arm like a football. Underneath the rust-spotted awning, surrounding the tour bus, were his old colleagues. Squat and Marck bent over, checking out the tires. Dave and Jeff stood facing the grill with their arms crossed, in discussion. Webb leaned against an I-beam, admiring the rig. They hadn't noticed him yet. Javier stared at their forms, trying to come to grips with their presence. It was like watching a familiar show with the sound off. There they were, looking and acting like they always had, but there was something foreign about their ways.

"There he is," Webb said, seeing Javier and starting to wave.

Javier wasn't sure what to make of them waltzing back into his life unannounced. A part of him, seized up with rust the past six months, broke loose and began to turn once again. The feeling wasn't necessarily good or bad, but it was one of blood and breath and effort, and that scared him. Something seemed to click back into place.

"What are y'all doing here?"

Jeff looked at the others, like he didn't know the answer and they were going to give it to him. His eyes finally met Javier's but didn't linger. He motioned over his shoulder.

"Surprised you still have that thing."

———————

Javier knew he would do the most time if they didn't go along with Ricky's plan. He was just the illegal immigrant turned coyote judges would lunge to make an example of. His was the face politicians would use in ads for a taller border wall. But if Ricky really played it that way, they would all go down. Hard.

He took in the desperation on the bandmates' faces while they waited for his lips to move. The wall clock's tick-tick-tick filled their ears. Javier leaned back in his chair and watched the second hand move in fits and starts. They needed him for this job, and not just because Ricky demanded it.

"Want a beer?"

He took their blank expressions for yeses and filled his hands with longnecks from the crisper. He set them on the table and took his seat. He didn't want to torture them, but there was a part of him that enjoyed seeing them squirm a little. Marck rubbed his stubbly head and crossed his arms impatiently. Nobody touched the beers. Javier felt the wheels turning, the swarm of possibilities once again in reach. He knew how he'd answer before they even asked the question.

"I'll do it."

"Oh good," Dave said. A sigh escaped behind the word. "We didn't know what we were gonna do."

"Nice," Marck said.

"Wooo," Squat said. "The gang is back."

Jeff murmured something, looking out the window into the crisp December sky. The bandmates slid their beers toward themselves.

"There's just one thing we need you to know," Jeff said after all the beers but his were uncapped. "We're a legit band now, and this is a detour. We're this close to being able to make our album." He pinched his fingers together. "We'll do this job, but once we get back to Texas we're picking up where we left off. And you don't fit into that."

The other bandmates wouldn't look at either of them, not backing Jeff up but not shooting him down either.

"Fair enough." Javier leaned forward on the table. "Now you listen—smuggling people across the border is my business. When we're in Mexico, what I say goes."

If they were drawing lines, Javier figured now was a good time to draw his.

"Fine." Jeff popped the top off his beer.

"To one last rodeo," Dave said and raised his longneck.

They toasted, and the room no longer seemed to be closing in on them. Squat gestured wildly telling Javier about their encounter with Jeff Tweedy, how he stopped by the green room after the show to say hello. How Jeff insinuated that they would make a good opening act for him, and Tweedy just chuckled and told them to keep on keeping on.

Dave's ringtone cut through their conversation. His cheerful face fell flat when he looked at the screen, and he left the room. They talked and drank, but something stuck in Javier's mind: What was to stop Ricky from pulling this again? Just *one more time* until their time was up. He had all the leverage, putting them in the position with all the risk. Something would have to change.

Dave walked back in. "That was Ricky." He ran a hand through his hair.

"What's up?" Jeff said.

"He wants us in Juárez tomorrow."

"Tomorrow?" Marck said. "What happened to coming up with a plan?"

"I don't know," Dave said. "He sounded weird."

That didn't sit well with any of them.

"I don't like this at all," Jeff said.

Webb nodded. "He don't seem like the type to make empty threats."

"No," Marck said. "We need more time. We just got Javier back."

"What choice do we have? Any of you want to go to prison?" Dave said. Nobody met his heated gaze. "I didn't think so. He said he'd call us tomorrow afternoon. Once we're there."

"Well, it is what it is," Javier said. "We'll take care of business and come home. Maybe we'll even beat the storm. It'll be all right."

The words felt flat and unconvincing, and he couldn't see any way the band heard them any differently. They sat in the quiet kitchen awhile, spacing out into their own worries and watching the light fade when cold gray clouds rolled in on the north wind. They made a plan to meet back at Javier's early the next morning.

Javier sat on the back porch again that night. He thought he heard a coyote yip, but it was too faint to know for sure. The whistle of the wind drowned everything else out. He figured he should be content. Another treasure map had been left on his doorstep. Another adventure awaited him. It was the kind of thing that used to make him feel like he had a golden light in his chest. That he was doing something honorable and could help others in the struggle. Maybe even help himself. But this time he didn't feel that.

Raindrops fell from the darkness and splatted on his jean jacket. Javier shut the porch light off and locked his door. His sleep was all tangled with memories, and when he woke he couldn't shake the feeling that some vital decision lay ahead, something just out of reach that could burn his whole world down to ashes.

When he got up to face the day, the righteous feeling he once had was missing, but he was powered by something almost as good: he had a job to do. The coyote had been summoned to rise up and walk the desert once again.

Chapter 13

1984

IN THE LAMPLIGHT OF THE BUNKHOUSE JAVIER LAY AWAKE and watched the shadows leap across the ceiling while the other boys traded stories in their second language. He still hadn't figured that out. Yolanda and Drew weren't around, but the boys still spoke in their best English, ranging from broken to near perfect.

Javier had exhausted mind and body. He hoed fields for people he never met, never getting to see any fruits of his labor besides the up-turned weeds he left in his wake. He missed the farm back home, where the work was hard but showed up as food on their plates. He came to the US looking for opportunity and adventure but found himself in a rut.

The boys cut loose a little in the bunkhouse, one of the only places Yolanda or Drew weren't over their shoulders, and they spent the eve-nings trading their best stories. The boys seemed to know each other in a way that went beyond words in either language. Javier never felt like he fit in. Adrián, the second oldest and most fluent, finished a story about his home in Sinaloa. How once walking home through the foothills he found a man's pale and leathery body decomposing in the dense brush. It was an area off the beaten path where he used to hunt for rabbits. The man's clothes were tattered and faded, but Adrián could tell they were nice once. A gold chain was still around his neck but had embedded into his rotting flesh. Whoever killed him wasn't too concerned about money. Eli looked like he might get sick.

"What happened?"

Adrián shook his head. "He was a drug dealer. In Sinaloa, they don't last too long."

The boys' expressions varied from open-mouthed awe to boredom from those who had heard the story before. Adrián answered more of their questions and then the topic faded out. "What about you?" Adrián said. The talking stopped and Javier could feel eyes on him.

"Me?"

"Yeah, you. What's your story?"

"No story," Javier said. But they kept staring, and he knew he had to tell them something. So he outlined his path from Coahuila to East Texas in as few details as possible, leaving out things like the money his mother left him. He mentioned the coyotes and the truck, but not the people that didn't make it. He tried to sound like he'd been brave and unafraid the whole time.

Adrián squinted. Doing stoop work all day had to have worn him out, but he didn't show it. He had his chair leaned back on two legs and his hands behind his head. "Bullshit," he said. "You didn't cross with no coyotes. That takes a lot of money." Adrián thudded his chair back on four legs. "Nah."

"Ni modo," Javier said, not wanting to make contact with Adrián's prison spotlight eyes.

"Maybe he came over in hees mamá's dirty panocha," said the fat boy whose name Javier couldn't think of. Ignacio or Emilio. His plump top lip curled, showing a mouth full of stubby teeth. His chubby cheeks dimpled around them. The boy's honking laugh entered Javier's head and pinched off the part of his brain that normally kept him rational. The boys all watched Javier to see what he would do.

He felt his heartbeat in his throat, in his head, in his fists. He landed on the floorboards, marched over, and struck the boy's nose with a solid jab and then connected a wild hook with his padded cheekbone. It felt good.

In a way he'd been waiting for this, for someone to do him wrong, so he could finally unleash all the hurt he kept inside, make someone else feel it for a change. The fat boy grabbed his nose and Javier had his fist cocked again when the other boys took him down. Javier yelled and twisted, but Adrián dropped a knee on his belly and covered his mouth. Javier gasped, sucking back against Adrián's warm, salty palm.

"Cállate, cállate." Adrián's eyes darted to the door. "Be quiet."

Javier couldn't speak if he wanted to. Adrián removed his hand and hovered it over Javier's mouth until he decided he wasn't going to yell again. Javier made a hollow noise in his throat, trying to find his breath.

"Are you trying to get us killed?"

Javier's anger had left him. He stared past Adrián to the fat boy. His head was tilted back and Jesús held a rag up to his nose, the top of it soaked dark red. Eli had his mouth open. Beto stood nearby with his arms crossed. He shook his head when the fat boy whimpered and blew a bloody mess onto the rag.

"Cálmate, Nacho," Jesús said.

"Don't call me that," he pouted. "Ese niño está loco."

"Ignacio, shut the hell up," Beto said. "I would've busted your nose too if you talked about my mamá like that."

Javier breathed a little easier. It helped that he didn't have a knee in his gut anymore. Adrián stared down at him. "No more. If they catch you fighting—" His eyes unfocused. "Bad."

Javier got frustrated. Nothing made sense here. What were they all so scared of? "Por qué está malo? Y por qué hablan en inglés todo el tiempo?" Javier looked around. "No están aquí."

"They're close enough," Adrián said. His anger had left him too. He stared out the window into the flat darkness. His voice dropped. "You don't get it, do you?"

Javier's blankness admitted he didn't. Adrián looked at him in a way he couldn't crack. There was some disappointment in it, some sympathy too.

"You like it here?"

Javier shrugged.

"Go ahead. Say the truth."

Javier sucked in his bottom lip. "I hate it."

"Uh huh. And what do you think about us. Do we like it?" Adrián turned to the others. "Anybody having fun?"

Nobody spoke. A couple shuffled their feet and looked on in solemn accord, their faces all shades of distress. Adrián turned to Javier. "So why are we still here if we want to be somewhere else?"

Javier's jaw tensed. He wanted Adrián to stop talking in circles.

"No veo cadenas," he said.

Adrián shook his head. "No chains, no barbed wire." He nodded to Jesús and motioned him over. He looked embarrassed when he approached, turning his back to Javier and pulling his shirt over his head. Between his shoulder blades was a cluster with four red lesions. Javier tried to make sense of it. The marks, almost perfect circles, were spread out like double-aught buckshot sprayed from a short distance. Three were scabbed over and brown, but one outlier was still white and puffy. All were circled by red rings. They looked like foul murderous planets, forever out of orbit.

"Cigarette." Adrián mimed rolling one between his fingers and touching it to Javier's forearm. Jesús didn't grimace when he put his shirt back down. Javier did.

"The new one," Adrián said. "Tell him why."

"I ran," he said.

Javier's heart dropped. His mind scrambled. *How did they catch him? Were they always watching? How long had this been going on? How did he get here? How. How. How.*

"And some will say you're lucky if it's Yolanda's cigarette that catches you. Drew's got other ways." Adrián shook his head and looked at the others. Eli got all fidgety, scratching at his elbows and staring through the beat-up planks beneath his feet.

"I don't know what they told you, but I bet it was close to what we heard too," Adrián said. "Dry place to stay. Protection from la migra. A paying job. An education." Javier didn't nod, but he didn't need to.

Adrián went on. "We get paid but they say it all goes to food, boarding, schooling," he chuckled. "And we're protected from la migra, I guess. If you want to call a couple of wolves saving you from a puma protection."

It felt like Adrián's knee had slammed into his gut again. How had he not seen this before? He felt so foolish for trusting them.

"But we look out for each other. You listen to us, work, you'll be okay," Adrián said. "Once you learn the rules, you don't have to worry as much. It could be worse."

Javier's jaw trembled, but he clamped it. He wanted nothing less than for the boys to see him cry. The thought that dying in the coyotes' truck might've been better floated through his head like a thick cloud over the moon.

The mood in the room had changed. Nobody talked or teased each other. Even Ignacio had gone silent, pressing the rag to his nose with hollow eyes.

"Time for lights out," Adrián said loud enough for everyone to hear. "Nobody says a word about tonight."

He nodded to Beto, who snuffed the kerosene lamp.

The night was long and sleepless. The next day loomed over Javier like a boulder balanced in the rafters. He cried silently into an old pillow, realizing he'd always been trapped, but how much worse it felt to reach the end of his chain and see how short it was. He curled up and wished the darkness would swallow him, that morning would find him gone.

2015

Javier didn't have to tell Webb to slow down. He gripped the wheel at ten and two and sat like he had a broomstick down his pants. They took the longer way, thinking that heading down to I-20 might let them bypass some of the bad roads. They were wrong. Black ice splotched the highway. Frontlines of pale gray mist swallowed up the horizon. Everything else looked white and sharp. They made their way southwest at fifty miles an hour, counting the cars that had slid into ditches.

They didn't have the luxury of waiting it out, and the forecast said the massive winter storm would stretch all the way from Chihuahua into Missouri. It had begun to drizzle overnight, and now pellets of sleet clicked on the windshield. The temperature flirted with the freezing point, warming up just enough to rain and then freezing over again. It would continue on that way, the ice building until its weight snapped trees and knocked down power lines. Javier had seen it before.

A silver Suburban on the shoulder was covered in a shell of ice. Its details were distorted and out of focus even up close. Icicles lined its running boards and fenders like jagged fringe. The flatland was almost a mirror image on both sides of the highway. Spindly mesquite and spiky yucca bowed under the layers of ice. A few Black Angus cows huddled near the fence. The frozen weeds looked wild and alien, like things that might take hold of your ankle and pull you off into the mist.

Somewhere around Midland cattle country faded, and pump jacks and natural gas flares began to sprout from the ground. The flares' tangerine flames leapt above the gray of the ice-swept brushland.

The bus's heater was out, so they kept their jackets on and eyed the flames with envy. Javier blew into his fist and wiggled his chilled toes in his boots. The sandpaper feeling in his eyes reminded him how little he'd slept the night before.

"Whoa," Webb said when a big patch of ice disappeared underneath them. The tendons in his hands protruded and went pale when he squeezed the wheel. He let off the gas and counter steered. It was enough to keep them from joining the fallen in the ditch.

"Holy shit," Jeff said. "Slow down."

"Which is it?" Webb snapped. "Not ten minutes ago you were telling me how we needed to make better time. I cain't do both."

"Drive normal," Jeff said.

"Look around," Webb said. "Is there anything normal about this?"

Jeff shook his head and cut his eyes to the window. The clouds and haze settled into a thick fog in the low spots. Javier heard Webb whisper, "God, just let us make it through this and I—I'll quit smoking, for real this time. Just dipping, nothing else."

Javier thought he should save his bargaining chips. The drive down was the least of their troubles. They were sliding into darkness with only a handful of matches to light the way. In Juárez, that's where they would need all the help they could get.

The four o'clock sky looked like dusk when they entered El Paso. The clouds had triggered all the streetlights, which made halos in the freezing mist. They stopped at a deserted filling station to diesel up and grab coffee. The clerk tried to chat them up like they were the last people on earth. Maybe they were. They hadn't seen another pair of headlights in a while.

They found them on the freeway. The bus stayed in the slow-moving right lane, where a path had been worn through the ice. A maroon sedan sped by in the slick white fast lane and disappeared into the building fog. Five minutes later they saw the car again, turned the opposite direction with its bumper hung on the guardrail.

Past the airport, the Franklin Mountains came into view. The city faded into its ice-crusted foothills. Only the dark of the scrub and ridges broke up the pallid slopes. Javier, still in a daze, followed the rise up to where the peaks should have been. In their place was a descending mob of white clouds. They stood out like cotton against the gray. Webb fumbled with the radio until he got it on a weather report.

"This is Mad Dog Peña with a KTSM weather advisory. It's thirty-two degrees in El Paso, Texas, and what started as another sunny week has taken an ugly turn. We are under an ice storm warning, folks. We have a frozen mix falling at the station right now and precipitation chances are hovering at 80 percent for the next twelve hours. All that rainfall we've seen should freeze over tonight and then we can expect between four and six inches of snow on top. We're looking at a complete impasse by daybreak. Unless you absolutely have to, do not drive—"

Webb snorted and cut the radio off.

"It's colder here than in Anchorage, Alaska," Squat said, looking at his phone.

"Not helping," Dave said, watching the storm continue down the mountain.

The border crossing was more active than expected, with everybody trying to get over in case the bridges shut down that night. Javier shook off the gnawing *what if* of that scenario. At the checkpoint, a wiry border agent hunched over in a navy coat approached the door with his hood up.

"Registros," he said, his breath making a thick fog in the frigid air. He barely made eye contact with any of them, shuddering from the cold and making a half-effort to look things over.

"Okay," he said.

"Do you know if they'll end up closing the—" Marck said, but the agent was already gone. And they were in Juárez again. Only a few blocks into the city, almost like they were being watched, the phone rang from a 432 number.

"Hello," Javier said. "Yeah. Uh huh. No. No complications. Just crossed the border." Looking out at the coming storm in the fading light, Javier nodded and listened to Ricky's directions on how to get to the warehouse on Calle Andrés del Río. He knew that the street was named after some long-dead guy and had nothing to do with the Andrés who prowled this area, but it added to the feeling that they were treading on hostile ground.

The Kentucky Club, which buzzed most nights, looked dead from the outside. Its green neon blurred in the haze. The movie theater and the taquerías looked just as vacant. Most towns in Texas and Mexico shut down for what Midwesterners would call a dusting, and they were already well beyond that. People were hunkered down by now, firing up space heaters, watching the local weather like a tornado was about to touch down.

The wind picked up and bowed the palm trees. Golden snow blew sideways under the freshly lit streetlamps. They turned down Tierra Blanca, a pale caliche road rougher than most alleys back home. The next road was paved but riddled with potholes, serrated where cars had broken off chunks of the weaker outside edge, following a cinder block fence tagged with crisp red graffiti.

"Plata o plomo?" Marck read aloud.

Dave shrugged and said, "I think plata means silver."

"It means silver or lead," Javier said. He turned to Marck. "As in take this bribe or you'll get a bullet in your head."

Marck's jaw clenched and he looked away from the wall.

"That must be it," Dave said, pointing at the off-white warehouse rising out of the haze.

It was a large windowless building with no signs or markings. Razor wire topped the fence. It was the sort of place that looked unremarkable in the daylight but took on a sinister tone when it was left alone each night. The bus nosed up to the automatic gate.

"Do you have a code?" Webb asked.

Javier shook his head. "He didn't mention one."

The gate lurched. Bits of ice fell from the chain-link as the little motor struggled with the extra weight. Webb gave a worried sideways glance and then carefully accelerated. The bus's wheels crunched over the chunks of ice and pulled up to the main entrance, where the parking lot had become one blank white space.

"Are we sure this is it?" Jeff said. "Looks deserted."

Tire tracks went across the lot and behind the building. Before they could follow them a sliver of light appeared. Nando, Ricky's partner, stood halfway out of the side door. The light from inside gleamed off the top of his scalp. He motioned for them to come inside.

Webb reached for the ignition, but Javier stopped him.

"You wait here," Javier said. "And leave it running."

Nando stared them down without a word. He led the way down a heated corridor. A rumble came through the wall, like the roar of a crowd from backstage, but this was harsher, like a machine capable of turning bones into gravel. The heavy door swung closed with a loud bang after the last of them. They pushed through a set of plastic flaps and the cold hit them. It was like being back outside. The warehouse had concrete floors and high ceilings. Steel racks with wrapped-up pallets and cardboard boxes and totes of unidentified liquids went all the way up to the fluorescent lights. Only one section was lit, and the lanes retreated into the darkness for what seemed like an infinite distance.

"What is this place?" Jeff said with his eyebrows arched.

"Food distribution plant," Nando replied.

Squat looked up at all the refrigerated cargo. "Mmm. I love me some"—he squinted at one of the boxes—"mechanically separated chicken."

A camera was mounted to the wall, but it was limp and unwatching. Going deeper and deeper into the facility, the thought crossed Javier's mind that they might not leave this place. It was a perfect spot for a murder. Cleaned and sterilized daily. The concrete floors had big drain grates in low spots. A thin stream of water went from the spray nozzle of a coiled red hose into the nearest grate. Ricky could shoot them, hose the blood down the drain, and then grind their bodies up to supplement the meat paste headed into the hot dogs of some middle schoolers in Aguascalientes. Javier tried to shake off the thought. He noticed half a dozen yellow forklifts, each one carefully parked between slanted yellow lines.

They stopped at a door with a keypad. Nando put his arms out to his sides, making a T. He held this pose, without speaking, until they knew to mimic him. He went down the line, frisking each person. Javier hadn't raised his arms when Nando got to him. The man's eyes flickered impatiently. Javier put his hands up and let him check for the gun he wished he had on him. Nando punched four numbers into the keypad and it clicked. The red-lettered sign on the door said

WARNING

ANHYDROUS AMMONIA ROOM

MUST WEAR PPE AT ALL TIMES

"Ándale," Nando said.

Javier eased it open. Only a single bulb kept the dim room from total darkness. There were tanks and pipes going every which way, and a loud hum came from somewhere in the back. Javier walked down the steel mesh steps with the bandmates close behind. Nando waited by the door. Javier's chest tightened. The room had shrunk to the size of a tomb.

He thought he saw something move and squinted into the faint outlines behind the ammonia tanks. An orange dot bobbed through the darkness and Ricky came into view. He let out a lungful of smoke and flicked his cigarette against one of the pipes.

"'Bout damn time," he said.

"Where are the migrants, Ricky?" Javier said.

"They're not here," he said, just loud enough to be heard over the droning machinery.

A wave of dread washed over Javier. "Not here?"

"Not here," Ricky said. He ripped the foil out of a fresh pack and let if fall between his boots. "As in somewhere else. Your money's there too." Ricky paused and rubbed his shoulder. "I keep getting these muscle spasms. Must be the weather." He pulled a cigarette from the pack with his lips and his eyes landed on Marck. "You got a problem, skinhead?"

Marck was all nerve, clenched up from frustration and the cold. He had as much as he could take. He found some courage and decided to put it to use. He stepped forward and snatched the cigarette from Ricky's mouth, crumpled it, and let the bits of paper and tobacco fall to the floor.

"Fuck you." Those first two words shot from Marck's tongue with precision, but then in the silent moment afterward, the machismo went out of his voice and left it sounding uneasy and pleading. "Do you know how long I've worked to get in this spot, how many shitty bands I've shuffled through? How many times I've slept in a van with rolled-up jeans as a pillow? Because I've lost count. And now, when I finally might be able to make a decent living at this again, you show up. You demand we work for you, you threaten to turn us in, and you keep us in the dark. It's not right."

"I don't have time for this," Ricky said.

"Neither did we," Marck said.

His bandmates looked on with a mix of pride and terror on their faces. Javier saw only foolishness. He tried to take Marck's arm, but he jerked it away. Ricky's patience was almost gone.

"I like your band dynamic. Kind of an early Beatles thing," Ricky said. "Three talented young guys and one stiff drummer keeping a seat warm for the next guy. Why is it that guy is always the loudest?" Ricky shook his head in mock uncertainty. "So little drummer boy, I'll drop a quarter in you the next time I want to hear you speak."

Marck's hands balled into fists and his face got red. He telegraphed a punch that swung wildly from his body. Ricky stepped inside of it and, in one fluid motion, pulled a hefty 1911 from his coat and slammed its butt on top of Marck's skull.

The solid thwack it made was sickening. Marck's face contorted and his legs went to jelly. He stumbled forward, sinking lower with each heavy step until he was face down by one of the tanks. He groaned.

Squat rushed over to him. "Marck? Are you okay?"

Marck groaned again and rolled onto his back. He kept his knees bent and used his feet to scoot himself backward on the concrete. He writhed and covered his skull with his hands. The pistol whip didn't knock him out like in the movies, but it did plenty. Squat and Dave got under each of Marck's arms and helped him up. A line of blood trickled down his pink forehead. Ricky pulled another cigarette out and lit it. He exhaled and a cloud of smoke rose and dissipated into the dim light.

"Glad we got that out of the way," Ricky said. "Can we get down to business now?"

Marck stood on his own feet now with Dave's wool hat pressed to his wound, resembling a dog that had been reminded of his place in the pack.

"Do anything like that again and we walk," Javier said.

Ricky tilted his chin up, narrowed his eyes. Then he nodded to Javier.

"Where's Ruiz?" Javier asked.

"Andrés found out about our plan." Ricky shook his head and for the first time, the bluster left his voice. "He killed them."

"Killed them? The wife and kids even?" Dave asked, looking as if he'd been slapped in the face with a severed hand.

"Yeah." Ricky covered his face with his hand. "It was a fucked deal. Señor Ruiz wasn't as rich as he led on. The Spanish mansion, the German cars, those were long gone. I assumed because of who he was, the way he dressed, he was still loaded. When it came time to put up, he pulls out a few hundred and says that's all he has left. Oh, I was pissed. He kept saying he had something worth a lot of money, some wild story about Sinaloa dope stashed in one of his safes, but I think he just made it up.

"Then he tells me about his cousin in El Paso, owns a couple gyms and an apartment complex. I figured we could still take them across and get the cousin to eat the cost. But then Andrés found the safe house I was keeping them at. They shot Ruiz, his ruca, and their two kids at the breakfast table. Blood and milk and Cheerios running down the wall. Fucking heartless, man."

Jeff grimaced and tugged at his hair.

"Now Andrés is after me," Ricky said. "I feel awful about the wife and kids, but Señor Ruiz, he was a coward. He'd do anything to save his own fat ass. I don't know what he said, but now Andrés thinks I have his made-up treasure."

The picture was still fuzzy for Javier, trying to connect all the names and motives. He also knew they were getting cherry-picked information, and he struggled to find Ricky's angle in it all.

"Don't worry," Ricky said. "I didn't bring you out here for nothing. I still have a job for you."

Javier nodded. "So *you're the one* we're taking across."

"No," Ricky said, brushing past them.

He led them back into the main part of the warehouse, where Nando and a little girl now waited by the forklifts. The girl sat on the nearest one, pretending to drive, tugging on the wheel and staring straight ahead with the focus of a race car driver.

"That's my niece, Cristiana," Ricky said. "She's your passenger."

"Her?" Dave said.

"She's not safe here," Ricky said. "Not around me. You're going to take her to my brother in Colorado."

Nando, who normally only frowned and grunted, showed her the levers and grinned and touched her curly hair gingerly. He was caught off guard when he noticed them approaching. He took her under the arms and set her on the concrete, helped her get her pink backpack on. She ran up to Ricky and threw her arms around his waist. Her purple down jacket made a whooshing sound when he ran his hand over it. He gave her a candy from his pocket.

"Think you can run one of those, mija?"

"Yeah," she said, struggling with the wrapper.

"Órale. We'll put you to work next time. What size uniform do you wear?"

She giggled and shook her head.

"So are you ready for your adventure?"

She pulled back from him and frowned. "Do I have to go?"

Ricky turned to Javier and smiled. "I only knew enough English to haggle with the gringos when I was a kid. Cristiana's nine and already speaks two languages perfectly." He turned back to her. "Yeah mija, you have to go. But you're going to have a lot of fun. Your tío Daniel will take good care of you. You know what he has?"

She shook her head. Ricky put his fingers on top of his head and whinnied.

"Horses," she said with the candy softening her S's.

"You love horses, don't you?" Ricky said. She nodded. "And I bet you can ride them whenever you want. These men are going to take you there," he said. "Javier and his friends will keep you safe. Son mis compadres."

Javier's mind had been idling, trying to run through all the potential scenarios, but now he could feel the RPMs rising into a whine. Without looking, Ricky stuck his hand out to the side and Nando put the bag in it. Ricky held it out to Javier. "Sixty thousand. Ten K each, or however you wanna split it."

"Up front," Javier said. "Just like that?"

"Just like that," Ricky said. "Look, I'm not simple. I know you could take the money and run. But for her sake, I hope you don't. You got integrity, Javier. I could tell that from the start. That's how I know I can trust you to get her to her uncle safely."

Javier undid the clasps and saw the three rolls inside. He handed it off to Jeff. The girl fidgeted and caught his attention. She looked at him without any apparent fear, her brown eyes flashing like torches that keep the beasts of night at bay. Brave because she was vulnerable, not in spite of it.

Javier was terrified. He had smuggled children before, but there had always been a parent along for the ride. Ricky expected him to step in and be this girl's protector? He doubted he could defend his crew against someone like Andrés, and they were more or less independent adults. What if she got hurt because he made a mistake? He didn't want that burden. All of a sudden the rehearsed walk into Texas had turned into a trip across a tightrope. Javier's vision narrowed. Feelings faded by years into fragments and fleeting sensations entered his mind in a wordless surge. Feelings of fear and helplessness, all telling him that life was completely and utterly out of his control. He thought he might drown in them. Then through the ripples he could see Ricky's hand jutted out, distorted.

"Javier." Ricky stuck his hand out a little further. "Do we have a deal?"

Javier inhaled sharply and reoriented himself. He glanced at the bandmates. Squat and Dave nodded. The others didn't object. As much as it scared him, he shook Ricky's hand and committed to the deal.

Ricky gave Cristiana a hug and said, "You have to go with them now. I need you to do what they say and stay really quiet when you get into your hiding spot. Like we talked about, remember?"

She had been looking around the room and landed on a wall-mounted eyewash station made of bright green plastic. Ricky put his hands on her arms and said sternly, "Me estás escuchando? This is important, Cristiana."

Her eyes darted back to him and she nodded with a hurt look on her face.

"What about you?" she asked.

"Don't worry about me," Ricky said. "I'll be right behind you." He brushed her hair back and touched her chin. "Everything's gonna be alright."

Chapter 14

1984

A RAINY START TO SEPTEMBER BROUGHT COOLER WEATHER, but it didn't last. The heat wave rekindled, and the mosquitos returned with teeth. Javier thought he would never get used to his new life, to being a captive, but little by little he did. The routine chipped away at him until he more or less accepted it. He kept his head down, made a hand. He became fast and efficient, rarely missing weeds and even helping the other boys with their rows whenever Drew wasn't around to discourage it.

His already passable English improved. He said and did what was asked of him and kept the rest to himself. Yolanda's rule was strict, and he mostly followed it. She had a way of keeping the boys in line, one that promised simplicity and grace in obedience. They knew the fury was there, would rise and strike them if they stepped over a boundary, but she didn't go around prodding for trouble. She could be pleasant, tender at times, when you followed her rules.

Drew was different. He was reckless, gristly, a man built for conflict. He'd try to rile the boys up when the mood took him, call them idiots when they made a mistake and wetbacks anytime else. One late August day he smacked Beto in the chest, knocking him in the dirt, for answering his question with "an attitude." When Beto scrambled to his feet with a scowl, Drew dared him to hit back. Stuck his dimpled chin out and stared with those unblinking blue eyes. His corny appearance with the bushy yellow mustache and potbelly and too-tight jeans only helped to conceal the truth hidden in those eyes: he was dangerous. The irises seemed to move when he locked on you, blue flames leaping around cellar-black pupils. That was the angriest Javier had seen him, but he realized that someone would eventually make a spark that would really set him off. He never guessed it would be him.

When Drew dropped them off in the field, they normally wouldn't see him again until he brought water. Javier worked hard, but his mind could unspool when Drew wasn't around. When those fiery eyes weren't over his shoulder he could also help out the weaker kids, the young ones like Eli and the ones who lost their wind easy like Ignacio. He wasn't supposed to do that. *Everybody has to pull their own weight* was the way Yolanda and Drew put it.

So when Drew's pickup rattled down the dirt road and he saw Javier swerving between rows, helping Eli, Drew slung the door open and marched across the turnrow. When Javier saw him coming he wanted to raise his hoe like a battle-axe. Instead, he threw it in the dirt when Drew approached, face red and eyes flame-blue.

"What the hell are you doing?"

"Working," Javier said. He felt the squeeze on his heart.

"How many times I told you boys to stick to your own rows? How is Eli s'posed to get any stronger if you keep doing his work for him?"

Javier would normally shrug and defer, but something in him wouldn't give. What he'd done wasn't wrong. It just broke one of their rules, their stupid good-for-nothing rules. You weren't supposed to act ashamed if you didn't do anything wrong. The impatient scowl that Drew wore only made him bolder.

"Eli will get strong." The words shot off Javier's tongue and exploded into the space between them. "Because he is out here every day. Not getting soft in the air conditioner like you."

The other boys' eyebrows chased their hairlines. Eli started hoeing a bare spot in the dirt. Drew's jaw tensed up and those serpentine eyes fixed on Javier. He knew he shouldn't have said it the moment it escaped his mouth. The full-bore punch crumpled him. A bolt of pain went through his jaw and down into his shoulder.

He thought he saw Drew and the young couple from the train and the mustached coyote standing over him and shaking their heads, whispering things that weren't quite words, but all that didn't add up. The people disappeared. He didn't exactly pass out, but everything after that came in flashes. The bumpy ride in the truck, the blood on his shirt like a maroon bib, the cussing Drew directed at both Javier and himself.

When reality settled back in, Drew was handing Javier a dishrag to hold to his busted lip. His mouth throbbed all the way through his teeth and gums. Drew retreated into the back bedroom with Yolanda. The hums of their raised voices came through the wall, but Javier couldn't make out what they were saying. When they came out, Yolanda went straight over to the counter and started cutting up squash from the garden into chunks. The muscles tensed in her wiry forearms when she cut through a tough piece.

"Do you know why we take you boys in?" she asked.

Javier shook his head. She kept on cutting with her back to him.

"I didn't have a good childhood, Javier. I suppose we have that in common. My father was a drunk, a mean one. My mother was a timid woman. She let him walk all over us until the day he died. I was born here in East Texas, but I felt like an outsider. The kids made fun of our accents, they made fun of our homemade dresses. But I excelled in school. I learned English better than those ignorant white kids. I learned to mask my accent, and do you know what? Things got better for me. It took a long time, but they did."

She raked the chunks into a pot and turned around to face Javier with the knife down at her side.

"I could make a living a lot of ways," she said. "But I choose this, to stay way out here in the sticks and teach you boys. It's my calling."

Her story made some sense, but he just kept seeing those cigarette burns on Jesús's back. She seemed to sense some resistance in him.

"Well," she said. "What do you have to say about that?"

Javier pulled the rag from his lips to check if he was still bleeding. Yep.

"You make a lot of money on us." Javier watched her face twist into a scowl.

"How would you know?" she snapped. "Why would you even say that?"

Javier shrugged.

"We have contracts with farmers and landowners, yeah," she said. "But that money goes back into this place, into *your* future."

"What about your new car? Drew's new boat?" Javier asked.

"You don't know what you're talking about, kid," Drew growled.

"Yes I do."

"Watch your tongue, Javier." Yolanda rotated the knife in her hand. She got up close to him, brushing his cheek with the broad side of the blade. "Or it might end up floating down the creek without you. Understand?"

Javier gulped and nodded. She filled a bag with ice and had Drew drive him back to the field. All afternoon he had her threat in his head. The sun made his head throb and the shade in that patch of soybeans was scarce. He stayed on the other side of the terrace from the boys, not wanting to catch them staring at his busted lip.

It was a hot day, especially scorching for fall. Not that East Texas got four real seasons anyway, he was learning. It was summer until proven otherwise. He wiped sweat from his face with his sweat-soaked shirt, the saltiness stinging his eyes. His lip and gums swelled and ached. And just when he thought he might break, a flash of inspiration cut through all the heat and pain.

He had come to see his bunk, along with these thickets and fields, as all the world had to offer. He'd been so scared of what might happen if he tried to escape that he stopped thinking about it at all. But now he remembered a whole world out there, a world so big he could get beyond Yolanda and Drew's reach. He saw some of it back in Mexico, and a little here, but there had to be so much more. He could get out of this muddy tangle of trees and vines and marshes and fields and run until he hit wide-open skies.

It wasn't enough to just save himself. He had to get all of them out of this mess. That night he reached into his backpack, into a small pouch that hadn't been opened in a long time, and found the special agent's card. The corners were bent and the edges had a fuzzy feel from the wear, but the name and phone number were still clear. Javier recalled Adrián's words about trusting a wolf to protect you from a puma, but he was desperate enough to try.

2015

Webb's hand snaked out to the wipers and then right back to ten and two. The blades sloughed off the snow but left more frozen residue behind each time. The avenue, lined with gas stations and American chain stores, showed more signs of life than the neighborhood they'd just come from. A few blocks later, Webb had to pull into an empty parking lot and use his long-handled scraper on the ice-scabbed windshield.

The band stood slack-jawed over the money, flipping through the bills and checking with each other to make sure they weren't hallucinating. Sixty thousand. It wasn't much to look at, just six fat rolls at the bottom of the leather bag, but it was more cash than any of them had seen in one place.

"Whoa," Dave said.

Marck held a bag of ice to his head, feeling the weight of one of the rolls in his other palm. Dave slipped the rubber band over his wrist and began counting Benjamins. Squat nodded absently and ran his thumbs over the bills' textured ink.

"This could change everything," Jeff said. That far-off look in his eyes said his imagination had already shot into the sky like a bottle rocket. Dave and Squat and Marck had all fallen into their own ideas as well. The money meant more options, no matter how you sliced it.

Javier felt the cold seep through his boots and socks. He hoped the blankets they gave Cristiana were enough to keep her warm. They had been moving at a trot for the last twenty minutes and still had a ways to go. It was almost nine. What were the odds the border hadn't already been shut down due to the weather? Then what? Stay the night in Juárez and try again tomorrow? Not ideal, but it might have to do.

Ricky's words entered his head again. About Cristiana not being safe. *How much danger was she in exactly, that they had to get across, tonight, through the worst ice storm in decades?* Ricky'd told them more than during their first encounter, but it hadn't registered how little he was actually saying about the situation. Ricky's problems were now their problems, and Javier was still trying to work out what that meant.

Stopped at the red light, through the haze of exhaust fumes and fine snow, Javier saw headlights behind them again. They had kept their distance, never slipping too far behind or veering off. Javier didn't want to call it to Webb's attention yet. No use in making him panic. A normal night in this part of town, there would have been dozens of lights behind them. It might be nothing.

The bus turned off the brightly lit avenue and came to a narrow street flanked with local shops, faded pastel buildings with disjointed signage and iron bars over their doors and windows. The streetlights were spaced out to the point that only the intersections were lit. They hadn't seen another soul since turning, and the headlights from earlier were nowhere in sight. The north wind whistled against the windows.

"Oh shit oh shit oh shit oh shit," Webb said, and the bus started to slide.

The back end swung wide, over the measly curb, across the sidewalk, and into the gray plywood that fronted an abandoned shop. It gave way in a dull snap, and they came to a rough stop. Javier met Webb's wide eyes and then both shot down. They had put Cristiana in the hollow space underneath the floor, lacking the time or seclusion to roll out one of the big road cases and put her inside. Plus, it would've been even colder down there.

"Cristiana, are you okay?" Javier asked loudly.

"What was that?" Her voice was muffled.

"We hit a patch of ice." Javier said. "Are you hurt?"

"No," she said, and then, "Are we in Texas?"

"Not yet. It's still going to be a while. Hold tight, okay?"

"Okay."

Webb eased off the curb, and they went outside to assess the damage. But there was none. Not even a dent. Just a scuffed place where the rear bumper had hit the old plywood. The sheet had broken in half, but it was only there to block off the space where a glass door had probably once been. Webb stuck his head inside the old building.

"It's a splinter museum in here."

Part of the roof had caved in. The floorboards and sheetrock had been ripped out long ago, leaving the decaying joists behind. Snow dusted the jagged gray wood. The bandmates stood off to the side cussing.

"What?" Webb said.

"This," Jeff said, pointing at the hissing tire and the mangled nail stuck in it.

"Aw man," Webb said. "First we spin out and now a flat tire."

"You," Jeff replied. "*You* spun out. *You* got us a flat. Are you trying to do this? There's no way you're this bad of a driver."

"Sorry, your highness," Webb said sharply. "Why don't you get back inside and let me take care of it?"

"Cause that's worked out so well for us," Marck said.

Webb pulled out his vape pen and inhaled deeply.

"Everybody chill," Squat said. "We're all stressed. Let's just take a breath and figure this out."

"Oh shut up," Marck snapped. He still held an ice pack to his scalp. "You mean well, you really do, but you're retarded and oxygen won't fix that. Maybe if you had a little more in the womb—"

Squat grabbed his collar and made a fist. "You're the one with the head injury. How bout I drag you down the ice a block or two? That might help the swelling."

"Yeah, go ahead and prove my point, moron."

Javier rolled the spare against the siding and started jacking up the bus.

"Stop it." Dave got between them and pried Squat's fingers loose. "What are we? Children?"

"Yes," Jeff said. "That's exactly what we are, Dave. So here's your chance to give us one of your big condescending lectures." Jeff mocked him with his swooping gestures. "Show us how wrong we are and how you're the only one with his shit together."

"You don't quit. Run your mouth all day and then you still try to act like the poor bass player." Dave shook his head. "Nobody's buying it."

"What are you talking about?" Jeff said.

"I get it, bro. You're on a roll," Dave said. "I haven't written a decent song in months. I can admit that. But don't pull that poor pitiful me crap anymore. You always complain how you never get to make decisions. You wanna lead? Well, go ahead. Make a call."

"Fine," Jeff said.

Javier got the spare seated and Webb handed him the lug nuts.

"Let's start with the record deal," Dave said. "Yes or no?"

"I don't know." Jeff fidgeted. "We'll have to see how—"

"How what?" Dave crossed his arms and took a half step back. "How it feels for the moment to pass you by while your thumb's up your ass?"

"No deal then," Jeff said. "We take this money and put it into the studio. Then we record the album."

That upset Squat. "Why haven't we recorded it already? We made enough back in the summer. We could have paid for time in some badass studio. We could have brought in that group from El Paso to back us on a few tracks. But no, we sunk it all into that rundown building."

Jeff's face went stiff. "This was the plan all along—to do it our own way. Right? With all we've gone through, we have to nail it, we can't miss our shot."

"I get wanting your own studio. That'd be so badass. But it's a luxury, man," Squat said. "We wrote all the songs. We can play them backwards at this point. I just want something to show for all that work. Is that too much to ask? What are we waiting for?"

"There's other things to consider," Jeff said. "The studio is already halfway done. It'd be dumb to abandon it. And then we have to budget money for marketing, distribution . . ."

"Holy Moses," Squat said. "And when are we going to hit that mark? A year? Five years? You keep moving the goalposts, man. It's always going to be *just a little more*. I think you're just scared."

Jeff shook his head dismissively.

Squat said, "If more money was that important, why didn't we keep rolling with Javier?"

"Are you kidding?" Marck said. "We'd either be in the penitentiary or a mass grave in the desert by now."

Squat ignored him and went on. "I went along with your plan because you were talking about going back to the old days, just us and a van and the open road. And it was going to be even better this time because people actually showed up. But you never enjoyed a minute of it. Always scheming. Always building a brand. Putting the cart before the horse, bro."

"That's not true," Jeff said.

Dave's jaw was set, his chin tilted up at a slight angle. "That's it. No more decisions for you. As soon as we get back, we're signing that deal. You make all these plans, but they don't work in the real world. You're clueless about the music business."

"You can't talk either," Squat said. His voice was warbly and vulnerable. "You'd sell us down the river for a chance at being popular. You'd step on your mother's face if it meant you got to live out your fantasy of playing Jim Morrison. It's all *me me me* with you two. Y'all never think about us, about the band."

"What-*ever*, Squat," Dave said.

"What happened?" Squat said. "I used to love playing with you guys more than anything. Now it feels like every show, every song, every idea, it's all just stepping stones. I want to make a living at this just as much as you guys. I want people to hear our music. I want them to buy T-shirts and tickets to our shows. I want a lot of stuff, but none of it means shit if we're always just looking for the next thing. If you're not enjoying yourself now, even a Grammy and a world tour won't change that."

"Squat," Jeff said with a patronizing headshake. "You're not seeing the big picture."

"I don't fantasize about Jim Morrison," Dave added.

Javier pressed the four-way into Jeff's chest, a little harder than he intended to, and he gave a little grunt. Dave looked at the changed tire and back at Javier.

"We have a job to do," Javier said, switching his eyes between all four of them. "Pull yourselves together. All that stuff will still be there for you to fight about back home."

Jeff started to protest. "Why do we—"

"Stop." Javier put his hand up. "You see that?"

"See what?" Marck said.

"Those headlights, at the stop sign a couple blocks back. How long have they been there?"

"A minute or two," Webb said, putting his hands on his hips and narrowing his eyes against the glare.

"So?" Jeff said. "Could be someone warming up their car."

"No, they weren't there when we got off," Javier said. "We need to go."

They didn't even have time to get back on the bus before the headlights, fierce high beams, came up faster than anyone had business going in these conditions. Javier wished he had his gun. The sedan's front doors flew open. Javier held a hand up to block out the glare and saw Ricky marching toward them.

"What are you doing out here?" Ricky asked.

"We slid off the road," Dave said.

"Yeah," Jeff said. "Our driver wasn't paying attention and—"

"Yuk." Ricky dismissed him with his hand. "I don't need your whole story. Is my niece okay?"

"She's fine," Javier said.

"Good. We're escorting you the rest of the way," Ricky said.

"Why?" Javier asked.

"Andrés thinks I'm trying to run. They trashed my place looking for me and Cristiana."

"Won't you lead them right to us?" Dave said.

"You think I'm simple?" Ricky nodded at the sedan. "We weren't followed. That's not my car."

"So you take her," Javier said. "If Andrés recognizes the bus, she isn't safe with us. Hide her in that car and gun it for El Paso."

"And then what? We can't cross in that car anyway. I don't have the papers for it." Ricky slapped the bus. "No, we have to beat them there. You just get across. Me and Nando will be waiting for his ass. I'm done looking over my shoulder for that cabrón."

Ricky motioned them into the bus and followed inside. "Nando's gonna tail us. I'll ride with you guys until we get close, just to keep an eye out."

They took off, and Nando followed at a slack distance. Ricky scrunched his nose up and sniffled, wiped it on his coat sleeve. They came to a stop sign, and he kept checking the mirrors. The exhaust looked like a steam engine in the cold.

The silence felt like a heavy chain around their necks. Webb compulsively turned on the radio and fiddled with the knobs, passing a weather advisory and several norteño songs in progress. He finally landed on a rock station and left it there. There was a telltale octave-jumping guitar riff and galloping drum beat and then Robert Plant went "ah ah ah aaaaaaah."

They went down another lonely street flanked by empty storefronts. Nando lingered a block behind them. The sole streetlight flickered like it might go dark any moment. The wind picked up again, sliding a cardboard box across the street. Something felt very wrong.

"Turn that shit off," Ricky said to Webb.

A sudden *pop pop pop pop* got everyone's attention, followed by screeching tires and a loud crash. In the rearview, Nando's white sedan collided with a streetlight and a red Tahoe with knobby tires sped toward the bus.

Ricky shouted, "Look out!"

They instinctively crouched. The SUV came up the bus's left side and on past them. It took a right turn and disappeared. Webb brought the bus to a stop.

"Stay inside." Ricky burst out the door, running back to Nando's crashed sedan.

"What was that?" Marck said.

"Are they gone?" Dave said in a pinched voice.

"I don't know," Webb said, his arms stiff as a corpse.

"Stay inside," Javier echoed and got off the bus. When he caught up to Ricky he saw Nando slumped over, his bloody face against the dashboard.

"No," Ricky shrieked. He slammed his fist on the cab. He took hold of Nando's shoulders and his head rolled back. "Not you too. You can't die on me, Fernando." Ricky gritted his teeth. He pressed the side of Nando's head into his chest and rested his chin there. Javier heard snow crunching behind him and spun around.

"I told you to stay on the bus," Javier snapped.

"What's going on?" Dave said.

"No way man," Marck said, seeing Nando's body.

Squat asked, "Is he dead?"

Ricky squeezed Nando tightly and then let him go. His body fell into the wheel, and the weight of it started the horn. Dave said something over the loud blare. Ricky's lips parted to show nicotine-stained teeth, and his eyes went feral. Javier turned to follow his stare and saw the Tahoe accelerate toward them.

"Get back," Ricky shouted and ducked behind the car with them.

Ricky drew his gun and fired at the vehicle, flashes of return fire coming from the open driver's window and tearing into the white sedan. The Tahoe kept on speeding down the street and fishtailed around the corner. Ricky ejected his magazine and thumbed in three .45 cartridges. Dave stood up and scanned the street.

"I wouldn't do that," Ricky said, shoving the magazine in with a click.

The Tahoe reappeared, its tires shrieking to find their grip. It slid to a stop and its occupants bailed out this time. The short, thick-necked driver and his young, wiry passenger raised their handguns and fired without hesitation. Javier and the others stayed hunkered down, hoping no lead would come clear through the sedan. Marck said *shit* every time another shot went off. Between the gunfire and the bullets piercing metal and breaking glass and the still-blaring horn, there wasn't much room to think. Then somehow Nando's body slid off the horn and the shots stopped. There was a brief ringing pause where they each patted themselves for wounds and looked at each other in astonishment.

Then Ricky sprang to his feet and fired two quick shots with his arms braced on the cab. He clipped the young guy in the shoulder, blowing away a chunk of his deltoid, and missed on the other one. He ducked back down, and the stubby man fired again. Ricky picked up a baseball-sized chunk of ice. He peeked around the bumper and threw it toward an abandoned shop on the far side of the street. Its big window, which had TALLER MECÁNICO shoe-polished in faded black, spiderwebbed when the ice hit it.

Ricky rose up in time to catch them looking where the noise came from. He put two quick shots into the driver's barrel chest and one more into his moaning partner. They crumpled onto the ice. Ricky looked back at Javier.

"Get out of here. I'll clean up the mess. Just make sure Cristiana gets across safe."

Javier felt a rush of guilt, realizing he'd forgotten about her. She had to be so scared. He brushed tempered glass off himself and came out from behind the bullet-riddled sedan. The Tahoe's back doors hung open now. They had been closed when the two men jumped out of the front and started firing. Javier was sure of it. He whipped his head around to find the others.

"Put the gun down."

The words came from over by the bus. Then Jeff appeared at the door. It wasn't Jeff's voice though. He took the two steps down onto the street with a short shotgun barrel pressed to the base of his skull. The man at the other end of the gun was built like a heavyweight fighter and stared down the sights with his lips clamped tight. Another man followed them both, staring daggers at Ricky.

"Andrés," Ricky said, walking closer but keeping his gun pointed down. Andrés was younger than Javier expected. He was handsome, sporting a fresh fade and a neatly trimmed beard, resembling some hotshot with bottle service at the club more than a narco or a cold-blooded killer. But going by looks could get you killed.

Andrés glided across the icy street, and his white sneakers never slipped. He held their leather bag of cash in one hand and a handgun in the other. His sharp eyes had no give in them. Ricky spat.

"Been looking for you," Andrés said. "You did a bad thing, stealing from me. And then you ran. How can I trust a man who acts like this?"

"Pobre-*fucking*-cito," Ricky said.

Andrés narrowed his eyes and his lips bent into a grin as friendly as a startled rattlesnake. The barrel stayed on Jeff's skull, but the heavyweight's singular focus was now directed at Ricky. The scowl on his face looked permanent.

"Well done, caballero," Andrés said. He looked at the men Ricky'd shot like they were potted plants that had been knocked over. The strongman whispered something to Andrés. The vise made a half-turn in Javier's chest. His eyes met Ricky's, searching for a knowing glance, a wink, something, but Ricky only stared blankly like he had just announced he wanted enchiladas for supper. The wind tugged at Javier's coat and whistled in his ears.

The driver of the Tahoe was face down on the pavement, blood pooling around him. His gun lay beside his half-clenched hand. The younger guy had fallen on his. Its black grip stuck out from under his thigh. They were both at least ten paces away.

"You went behind my back with Ruiz. Now you're going to make it right." Andrés jostled the leather bag. "Chump change. Where's the stash, Ricky?"

"I don't know," Ricky said.

"Mentiroso," Andrés snarled. "It wasn't at your place. You have it."

"No lo tengo, cabrón."

Andrés ran his tongue along the inside of his cheek and nodded.

"Is it with your little sobrina?" He motioned with his gun to the bus. "In there?"

Ricky's eyes flashed briefly before he could stop them. Javier saw it. Andrés saw it.

"Órale," Andrés said, his trigger finger tensing.

Ricky's eyes darted back and forth. Javier could see the motor whining in his mind. He must have come up with something, because his eyes relaxed and he put up a hand in deference. "Take it e-see, jefe. I'll show you where it is."

Ricky bent at the knees and began to lower his gun. Javier's heart dropped. He couldn't imagine Andrés showing them any mercy. That gun held every bit of their remaining leverage. But just before the steel touched the ground Ricky dropped to one knee and jerked it up. He fired a shot that whizzed by Andrés, close enough to make him duck and cover. The heavyweight swung the shotgun from behind Jeff's head, and it erupted in a flash that rattled the shop windows. The empty buildings trapped the sound and threw it back at them. Jeff cowered and covered his ears.

Ricky's limp body landed on its back. He took a few stunted breaths while blood leaked out of him like motor oil. Javier's fight or flight response had kicked in, but his body had chosen the third option and froze. The band had done the same.

A siren went on and on in Javier's head like an air raid was underway. His perception came in snippets between rapid heartbeats. All eyes were on the gunman, who brought the smoking barrel down to chest level but gripped a handful of Jeff's coat to keep him in place. Andrés watched Ricky bleed out the way a cat watches an addled mouse he has no intention of eating.

A clicking noise came from deep in Ricky's throat though his hollow eyes showed he'd already given up the ghost. Javier and the others grouped together. Their safer-in-a-herd instincts, which might have served their ancestors well against mountain lions and bears, now just made them a perfect cluster for a few shells of double-aught buckshot.

"Where's the girl?" Andrés shouted, and his partner aimed the shotgun at Javier.

"Girl?" Javier said. He felt the panic spread through his body. The heavyweight hoisted his shotgun in the air with his free hand and cycled it. The spent shell tumbled to the pavement with a hollow plastic sound.

"Don't fuck with me. Tell me where she is, or I'll kill all of you. It won't be quick like your boy there either." Andrés took turns aiming his handgun at each of them. "I'll shoot you in your kneecaps. You in your stomach. You in your dirty little dick. Then we gag you and tie you up in one of these buildings. You cry and slobber and bleed and not a soul will hear you."

Jeff had a steely look on his face, but when he didn't blink, Javier knew he was only frozen that way. Andrés made Dave kick the 1911 over to him, sliding as easily as a hockey puck on the ice.

There was a tiny gap between fear and more fear where Javier realized he had a choice. He could give Cristiana up or he could refuse, getting everyone else shot. The options filled him with dread. It crossed his mind that if he refused to talk, they'd be killed, and then Andrés would find Cristiana anyway. Maybe Andrés wouldn't hurt anybody if he just came clean and told him where they'd hidden her. He'd see she didn't have the stash and let them all go. The thoughts came quicker than he could make sense of them. Javier felt like he was drowning.

Their eyes met then. Andrés was motionless, unblinking. His stare was as cold and vacant as deep space. The vise bore down on Javier's heart and he watched Andrés's patience slipping. The man had already proven himself willing to kill women and children if they got in his way. Javier realized he couldn't give Cristiana up. Maybe Andrés would find her anyway, but he had to give her a chance.

Javier's mind scrambled for another way to proceed. Come on, Javi. Think. An idea crashed like a meteor into his brain. There wasn't time to process it. He pointed at the storage compartment, where they kept the road cases. Andrés's lips twitched.

"She's in there," Javier said.

"Open it," Andrés said.

The heavyweight scowled and motioned with the gun. He and Andrés stayed back, ready to fire if something went wrong. Jeff opened his mouth like he was going to say something, but stopped. Dave and Squat were hollow-eyed and shaken. Some of Javier's composure returned when he felt the burden of action settle on him.

Javier fished the key from his pocket while holding up his free hand for them to see. All he knew was that this would buy them another minute. They'd be killed for sure when Andrés found out she wasn't in there. He felt the solid ground under his feet, the frigid air slice across his face. He focused and took in his surroundings. The white sedan and the Tahoe were behind them. The bus wasn't blocked in. He caught a glimpse of Webb through the window. He must have hidden when they came in and grabbed Jeff. He stared out at the carnage, just his eyes and forehead visible. His nervous pupils fixed on Javier, who was hit by another idea.

Javier mouthed *go* and motioned his fists like a steering wheel, close to his chest so the men couldn't see. Webb ducked out of sight. Javier unlocked the compartment and pointed at the road case way in the back. The heavyweight shoved Jeff away and leaned inside. Javier stared at the bus's empty window, figuring they only had a few seconds until the man realized there was nothing in that case. The bus revved wildly, tires scrambling for traction, and fishtailed.

"Ay," the heavyweight shouted. He lost his footing and stumbled.

"Alto," Andrés growled.

This was it. Webb had their full attention. The heavyweight got his feet under him and fired toward the bus's long side mirror, shattering the glass and knocking a chunk out of the plastic backing. Javier flinched. Terrified, he rushed him. He blocked the trigger guard with his palm and forced the barrel in the air.

Webb threw it in gear and swung it around. Andrés saw it coming and moved to get out of the way, but his foot slipped. The bus wasn't moving fast, but the front bumper hit him solid. He fell on his ass and his head whipped into the hard ice. It was the type of fall that gave football players concussions. Andrés had no helmet, and this wasn't turf. He was out cold.

Javier wrestled with the heavyweight, both of them trying to push the short barrel toward the other and get control of the trigger guard. Squat ran up flat-footed so he didn't slip and got the man in a headlock from behind. The heavyweight used the gun to shove Javier, who landed on his back and slid away. Dave grabbed the shotgun by the stock. Javier scrambled to his feet and swung a left into where he hoped the man's liver would be. Between corded muscle and ribcage there wasn't much give. The heavyweight grunted, but he withstood the three of them like a tank. Using both hands Dave couldn't pull the gun away from his one. The man punched Javier in the jaw with his free hand, and he fell down again.

Marck searched for one of the unmanned guns. Jeff just stood watching, his eyes nervously switching between the bedlam on ice and the idling bus. He tapped at his ear like he was trying to get water out of it.

The heavyweight was able to get both hands on the gun. His face was purple from Squat's chokehold. Jeff was too scared to jump in, but he couldn't run away either. He took one step toward the bus and stopped. He took a step toward his bandmates and stopped.

Marck ran up with a dead guy's handgun. He stared at it a moment, then knelt down to offer it to Javier. Javier took it and pointed it at the heavyweight, but he and Squat and Dave kept shifting around. He couldn't get a clean shot.

Jeff squeezed his bony fists, bounced in place a couple times, and ran toward the fight. The heavyweight slammed the butt of the shotgun into Dave's nose. Just as the heavyweight angled the barrel toward Squat's head, Jeff got his hand on it and pulled it away. The gun went off. There was a flash and another deafening boom. Jeff fell to his knees, covering his ears once again. A couple inches closer and pieces of him would have been pattering down on the ice.

"Squat, get down," Javier shouted.

Squat let go and dropped on his belly. The heavyweight's head swung around in time to see Javier fire. His first shot missed, pinging and zipping as it ricocheted off steel. Javier cringed but squeezed the trigger again, and the second bullet connected with the heavyweight's torso. So did the third and fourth, and the big man went down.

Marck put his hands behind his neck and started to mumble. Dave went to check on Jeff. Javier lowered his gun, feeling the weight of it in his hand. Another shot rang out and he felt a bullet whizz by. They all turned to find the source. Andrés clutched his busted head with his left hand and held a gun in his right. He bled and shook. He fired again, and Javier felt the bullet punch through his forearm and exit the other side. Adrenaline numbed the pain, made it so much less than he expected from a gunshot.

Though it couldn't have been more than a second, Javier felt frozen there for a long time, seeing the blackness in the muzzle and the wild bloody man holding it. He felt heat and gathering pain. Javier aimed and squeezed the trigger again and again.

Andrés collapsed on the street. An empty feeling rushed through Javier like the fierce north wind. His arm went limp again, but he held onto the gun. He stared at Andrés, whose skull was making a dark puddle on the ice.

"Get in," Webb shouted from the bus. Dave plucked the bag of cash from the street. Javier felt Squat's hand clamp on his shoulder and came to. He let the handgun clatter on the street. Squat wiped it down with his shirt and tossed it on top of the nearest building.

The smell of spent gunpowder swirled into the thin freezing air. There were no flashing lights. There were no sirens. There were bodies scattered on the streets, beginning to collect snow, and it was quiet as a morgue after all the living had gone home.

Chapter 15

1984

THEY WEREN'T ALLOWED TO USE THE PHONE, FOR OBVIOUS reasons, but the next day was chore day. Javier and Beto had window duty. When Yolanda made her run to the store and Drew went into the shed to work on his transmission again, Javier saw his opening. He told Beto he was going around the corner to take a leak and slipped inside the house.

The phone call was short. Agent Haskins wasn't in, so he told the lady who answered that a bunch of Mexican boys were being held captive. He gave them the address he found on a mattress sale advertisement by the ashtray. She told Javier that she'd pass the information along to Haskins and be in touch.

"You're not coming now?" Javier asked.

"We have procedure to follow. If you're in immediate danger I can contact the local police."

Javier shook his head, silence on both ends of the line. The woman promised to get Agent Haskins to call him back, but Javier told her that wasn't a good idea. He knew they'd be the ones to answer the call and it would be twice as bad. By the time he hung up, Javier felt deflated.

The next morning he pushed the call to the back of his mind, preparing for the weekly English lesson and wondering what they'd have for lunch. He took his place at the long table and began to copy and correct the sentences Yolanda had written on the chalkboard.

> 1) *Their are fifty states in our country.*
> 2) *"Your a big jerk," the woman said.*
> 3) *The wind blue hard enough to rip the shingles off.*

There was a knock at the front door. Javier almost fell out of his chair when he saw Agent Haskins and his partner on the front porch. Yolanda had them trained well enough that most of the boys went back to their work, but Javier put his pencil down, realizing it wasn't going to be that kind of a Sunday.

Yolanda stayed calm, perfectly polite, asking what she could help them with. But Agent Haskins was already looking over her shoulder at the seven boys inside. Javier made eye contact with him, not fully believing his call had brought him here. Haskins nodded. Javier nodded back, not sure whether to be elated or terrified by what might come next. He caught Adrián staring with a wild look in his eyes.

Haskins flashed his INS credentials. When Yolanda realized her smooth talk was going nowhere, that the men were going to investigate, fear gathered in her eyes like storm clouds. It was a look Javier hadn't seen on her before. She was usually so confident and composed. Haskins asked if they could come in, stepping across the threshold before she could reply. Drew stood back with his arms crossed.

"Javier," Haskins said. "You doing alright?"

"Yeah," Javier said, even though they both knew it was a lie.

"Can we talk outside?" Yolanda said.

"Here's fine," Haskins said. "How long have these boys been here?"

"We're their legal guardians," Yolanda said. "I assure you."

"I assume you have the paperwork to prove that."

"Well," she said, "the paperwork is in progress."

Haskins shook his head. "Not how that works."

His partner, a stout woman with a long black ponytail, looked at Yolanda in disgust. Only Javier and Adrián seemed to grasp what was happening. Javier avoided his scalding stare, but Adrián kept daring him to look his way. The others were confused, didn't seem to know what to make of it all. Antonio kept on correcting the sentences like Yolanda was about to come back over and check his work.

"While we sort all this out," Haskins said. "We're going to take the boys back to Houston, see if we can contact any family members."

"No," Yolanda said.

"You can't do that," said Drew.

"Agent Lopez," Thomas said. "Would you mind taking the boys outside?"

Lopez motioned to the boys. "Chicos, vengan aquí."

Yolanda shoved Drew. "Do something."

Drew looked confused but obeyed, grabbing the female agent's arm. She stared daggers at him and then swam her arm under his. She shoved him off balance and slid behind him, locking her arm around his neck. Thomas had his hand on his gun holster, watching both of them. Drew's face started to go purple, and Lopez asked if he'd had enough. He nodded feebly and she let go. He fell on his butt and gasped for air. She slapped cuffs on him, and Thomas did the same with Yolanda.

"It's alright," Agent Lopez said, retucking the hem of her shirt. "Todo está bien."

"Hold tight a minute," Haskins said. "We'll sort all this out."

The confused boys sat at the table while they took the couple out to their car.

"Those two aren't going to hurt you anymore," Haskins said when he returned.

"Where are you taking us?" Beto asked.

"Well, home eventually," Haskins said. "For now a detention center." Noticing their wild-eyed looks, he went on explaining. "That's just temporary. Who knows, you may get to stay in the country. Right now we just need to get you out of here."

This wasn't what Javier had in mind when he called for help. He didn't want to be around Yolanda and Drew, but he didn't want to be put back in a cage either. There was no winning. He felt betrayed. The harsh scraping of wood made Javier jerk his head around. Adrián's chair was thrown back, and he climbed over the table.

"You did this," he shrieked. "Pinche cobarde. Vete a la mierda."

He lunged at Javier, but the woman caught him around the waist with one of her thick forearms. Adrián squirmed in vain, tears running down his cheeks. Javier had put his hands up when Adrián dove. He lowered them now. Adrián tried one last jolt and then gave up.

"I can't go back home," Adrián said. "*You ruined it.*"

Javier was still in shock, but the way Adrián's voice cracked on that last part got to him. The agents herded the boys out the door and toward the white van they had parked in front of the house. Javier finally saw Yolanda and Drew, in the back of an unmarked black sedan behind the van. Drew's eye was scrunched up, that side of his face red and puffy. Yolanda's mouth didn't move, but her eyes snarled, "You did this."

An impulse gripped Javier. Struck with a clear vision of what to do next, he took hold of Eli's hand, turned, and ran. Eli stayed with him a few steps and then dug his feet in. Javier pulled him forward, but Eli yanked back his small hand with all his might. His brow was set hard over his wet brown eyes. His lips were drawn tight so that you could tell his teeth were clenched underneath. Javier released his hand, not understanding. Didn't he want to escape?

"What are you doing?" Eli said. "They will help us."

Agent Haskins noticed and marched their way. What came next didn't even feel like a choice. It was instinct, Javier's fight or flight response recognizing that these adults were much too big to scuffle with. He planted his right foot and took off, around the house, through the garden, and into the tall bluestem grass. His labored breath and the rustling of the grass were all he could hear. The tangled woods were just a strong stone's throw away.

He looked back and saw Haskins and Lopez coming around the corner, through the garden. Lopez stumbled on a furrow and went to one knee in her slacks. Haskins shouted for Javier to stop and ran with high knees and elbows bent at right angles, much faster than Javier suspected a man in a suit could.

Javier turned sideways to fit through a clearing in the brush, limbs scraping his arms and legs. His jeans ripped. He kept going. He came to a hip-high deadfall and the adrenaline helped him clear it. He ran, zigzagging around the trunks and stumps until he absolutely couldn't anymore. He dropped to his knees and rolled over onto his back. His breath ragged, his heart booming, the pain in his mouth returning in steady pangs.

He lay there for a long time listening, and when he regained a little of his wind he crawled into a hollowed-out spot at the base of an oak tree, the kind of place a mama coyote might keep her pups. He heard voices off in the distance. They got louder, and his heart kicked in his chest. He hunkered deeper into the dirt. All he could do was wait.

———————

2015

Marck fumbled with a picked-over first aid kit they had hidden away. He cast aside the futile things, the expired aspirin and paper-cut bandages, until he came to something useful. Squat pressed a gauze pad to Javier's wound, and they all unsuccessfully tried convincing him to go to a hospital.

Javier shook his head and watched his dark blood seep into the lily-white dressing. Squat held firm pressure, and when the bleeding slowed he put on more gauze and taped around it. Dave twisted up tissues and stuffed them in his nostrils to stop his own bleeding. The cut on the bridge of his nose had already started to scab around the edges. Jeff sat on the couch snapping his fingers repeatedly into one ear and then the other.

"You're shot," Marck said. "You need—stitches or something."

"I'm alright," Javier said. The adrenaline was wearing off, and he felt like his forearm had been branded.

"Webb, turn left at the light," Dave said, looking at his phone. "There's a hospital 1.1 miles from here."

Webb glanced back for Javier's approval.

"Put your phone away," Javier said. "The only place I'm going is Colorado."

"Look at your arm," Dave said. "You don't think they'll ask questions at the border?"

"You don't think they'll ask questions at a hospital?" Javier swung into his jean jacket and kept his arm above his heart. "Good as new."

Marck shook his head. "This is insane."

"What?" Jeff shouted. "What are you saying?"

Squat and Dave shared a concerned glance.

"My ears won't stop . . . ah, this damn droning," Jeff half-shouted. He snarled and his eyes darted in pained confusion.

Dave nodded. "Your ear was almost touching the barrel when it went off."

"What?" Jeff whined. "Sounds like you're at the other end of a cave." He shook his head. "I can't lose my hearing, man. I'm a musician. I can't. I can't."

He started to cry, and Dave put an arm around him.

"It'll be okay, buddy," Dave said, patting his shoulder. "This'll pass."

They turned on the avenue that led to the bridge, back into the well-lit districts. Javier had asked Cristiana if she was hurt, and she said no, but he knew that wasn't enough this time. They removed the panel and saw her, curled up under the wool blanket with her backpack clutched to her chest, squinting into the light. She scrambled out with mussed hair and a wild look in her eyes.

Javier said, "Are you sure you're—"

"Where's my tío?" she said.

Javier's instinct was to keep what happened from her, for now, but when she turned that fierce look on him, it reminded him of how he'd felt, being the one in the shadows. Everything was not fine, and she knew that. Lying would only prolong the confusion and delay the pain.

"Did he ever talk to you about his work?"

She scrunched her eyebrows and scanned the floor.

"He said he helps people."

Javier tightened his lips.

"Did he ever talk about needing to run away, about people looking for him?"

She nodded, not liking where the conversation was leading.

"He said it wasn't safe here. That we needed to go north for a while."

"He was right. Some bad men showed up," Javier said. "And your tío fought them off, to protect you. That was the loud noises you heard."

"Where's my tío?" she repeated.

"One of them shot him," Javier said. The next two words were unavoidable, but Javier still had a hard time getting them out. "He died."

He watched her heart break in the dark recesses of her eyes. Her mouth fell open and she covered it with her little hands. She looked lost, slipping into a black inner realm of sorrow. He felt awful for speaking that feeling into existence, for being involved in any of this mess.

"No," she cried. "He can't die. He was gonna come with me. He said he always had my back. He said always!"

"I'm sorry," Javier said.

"I want to see him," she said.

Her voice, the intolerability of her uncle's absence, felt worse than the sharp pain in Javier's arm.

"I'm sorry," he repeated and his voice cracked.

"Where is he?" she shouted and smacked the side of her fist into Javier's leg. "I want to see my tío!"

Tears burst forth, running down her chubby cheeks. Webb's eyes jumped from the road to his mirrors. Marck went over to her and knelt down. She tried to speak again, but choked. He put his hand on her shaking shoulder, and she leaned into him. He stroked her hair and soothed her, the way he'd done for his own daughters a lifetime ago.

"You're safe here, sweetie."

The bus pulled into a truck stop where several semis had weathered the storm, icicles skirting the cabs and trailers. The ground was entirely white except for the concrete under the canopy, where eerie fluorescent light shone on the pumps. There was something unsettling about a gas station late at night anyway, and between the shock and the desolation of that place, it seemed like they'd slipped into another dimension.

While Webb dieseled up, they tried to comfort Cristiana as best they could. She wouldn't eat anything, but they got her to drink some water. Her backpack dangled from the strap at her elbow. When Javier reached to readjust it on her, she jerked away from his touch and hiked the straps up on her shoulders. He held his hands up to show her he didn't mean any harm.

Webb got back in and said, "We need to get a move on. A cop car just went by and the boys inside gave us a long, long look."

"It's time to go now," Javier said to her.

Cristiana didn't respond.

"It's what he wanted," Javier said. "For you to be safe. To do that, we have to take you away from here."

Cristiana wiped her nose on the back of her hand. "He killed people," she said wearily. "And they killed him back."

Javier didn't want to respond, but realized it wasn't a question anyway. She let them help her into her hiding spot, and they departed. The snow was patchy, beginning to stack up. The tire tracks ahead didn't even go all the way to the asphalt, and beneath all the powdery stuff, layers of ice remained. They were almost six hundred miles away from their new destination. None of that mattered if they couldn't make it out of Juárez.

Javier wondered how long before somebody somebody stumbled on that grisly mess they'd left behind. He puffed out his lips as the thorny pain churned through his forearm. Some deep part of him was grateful, though, because images of Ricky's open chest, of his own finger pulling the trigger on Andrés and his compadre, began to creep back into his head. When the pain surged, they faded into the shadows.

The streetlights over the bridge were out. Orange cones merged all the lanes into one. The displays normally full of green arrows and red X's were all blank. At the checkpoint was one idling car, an older model sedan. One dark figure was leaned into the driver-side window and another stood back a few steps. A moment later they waved the car on and studied the bus through black ski masks. They calmly motioned for them to pull up.

Javier got the documents from the glove box. He looked at the bandmates, who all had the same pummeled daze of a boxer barely hanging on in the tenth round. He didn't have a speech. He didn't have a plan other than to deflect the agents' questions about their haggard appearance as best he could.

The masked figures entered, the federal decals on their jackets the only thing separating their look from that of bank robbers or terrorists. The distinction didn't ease Javier's mind. Their disembodied features, patches of pale skin around their intense eyes and stern mouths, chilled him. They rolled their masks up. The faces lost most of their sinister qualities when seen in full. The woman had a long nose with a slight crook in it. The man's lips were cracked, his cheeks shiny and wind-bitten as if he hadn't put on the mask in time. He already looked irritated.

"When I heard I got transferred to El Paso, I thought at least it'll be warm there." He shook his head. His accent came from one of those overcrowded northeastern cities where the winters ground peoples' patience into a fine powder that would scatter in the wind. "Might as well be on the Canadian border for crissake. At least my blood pressure would be lower."

Javier knew he should chuckle, make small talk about the weather, but the words required to do that made no sense to him. The man didn't seem to notice or care. He went on and asked the standard questions and they gave him the standard answers. Javier could answer them on auto-pilot. They all could now. They were The Texas Velvets—Jeff thought that one up on the way down—and they were headed back home for another show. The man licked his thumb and flipped through the documents Javier handed him.

"Anything to declare?" the woman asked.

Javier shook his head. "No, ma'am."

"What happened to your windshield?" she asked.

"Semi threw a rock," he said. "We'll get that fixed."

She nodded in a way that didn't suggest she agreed. "And your mirror?"

Javier leaned and looked at the long right-hand mirror. The shotgun had done a number on it. The glass was spiderwebbed and missing a big chunk that exposed the jagged plastic backing.

"Hit a lamp post backing up," Webb said.

"Ah," she said. "Need to be more careful. These things don't turn on a dime."

"No ma'am," Webb said.

The other agent stared at Dave's nose for a measured moment.

"Nose bleed," Dave said. "Must be the altitude."

The agent raised his eyebrows in a manner intended to make him uneasy.

"Well, you've answered all our questions. I guess you can be on your way." He turned to his partner. "I forget anything?"

"Yeah," she said coolly. "The border is closed."

"What? No," Dave said. "I mean, please, we have to get back home."

"Sorry to tell ya," the man said. "All that ice is snapping electrical poles like breadsticks. Nobody gets through until the power's back on."

"What about that car before us?" Squat asked.

The agent looked at his partner, sharing an inside-joke glance.

"Atypical circumstances," the woman said.

Javier nodded. He knew where this was headed.

"How much?"

The man stared at Javier with manufactured confusion.

"How much what?"

Anger bubbled up in Javier. They knew exactly what they were doing. He'd come to expect this from the cops and federales in Mexico, crooked as the Rio Grande, but it surprised him coming from the US side. Not that they were any more moral or had a loftier sense of justice. There was just a stronger system in place to tamp down this sort of corruption. But the system was down.

"I won't say it again," Javier said.

"You won't, huh? Well I guess that's the end of it," he said.

"Five thousand," Javier said, throwing out a large number in hopes of overwhelming them.

"Hmm," the man said with his best poker face on. He tapped his lips with his finger. "Think we should call Soto?"

"Maybe," the woman replied.

"Ten," Javier said through gritted teeth.

"Most of them start around a hundred bucks," the man said to his partner. "We've got a high roller here."

Javier could feel the heat from the bandmates' stares. The man's eyes twinkled like a car salesman. His partner grinned and nodded.

"The maximum you can carry across the border is ten thousand dollars," she said. "Unless you've officially declared it to Customs. And as I recall, you declared nothing." An upper-hand grin came and went on her thin lips. "So if we found, I don't know, a penny more than ten thousand dollars onboard we would have to confiscate all of it."

"Hmm," the man said. "Flush with cash and in a hurry. You don't think these nice gentlemen could be hiding anything, do you?"

"I'm afraid we can't rule it out," the woman said.

"Damn." The man jerked his thumb over his shoulder. "I really wish the power would come back on. The generator doesn't make enough juice for our new toy."

Out the window, across the empty lanes, sat a squatty white vehicle that looked like an unmarked delivery van. It had a weird shape to it though, like a kid's drawing of a van.

"That's a backscatter X-ray," the woman said. "It can penetrate through solid steel and reflect off hidden objects to give us a nice clear image of what's inside."

"Just got it last week. Scans the thousands of vehicles that pass through here every day," the man said. "We can spot a bundle of Mexicans or a measly kilo of coke like a neon sign."

"You don't say?" Squat said in an admirably casual tone.

"Smuggling through these ports of entry will become a thing of the past," she said. "The future is container ships and tunnels and drones. Crossing in a vehicle—only ignorant low-level crooks will continue to attempt that."

"No more human error. No canine error even," the man said. "The machines are gonna see everything. These backscatter rigs, they barely got here and they're already almost outdated. You oughta see what they have coming out next year." The man shook his head in weary awe.

"That just leaves common people the option of crossing the wilderness on foot," the woman said. "But we're not too worried about that. There are patrol units on the high traffic paths, and we have our own drones to keep watch. Besides, the desert is an effective deterrent all on its own."

It sounded like the kind of speech the villain in an action movie would give while keeping a pistol aimed at the main character, but neither of them had even put a hand on their firearms. Javier felt weaker than any of the heroes ever seemed to.

"And technology is great and all, but I can't wait for that big-ass wall," the man said. "So what if it's more a symbol than an actual barrier? Who cares, it makes our job easier. Sends a clear fucking message: no place for you here. Safer for everybody that way."

"So, in theory," the woman said. "This could be one of the last times that human judgment outweighs surveillance and algorithms and bureaucracy here on the border."

"Better make it count," the man said.

Javier felt trapped. The agents knew they had to get across, they knew they had more than ten thousand. They would take all of it. What would that do to the band, having put themselves through hell without even gas money to show for it? Jeff rubbed his ear like he could massage it back into working order.

"So how does this work," Marck said. "You shake us down and then let us go?"

The man shrugged. "It's better than prison, isn't it?"

"What if we do something like this again?" Squat said.

"Squat," Dave hissed. "Shut up."

"What? For real. Say you let us go and then we turn around next week and smuggle a half-ton of meth into Texas. That wouldn't bother your conscience?"

"I'll sleep just fine," the man said. "On a brand-new king-size bed. Plus, you come back and we'll catch you. We did it just fine without the X-ray. What makes you think you'd get by that?"

Squat shook his head and crossed his thick arms.

"And don't take the high road with me, any of you. We just thought you boys might like to make a deal is all. If not, no biggie, I'll just call up my supervisor and let him sort all of this out."

Dave's eyebrows pinched in as he picked at the scab on his nose. Javier showed his hands to the agents and slowly reached for the cabinet. He took out the saddle-brown leather bag, noticing the dried blood drops when he reached inside for one of the rolls.

"Nope," the woman said. "Hand it over. All of it."

She rummaged through it without taking anything out and then let the man look inside. She leaned in and whispered something in his ear.

Javier decided they could take it all, so long as they let them through. He didn't care about the money, about how much the band might hate him for giving it up. His goal was so much clearer and more crucial. He had Cristiana to think about now.

At that point, Jeff was thoroughly out of the loop and frustrated. Javier didn't like the way he was looking at the money. Jeff didn't just see a leather bag with sixty K inside. He saw all his dreams, his studio, his hearing, his effort and time perfecting his craft, clenched in that agent's hand. And he got a little crazy.

He lunged for the bag and got a hold of the strap. He jerked at it and took the agent by surprise. When it was slipping out of her hands, her partner jumped in and started pulling back on it. The tug of war went on for a few seconds, with everyone yelling at Jeff to stop and him digging in further. Squat finally got ahold of his fingers and pried them off. The two agents stumbled backward with the bag. Squat grabbed Jeff under the armpits and held him back.

"What the hell was that?" the woman demanded.

"Let's take it easy," Javier said. "You have the money. That's what you wanted."

"Oh you little punk. I could knock your teeth in," the man said, pointing at Jeff. "I oughta cuff you right now."

"No," Dave said, focused and mean. "You're gonna take the money and let us go. That's what you'll do. Because if you don't, you go down with us. You don't want that. Do you know what the Mexican Mafia does to guys like you in prison?"

"I'd show a little more respect if I were you," the man said, framing his gun.

"Go ahead," Squat said. "But you're gonna have to shoot all of us."

The woman already had her eyes on the door, holding the bag tightly against her body. The man stared at it. His hand dropped from the gun and his shoulders sank. Javier knew then they were going to let them go.

"This is an unforgiving job, you know," the man said. "We're an annoyance to tourists and commuters, demons in the flesh to immigrants.

The other government agencies look down on us. We put our lives on the line to keep the country safe—and we don't get paid shit. It's a raw deal, if you ask me."

No one responded.

"We all do what we have to," the woman said.

They had moved past intimidation and into rationalization. The agents shared another look, this one with a hint of shame. The woman zipped her jacket around the bag. They departed without another word, retreating to the booth with their grand prize. When the bus rolled past, snow crunching under its tires, they could see the man talking excitedly to the woman. She watched him cynically, cradling the bulge in her jacket like a pregnant belly.

The frosted WELCOME TO TEXAS sign shone in their high beams, and the tall streetlights looked fuzzy in the wintry haze. Javier felt none of the usual relief when they crossed the line. The heaviness in his chest had followed him into another country, and his gunshot wound once again began to pulse in excruciating bursts, making him wonder if the bullet had struck bone on the way through. His bandages were sticky, saturated with blood now.

Javier spoke through the vent, telling Cristiana they were in the US but she would have to stay hidden a while longer. The checkpoints went as far as seventy-five miles inland, and they were all too haggard to take another risk. They made it to a twenty-four-hour drug store in Las Cruces after midnight, where they bought disinfectant and bandages and inadequate painkillers.

Chapter 16

1984

THE MEN'S VOICES, GRUFF RUMBLINGS MUTED BY THE trees and thick brush, neared. Javier knew there would be no fight or flight if they found him this time. He was out of gas. He stayed low and quiet, trying to contain his rushing breath.

When the voices trailed off, Javier still didn't leave his hiding spot. He stayed low until he got a strong urge to rise up and look around, and then stayed another long while. He had more time than he needed to think, struggling with whether he'd done the right thing. It sure felt like it before, but now he replayed Adrián's cracking voice, Eli's refusal to follow him. He didn't know why he chose Eli to take off with. They weren't that close. Maybe because he was the youngest, the meekest, Javier felt he could save him.

When dusk and its inky blue light started to seep in, Javier got up and brushed himself off. Night hurtled forward and darkness out there ran deep. It was no time to get caught out in the woods without even a pocketknife or a book of matches.

A chorus of cicadas and crickets had overtaken the silence. He staggered in the direction he thought he'd come, but the thick underbrush seemed to loop back on itself the further he went. The treetops filtered out what was left of the pale light and left him feeling his way through the woodland. He came to a creek he knew he hadn't crossed before. Black water drifted along banks knotted with thick roots. He put his hand on a half-sunken oak and squinted into the darkness. He recognized a big rock shaped like an egg. The boys had fished nearby. The creek ran east and then bent around to the south.

Javier followed the bank around the bend and found a shallower part of the water to cross. He took off his boots and socks and rolled up his jeans. The dark water, ripples lit with blue moonlight, was cool, and the mud felt good on his feet. Then Javier caught himself mid-step and froze. Cutting through the glimmering ripples, a long black water moccasin slithered across the surface, its head poised above the water within kicking distance. Javier held his breath, and it slipped on by. Two more menacing heads emerged from the creek, making blue ripples of their own, and lithely followed in search of prey they might corner and devour.

On the other side, Javier caught his breath and pulled on his boots. He veered off from the creek. He tried to keep his path straight, but each time he dodged a fallen limb or wove through a cluster of slender trunks he doubted his accuracy. He should have been in the clearing by now. His boot got caught in an arching ground root and he flung forward, the hard-packed earth scraping his palms when he tried to catch himself. He slapped the ground in anger and began to cry.

He sniffled and blurrily eyed the ever-darker woods. He wiped his eyes, blew a snot rocket. Behind all that fear and pain and raggedness, he felt a sturdy force holding him up. And even though getting back to the clearing was only step one in a long and often illegible list, he knew it was all he could do in that moment. He got up and kept trudging along.

He pumped his fists in the air when he finally came to the waist-high tangle of deadwood. He climbed over it this time, taking care not to get snagged on the small branches. He located a point of light, which turned out to be the back porch's yellow glow, and used it to guide him the rest of the way.

He stayed in the shadows and made sure the driveway was empty. No lights were on inside the house, and Javier left them that way in case anyone drove by. The floorboards creaked under his boots. He found a flashlight in the junk drawer that he had to bang with his palm to keep lit. The house was creaky, and everything in the flashlight's beam looked sinister. The scattered notebook paper and pencils from their unfinished English lesson. The ashtray full of butts and the kitchen faucet dripping into a dirty skillet. Javier went into Yolanda and Drew's room and saw their bed unmade, like they had just gotten out of it. A chill went down his spine.

Javier heard a crash and spun with the flashlight, but the movement snuffed it out. He banged it on his palm but it wouldn't even flicker. He smacked it harder. Whoever made that noise, they were about to get him. He twisted the base and the bulb flashed on. In the doorway the smoky cat's eyes glowed. Staring into the light, its pupils were razor-thin slits. It hissed and bared its teeth. Javier shouted in the deepest voice he could muster and took two stomps toward it. The cat bounded down the hall and disappeared into one of the other rooms. When Javier let his breath go it was like pulling the valve stem from a tire.

Javier's stomach gurgled. All he'd had was a bowl of oatmeal all day. He rummaged the fridge and ate two bologna and cheese sandwiches. When he went to put the stuff up, he spotted a battered tin of saltines at the back. He cocked his head. He lifted the lid and in place of the crackers was a mess of loose bills. He couldn't believe it.

He spread the bills on the counter and counted, twisting around with the light when the cat knocked a vase of plastic hydrangeas off the end table. There were eight hundred and seventeen dollars. He stared at the rumpled bills in his hand, the guilt of stealing still tugging on him even after all they'd done. But he took the cash and shoved it in his front pocket. These were his wages.

He knew that he had to leave right then. He was tired and would have a hard time finding his way in the dark, but to stick around until morning was too risky. There was no way he'd get much sleep in the house anyway. Javier scavenged the cabinets and added crackers and cans of Vienna sausages and sardines and filled a big insulated mug in the sink. He found the bag of cat food and poured it out on the floor.

He walked down the drive and onto the dirt road leading south. He spent the night in a dry ditch, shielded from view by tall grass and cattails, not far off the highway. He couldn't shut his mind off, wondering what would happen to the other boys, if it would have been better to simply run away and leave all of them out of it. He bolted upright in his sleep that night, sure that Yolanda and Drew were standing over him with ropes and knives.

Javier walked a couple of miles the next morning before a white-haired couple stopped and offered him a ride in the bed of their single-cab pickup. They dropped him off at the Huntsville bus station just before noon.

The board was full of destinations and prices, places as far as LA and as close as Houston. He could afford a ticket to any of them. He stared at the list a long while, running his tongue over the swollen split in his lip that still held the taste of iron. Not too long ago, the possibilities would have filled him with joy, each city its own dreamworld in his mind. Now it was too easy to imagine how he might be beaten down and chased out of each one.

After everything, he still didn't want to leave Texas. The image of it that formed back on those early mornings in the fields with his mother still outweighed his experiences so far. It was a big state. There had to be a place for him. Where though? Houston and all its rain-drenched offshoots had lost their appeal. All he knew about Dallas was that it was big and the Cowboys played there. Then there were the cities with Spanish names: San Antonio, El Paso, and Amarillo. Those seemed like possibilities, cities where his accent might not stand out so much.

The map illustrated how different the western part of the state was, little spaced-out dots and skinny highways, compared to the tangle of towns and interstates back east. His father had said that he had a cousin in Lubbock, but Javier had never met her. It wasn't much on paper, and he had no idea what it was like. But it was all the way across the gigantic state and probably looked nothing like overgrown East Texas. Those felt like positives.

He bought the ticket and got a window seat in the back. He caught a few stares walking down the aisle. His jeans were ripped and dirt-stained.

His hair was sloppy and uncombed. The people just glanced though. Everyone had their own problems, couldn't think too much about the grimy eleven-year-old by himself in the back row. About what his yesterday might have looked like.

The bus rolled onto the sunny two-lane highway and eased into that steady hum. That was the one feeling Javier had really come to enjoy, the sound and feel of going somewhere, the road noise and the weave of changing lanes. Knowing that the fields and the detention center and that graveyard of a parking lot in Houston were all disappearing in the rearview mirror eased his mind. It wasn't long before he fell asleep, his body finally demanding he catch up on all that he had missed.

He woke to a sunbeam stretching over his face. He blinked a few times, keeping his head against the seat. A passing sign said Lubbock was forty miles away. He'd ridden the bus for a whole day and still hadn't made it across the state. He sat up slowly, leaned toward the window. It was flat and sparse country, not pretty or green. In the distance to the north, Javier traced the meandering line where the rolling hills and mesquite stopped at the caprock escarpment, where the land flatlined into an endless horizon, perfectly framing an ocean of sky.

A golden ripple of clouds, shaped like a wide eye, hung over the highway ahead. The thin clouds above it, blends of gray and lavender, dissolved into the darkening heavens. These high plains reminded Javier of home, though they looked like something from another world. He thought about what it would be like to live up there, if the clouds didn't give way under his boots. To ride on the crest of that golden eye, the light just filling him, driving out the emptiness, casting aside all his bruised parts. The wide-open sky and its grand brushstrokes helped him see the bare-naked truth.

He had thought himself weak for failing so many times on his journey, for stepping into so many snares. But he wasn't weak. He really felt that now. He'd been knocked in the dirt until he could taste grit in his teeth, but he made it all the way to Texas. Like Mamá always said he would. The fear and the doubt weren't gone for good, he knew, but he welcomed a break in the clouds. He took another ragged breath and prayed that he would be okay in this new place. He asked God for strength and for grace, for another door to open. He unfolded his hands and leaned back in his seat.

The sun went low, its retreating light coating the earth in rich blue. The clouds retained its light like a memorial, swirling in shades of pink and purple and indigo. The first few stars made little pinpricks overhead, and Javier watched the highway spill into the last-ditch flare of the western sky. He didn't know what else to ask for.

2015

The Colorado plains were blanketed in snow, but the highway was clear. By the time they made it through Pueblo the sun was just below the horizon, shining fire onto the underbellies of cloudbanks. The glacial mountains loomed large to the west, but their exit took the bus east, where only black shapes of bare trees and electric lines broke up the uniformity of the horizon. The snow still looked blue in the gathering light.

A dually pickup sat in the house's caliche drive. Javier double-checked the address Ricky gave him with the one stenciled on the mailbox: 4401 County Road V. It was a newer ranch-style house with a long, covered porch strewn with rustic furniture. Several horses—from a dark bay gelding on down to an exquisite paint filly—munched from a hay feeder out back. A shaggy blue-eyed cowdog lowered its front end and barked through the gate.

"Does this look right?" Javier asked.

Cristiana shrugged, eyes fixed on the dog. Javier noticed her bag on the floor and reached to pick it up. The zipper had partly worked its way down and when he lifted up on the strap it yawned open, spilling out a set of clothes and four tightly wrapped packages.

"No," Cristiana shouted, scrambling for the items. "You can't look in there."

She scooped up the clothes and packages, stuffing them back into the pink backpack, but Javier got a hold of one first. He tilted it until it caught the faint light. Through countless layers of plastic he could make out a mass of bluish pills. Javier had no idea what they were, but correctly appraised them as illegal and expensive.

"Whoa," Marck said. "What the hell is that?"

"Drugs," Javier said.

Cristiana was still struggling with his good arm, trying to get it back, when they saw motion near the house, just the flash of a figure going inside and the screen door slamming behind it.

"So Ricky was using his niece as a mule?" Dave said. "Bro. That is *low*."

"Keep your big nose out of it," Cristiana shot back, taking him off guard.

Javier waved the package at her. "What is this?"

She shrugged.

"Don't give me that," Javier said.

She stiffened her lip and crossed her little arms.

"Alright Webb, turn it around. Back to Juárez," he said, hoping the tactic would work on a nine-year-old. Webb made a slow show of reaching for the gearshift, thunking it into reverse.

"I don't know," she cried. "I don't! He just told me not to open it. To make sure it got to Colorado. He said that it was going to help us start a new life."

Javier squeezed his fist and his arm went to throbbing again. He felt so stupid. He nodded to the house. "Is this even your uncle?"

Her eyes shifted about, quicker and quicker, until they clenched up and began to water. "I don't think so," she said. "This wasn't supposed to happen. Tío Ricky was going to come find me. He said we were gonna start over."

"Where's your mom?" Squat asked. "Wouldn't you rather be with her?"

"She's gone," she said flatly. "Tío Ricky was my family. All my family."

Javier squinted out the window, catching only the gentle bend in the tree limbs and the lazy swish of the horses' tails. The dog had stopped barking, but it watched them intently from the gate.

"What if we took her to the police?" Dave asked. "She won't be in any trouble, right? She's just a kid. Maybe they can find a place for her."

She shook her head and flicked her hands dismissively at him.

"Just give me a minute to think," Javier said.

"Hey uh," Webb said. A man came from the house and was marching up to the bus. Javier didn't even try to hide the package in his hand when the man stepped inside. He bore no resemblance to Ricky. Gray-streaked hair, shaggy for a guy his age, stuck out of his faded Broncos cap. He looked them over for a minute.

"You must be the crew," he said.

"Who are you?" Javier asked.

"Daniel Zavala," he said. "I'm a friend of Ricky's."

"He's dead," Cristiana said bitterly.

"Oh no," Daniel said. He removed his cap and looked down. "I'm sorry for your loss, Cristiana." He paused and grimaced. "But your tío knew this might happen. Me and him, we set up a plan. I'm going to take care of you now." He eyed the package in Javier's hand and then her again. Her purple jacket had a snag with white fuzz spilling out. He touched the backpack hanging on her elbow. "Can I borrow this?"

She held it out to him.

"Thank you, mija," he said. "I need to talk to these guys for a minute. Can you wait outside? When I get done, I'll get Natalie to make whatever you want for breakfast. How does that sound?"

She froze there, looking around at all the men straining to appear strong and in control. Javier wished a different life for her in that moment. She was already caught up in her uncle's business. Men who valued their interests over her safety made decisions for her. And how was he any better? Had he brought her across on charity? He felt hollowed out and nauseated.

"Go on," Daniel said, quiet but forceful. She got off the bus.

Daniel glared at Javier. He held out his hand for the package and Javier took a step back. Daniel lifted his shirt to reveal an appendix holster. Javier's nerves were exhausted, so watching Daniel's fingers brush across his pistol grip ruffled him about as much as if he were watching it on TV. For once, he didn't have a plan and his mind wasn't scrambling to cook one up.

"You should go to the hospital," Daniel said, tucking his shirt back in. He motioned to Javier's arm and the bloodstain bloom on his jean jacket. "You could get a nasty infection."

Javier readjusted his arm. The pain had gone into a tolerable whine, but it screeched again when called upon. The power of the mind, Javier had wondered, or the weakness of the operator?

"I'm sorry," Marck said. "Are you a doctor?" His forehead vein was bulging the way it did when he got really angry. "Keep your medical opinions to yourself."

"Yeah," Dave said, feeding off him. "Start answering some questions. First off, what is this stuff?"

"Fentanyl," Daniel said. His brown eyes were uneasy, lacking the wild edge of Andrés or Ricky. He didn't want the situation to escalate.

"Like what they dope up cancer patients with?"

He nodded. "But just a taste in each pill. I mean, that's what Ricky said. Sell it as Oxy. Easy."

"You risked that girl's life," Javier said. "For this?"

Daniel opened his mouth, stopped himself, and started again. "It just worked out that way. They weren't safe in Juárez anymore. Look, I'm no narco. I'm a welder. I got out of the game a long time ago. But Ricky came to me with one of his old schemes. He said we could sell this and make a ton of cash. And Cristiana, I'm going to use some of that money to help her out. That's the way Ricky wanted it. I'm a man of my word."

"She could have been killed."

"But she wasn't. Thank God," Daniel said.

"You don't care about her." Javier waved the bundle of fentanyl. "You only care about what this can get you."

"You don't know nothing." Daniel spat. "I provide for my family. I put a roof over their heads. My kids never have to worry where their next meal is coming from. They ride horses and four-wheelers, stuff I never got to do growing up. And Cristiana? Once we sell this, she'll be set for a long, long time. Seems like that was worth the risk."

"That right?" Javier said, his gaze burning.

"It didn't have to be this way," Daniel said in frustration. "Ricky got reckless. He could have worked out a deal with Andrés, but no, he wanted it all. Stubborn ass."

Daniel couldn't go more than a few seconds checking on his last package, still warm in Javier's hand.

"But what's done is done. So just give me the package and this will all be over," Daniel said.

Javier rotated it in his hand. "Ruiz is dead. Ricky and Andrés too. But do you really think they were the only ones that knew about the dope?" Daniel rolled the question over in his mind. "The cartel will come looking for this. You know that, right?"

"How bad do you want all that money?" Javier went on. "Is it worth dying over? Is it worth your kids dying over?"

"You don't know what you're talking about," Daniel snarled.

"How about killing?" Javier went on. "Who would you kill to keep it? *We* know your dirty secret. Would you kill us? What if Cristiana lets something slip at school? What then?"

Daniel got all squirmy, and he got that tunnel-vision look in his eyes. The bandmates were stunned into silence. Javier nodded to himself, understanding where everyone stood. He tossed the package at Daniel's feet and he left it there.

"Where's your line in the sand, Daniel? How far can this go and still be *worth it*?"

Javier and Daniel stared at each other for an amount of time that seemed uncomfortable to everyone else.

"Cristiana," Javier called. She stood near Daniel's fence, watching his dog pace back and forth.

Once she'd climbed back in, Javier knelt down to look her in the eyes. "Are you sure you don't have any other family? Anyone else to stay with?"

She said, "I know I have family on my dad's side, but I never met them."

"I know all this has been hard, but I need you to make a decision, okay?" She nodded and squinted in concentration. "You can either stay here with Daniel or you can go with us. I don't have much, but I can take care of you. And it'll just be temporary, until we track down your family."

"That wasn't the deal," Daniel said as more of a statement than a complaint.

Javier ignored him and waited on Cristiana's response. It didn't take long.

"I don't want to stay here," she said. "I'll go with you."

Javier watched her for any sign of uncertainty. Then he clapped his good hand on his thigh. "Okay, then. You heard her."

Daniel didn't seem too shook up about her leaving, especially with Ricky no longer around to enforce the deal, but he was obviously doing some internal math to figure out what it meant for him.

"Wait here a minute, all right?" Daniel headed for the house.

Dave watched and said, "What if he's getting backup?"

"Yeah," Marck said. "Let's just bail."

"Don't you see? There's no running anymore," Javier said. He was spent, but the words kept coming from a place deep inside him, easy as water from a natural spring. "We can't run far enough for things to go back the way they were. If Daniel wants to find us, he'll find us. And that goes for the rest of them back in Juárez too." Javier shook his head, feeling the sadness rising to the surface. He spoke candidly, in a voice the others had never heard. "I'm sorry. I didn't do enough to make that clear from the beginning. I didn't care if you understood the consequences or not. I just wanted you to go along. You get to a certain point, no matter what your intentions are, and there's just no going back. You have to carry it with you the rest of your life. Like last night."

"You did what you had to do. Those guys were gonna—" Squat stopped himself, remembering Cristiana. "You know."

"And what does any of this have to do with right now?" Dave asked. "We're right, we're wrong, who cares? We can figure all that out later. We need to go."

"Go on if you want to." Javier stepped down onto the driveway.

The bandmates packed near the window, watching him stand there all alone, clutching his hurt arm to his midsection like a broken wing. Daniel came out of the house and let the screen door slam behind him. He had something in his hand.

"Oh shit," Dave said.

Squat was the first one out, and then the others. They all piled out and lined up shoulder to shoulder with Javier. Daniel cocked an eyebrow and stopped a few feet in front of them.

"Here." He handed Javier a roll of hundreds. "I'm low on cash until I make that sale, so it's all I got. And it's all you get. I'm not gonna track you down and bring you Ricky's cut just cause you're taking the girl."

"Wouldn't want you to," Javier said. "Don't ever track her or us down, under any circumstances. Understand?"

Daniel narrowed his eyes and leaned on his back foot.

"Go on and sell your dope. We won't stand in your way," Javier said. "But if anybody from down south comes looking for it, that's on you. Keep our names out of your mouth. I don't ever want to see you again. But if I hear of anybody on our trail, I catch so much as a whisper, I'm coming for you first, Daniel Zavala, 4401 County Road V."

He let the words hang there, and Daniel squirmed a little under the weight of them. Javier knew those packages would ruin him, one way or another. Jeff might struggle to hear what was being said, but he didn't really need the words. He sensed it too.

"De acuerdo?" Javier asked.

Daniel nodded quickly. His eyes met Javier's for a second and then trailed off to the snowdrifts in front of the home. The sun was up now, and the powder glistened with dazzling light.

An old memory, too sun-faded and brittle to be replayed in the waking hours, had been coming back to Javier in his dreams, where his subconscious could dance over the gaps, spinning a form in motion more real than anything a photograph or waking thought could produce.

He was ten years old, back on the farm, doing his morning chores. It was a typical October morning, cool breeze and deep blue sky. The sun was up, filling him with that soft golden light that only the nearing of winter can bring. He tended to the chickens, letting them out of their ramshackle coop, raking the mess, and collecting the eggs.

His mother was nearby, picking black-eyed peas and stuffing them in a burlap sack. She stood up and looked at him, shading the sun with her hand. He was looking back in time, before the cancer, when she was so young, so full of life. Javier had almost forgotten her how she was then, because the other image, of the gaunt and defeated woman, barely recognizable, dying in a rural hospital, was the one that dominated his memories.

But in the dreams, she was as she had once been. Her honey-brown eyes, which she had passed down to him, were bright and hopeful. She was slender but had that wiry strength. Her hands could open any jar and stung like hell when she spanked him. She was never the "wait 'til your dad gets home" type. She was also the most comforting person Javier had ever known, wiping away his tears and wrapping him in a warm hug, making him feel absolutely loved and accepted.

Javier carried on to the goat pen, whistling an old tune. Something began to feel off, a moment before the sunlight drained from the sky. He felt like he couldn't catch his breath. The sky turned gray and a cold wind from the north blew in, turning the day on its head. Thunder rumbled in the distance. His mother finished picking and then slung the bag over her shoulder.

A flash of lightning spread across the sky like roots growing in hyperspeed. The small glimpse of the storm's power made Javier's spine tingle. Thunder crashed around him and then retreated to a low rumbling threat on the horizon. His mother called out to him, but he couldn't make out her words.

Dark clouds, like smoke from thousands of burning tires, hovered over the farm. The goats were spooked, climbed up on hay bales to get to higher ground. In the dreams this was where it branched off. Once he was struck by the lightning. Once a giant tornado sucked them into its vortex, a swirling mass of splintered wood and flesh and hay. Once great streaks of fog fell from the sky, separating him and his mother. The constant was the storm, black and seething. And Javier always awoke with a gasp, sweaty and disoriented.

Javier dreamed one of these dreams the night before their trip to Juárez. The storm was as fierce as ever, the frigid wind blowing so hard it made his eyes water. The dark clouds swooped down on the farm, cutting Javier off everywhere he tried to turn. The basket of eggs dropped from his hand and made a dull crunch. There was a loud clap of thunder, and it began to rain. He spun around—or was it the storm spinning around him?—dizzy and scared. He called out for his mother. He had just seen her at the edge of the garden, but he could no longer tell what direction that was.

Then, in all the darkness and swirling terror, he saw a gap in the darkness with new eyes. He struggled against the wind and the mounting rain, focusing on that one point of light. He leaned into the storm, acting in spite of his fear, going the only direction he could. The wind knocked him back, the sideways rain pummeled him, but he kept going. He was so determined it took him a few seconds to recognize that when the rain had slowed, when the wind had died down, he had made it to the clearing.

When his eyes adjusted to the light, he saw his mother. She had an unearthly lightness, like she was just barely floating above the ground, and a glow in her face and eyes. Javier looked down and found his clothes dry. Then it was a perfect October day once again, like the storm had never happened. He was confused but no longer scared.

His mother was smiling when he approached her. She wrapped him in her arms, and it felt like coming home. Then she whispered something in his ear. He shut his eyes and nodded. He didn't want to, but knew he had to. He let go of her and watched her fade out of sight. He was at peace with it this time. Then he woke up.

———————

"Where's she gonna go?" Squat asked, after Cristiana had fallen asleep on the couch. She was exhausted, out cold after a sleepless night. Her lips were parted slightly while she breathed deeply, the most peaceful look on her face since she hugged her uncle for the last time back at the warehouse.

"She'll stay with me," Javier said. "Until we can find something better."

"With you?" Marck said. "What do you know about taking care of a kid?"

Javier shrugged. "Well, we don't know where the rest of her family is. We can't take her to the police. We can't just drop her off on somebody's doorstep. If you got a better idea, let's hear it."

Marck went quiet, thinking on it, and then just shook his head.

"We can help you out, Javi," Squat said. "We can get her into school. And when we're on tour we can tutor her. We can each do a different subject. Jeff's super smart at English. I can teach gym. Or music."

Dave stopped writing in his notebook and set the pen down. "Don't get too ahead of yourself, Squat. We don't even know where we're gonna be in a few weeks."

"I appreciate that, Squat," Javier said. "But you do what's best for the band. I'll be alright. This is just until I can track down her family."

"What if they're shitty people though?" Squat said. "Like that Daniel dude."

Javier hadn't thought that far ahead. "Well—I don't know."

They passed Trinidad and then Raton, where their words as well as the mountains and pines receded into the vastness of the Llano Estacado, where the long horizons laid bare all that had ever been. Javier had gotten back to reading the book about Quanah Parker. These were once the lands of the great Comanche Empire. The best horsemen the world had ever known, a fact that rival tribes as well as Mexican farmers and white settlers learned the hard way. Their raids were the stuff of legend. Their way of fighting baffled enemies for a hundred years. Javier had read that a young Comanche on a horse was the least fenced-in a human had ever been.

As humans make war and seize, take back and defend, drawing and altering invisible lines in the dirt, empires fall and new empires rise. The relatively small-scale brutality of the Comanche was eventually flattened by the massive American machine, that westward expansion accelerating until it had the momentum to crush all obstacles. Though they held out the longest, the Comanche too were fenced in, driven into Oklahoma like so many other tribes.

And for all the tenacious settlers and the Texas Rangers did, they were never who the Comanche hated most. They were the enemy, but their desire was understood. It was the same desire that the Comanche harnessed to drive out the Apache, to protect and expand their own vast empire. Who they really despised were the buffalo hunters, men who would come in and kill hundreds of buffalo in a single day. They left hills of usable meat and tendon and bone to rot on the open plains, driving the animal to the edge of extinction and forever altering the Comanche's nomadic way of life, all because they could get two dollars apiece for the hides.

The buffalo hunters were long gone, but their spirit continued on in people cruel and indifferent— like Andrés, the agents at the border, Daniel—who saw the world only in terms of what could be hacked off and sold. Javier recognized it in himself too: the desire to take, to choke out your conscience until it can't stand in the way. And then what? Is a man without a conscience still a man? Or has he entered a new realm, too savage for men, too vain for beasts?

Javier watched wintry pastures and barbed wire zoom by to the east. White-faced Herefords were clustered up by the fence, the mamas shielding their calves from the harsh winds. It was December's picture on a calendar if there ever was one. The ground sloped at the slightest of angles, barely perceptible as changes in elevation.

They could see forever now, with the clouds beginning to lift. Despite all the bloodshed and progress that had come to the land, the people come and the people gone, the flatness of the plains was still its best feature. It was here that Javier felt he could breathe best, where he could expose his wounds to the light of day. It was a place where time shook loose its shackles and distance wasn't just a measurement. It was a thing you lived in.

Cristiana groaned softly and looked around her with blinking eyes.

"Where are we?" she asked.

"We just passed through Hereford," Webb responded. "The town you can smell from three counties away."

Cristiana squinted at him.

"We're not far from home now," Javier said.

"Where's home again?"

"West Texas," Javier said.

"Huh," she said. "Do they have horses in West Texas?"

"Yeah." Javier chuckled. "There's a few around."

"You really like horses, don't you?" Squat sat down beside her.

Cristiana nodded and rubbed her eyes.

"My family has a little spread not too far away," he said. "There's not any horses out there anymore, since my abuelos passed, but it's a perfect spot for it. That's where I learned to ride as a kid."

"I bet we could scrounge up enough cash for a horse," Dave said. "If Javier has the space to keep it."

Cristiana was awake now, her eyes bouncing between them, landing on Javier with great interest.

He nodded and grinned. "I think we could make that happen."

Cristiana nodded with a half-smile.

Jeff was still in his own ringing world, but his spirits had been lifted with the rest of them. He rested his elbow on Dave's shoulder and they all watched Cristiana. It made Javier feel good, seeing her excited about something.

The bandmates crowded onto the couch with her, looking up pictures of horses for sale on Jeff's phone. They looked and compared and dreamed for a while, but her lack of sleep caught up to her again. She dozed off, and Squat gently moved her from his shoulder and tucked her in with a wool blanket.

Javier's grin faded and his thoughts picked up steam. He had spoken the truth. There was no going back to how things were. Spanning great distances made Javier feel alive, but even this reminded him of the unwinding of his time. The days and months ahead would hold conflict and retribution. People would come for those drugs and they might come for him.

Javier stood at the front of the bus and stared out the windshield. The anxiety was still there, but it didn't seize him up like it normally did. There was a booming in his soul more powerful than the gunshot, enough to stifle the fear of the next one fired at him. He wasn't bulletproof, but he wasn't scared of dying, and that was close enough.

He had worried all these years about whether he was doing right by his mother, whether her final sacrifice was in vain. Even his good deeds had been done fearfully, things he thought he had to do to measure up, to be worthy of love. And when that didn't work, he leaned hard in the other direction. He hardened his heart and toughened his skin, keeping his weaknesses secret.

But now he knew he was worthy. He always had been. And it was up to him to live, not just to check boxes but to really use what he had and do right by people. That started with Cristiana. Maybe it was just temporary, but he was going to take care of her the best he could, pass on some of the lessons his mother had taught him. He felt more hopeful than he had in a long time.

Javier sat down at the little table with Dave, wincing when he laid his forearm on the surface. He couldn't say the weight had been lifted but he did feel better, even with the hole in his arm. He looked out the window at patches of pale-yellow grass poking out of the snow and ice, moving stiffly in the wind. They were right back where they started, with no money, no album, and a ramshackle bus.

"I have a new song," Dave said.

"That right?" Javier replied.

"Yeah. I wrote the chorus a few months back and didn't know what to do with it. Then for some reason, it just came to me. I finished it about the time we got back into Texas."

"I'd like to hear it," Javier said. He knew before he listened to it that it wouldn't be a hit, probably wouldn't make it on any chart, but somehow that just made it more true. Dave laid his notebook open, reached for his guitar, and the others gathered around.

Webb mashed the accelerator, speeding down the home stretch. Thin boundless clouds streaked across the pale blue sky like the lines on a staff. The road noise hummed its familiar refrain and another new-born song, majestic and a little clumsy all at once, rose above the hard winter air.

Windswept

Each time the wind blows I roll
Each time the wind blows I ro-oh-oll
On by the mesquite trees
On top of that sweet breeze
Each time the wind blows I roll

All my best lines are borrowed
All my stories are staged
I had something special
But I chased her away

I don't expect forgiveness
I don't expect sympathy
This road will end somewhere
But it won't end with me

Each time the wind blows I roll
Each time the wind blows I ro-oh-oll
On by the mesquite trees
On top of that sweet breeze
Each time the wind blows I roll

Acknowledgments

THANK YOU TO THE FOLKS AT UCR Palm Desert for the encouragement and feedback y'all gave in the early stages of this book. Thanks to Sandra Spicher, Kathy Walton, and Abigail Jennings for their sharp eyes and editing expertise. And thanks to the regulars at the Writer's Roundtable in Kansas City, especially our host Camilo and fellow writers JB, Robert, and Brandon. I had no desire to lead a writing group, but the opportunity just kind of fell in my lap and I'm so glad it did. Writing is a lonely task. It helps to find people who get it, people who understand the endless cycle of excitement and frustration and can talk about that and all the nuts and bolts of storytelling.

I am grateful for all the great teachers I've had, starting with my mom, who said the only time I sat still was when she would read to me. That love of storytelling started with you, mom. Thanks to Mrs. McKinney and Mrs. Sims and Mr. Patterson and Trampas Smith and Stephen Graham Jones (who also came up with the title), teachers who pushed me to read more, write better, and shared my enthusiasm for stories, who made this book grow and take shape in their own ways.

And thanks to the great authors who wrote about the old country. S. C. Gwynne and Cormac McCarthy were my big two on this project, but many skilled writers have set their sights on West Texas. It took reading their books (along with moving away for several years) to remind me how interesting my roots really were. Even when I left, West Texas was always on my mind. It doesn't take much to make a mountain seem majestic, but those flatlands—that's an acquired taste. Good writing reveals the beauty and the bitterness in those places, gives you fresh eyes for all that you saw without really seeing. I saw my home with awe again, and my appreciation for that goes far beyond what you read in this book.

Thanks to my parents, who never tried to talk me out of going to school for creative writing or making up my own weird stories or any other interest of mine. As long as I worked hard and didn't give up, they were in my corner. Thank you to my wife, my better and kinder half, who loves me for who I am, gives me strength to dust myself off and try again when I fail. I thank God for more blessings than I deserve, for guiding me on this path, for the way writing allows me to express myself in words I'm not articulate enough to say out loud.

Music Acknowledgments

I LIKE TO WRITE WITH MUSIC ON. A teacher once told me that writing rituals—having to sit in a certain chair, drinking coffee out of a certain cup, listening to a certain playlist—become built-in excuses when they aren't available. Serious writers write on folding chairs and park benches and in airport lobbies. They write with roofers hammering away next door and kids fighting for the last ice cream sandwich. I don't doubt that, but man is it nice to slip on the headphones and cruise, to the point where the songs are clouds appearing and disappearing in the big blue sky, with a two-lane highway stretching as far as the eye can see. Maybe the bandmates were listening to some of this music on the open road. These were the albums on repeat at various stages of writing the novel:

Cody Jinks, *Lifers*
Espinoza Paz, *No Pongan Esas Canciones*
Frank Ocean, *Blond*
Jason Isbell, *Southeastern*
James McMurtry, *Complicated Game*
The Killers, *Battle Born*
Los Lobos, *Kiko*
Turnpike Troubadours, *A Long Way from Your Heart*

About the Author

TRAVIS BURKETT was born and raised on the flatlands of West Texas. After several years in Kansas City, he recently returned to his hometown of Lamesa, where he farms cotton, writes, and raises his two sons with his wife. This is his first novel.

Printed in the USA
CPSIA information can be obtained
at www.ICGtesting.com
CBHW022149180424
7180CB00002B/122